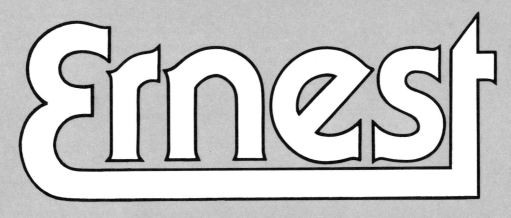

Ernest

by Peter Buckley

The Dial Press New York

Published by The Dial Press, 1 Dag Hammarskjold Plaza,
New York, New York 10017

The photographs in this book, except those taken by the author,
appear by the courtesy of the John F. Kennedy Library.

Every effort has been made to identify the photographers whose
work appears, in order to give them the credit which they deserve.
These credits appear on page 258.

Manufactured in the United States of America

First printing

Library of Congress Cataloging in Publication Data

Buckley, Peter.
      Ernest.

      1. Hemingway, Ernest, 1899—1961—Biography.
2. Novelists, American—20th century—Biography.
I. Title.
PS3515.E37Z58414   813'.5'2   78-17729
ISBN 0-8037-2392-X

For Susan, who makes me very happy.
With my love, always.

My family and my friends helped.

My wife Susan did her best, as wife and editor, and you can't do any better; Michael corrected my spelling; Annabel offered her good taste; David was enthusiastic, and Elinor encouraged me.

Vera was always full of good ideas, and she gave them all to me. Mira was always there to answer my questions and to tell me I was wrong, and she was also there to tell me when she thought I was right.

Bridget was fine, I could always count on her. Dick gave me very good advice when I needed it. Hilda made excellent prints in her darkroom. Jo kept her archives in order and made my work easier. Bill acted as a judge, and he was a very fine one.

Americo gave me more than he will ever know. Ira took the time to teach me. Carlos shared his scholarship with me.

John Gehlmann remembered what happened over sixty years ago and Frank Platt remembered what happened in the nineteenth century.

You all helped, and because you did, this book is a better book.

Thank you.

With all my thanks to Mary who has been a generous friend for twenty-five years, ever since we met on a hot day in Spain a week after Ernest's fifty-fourth birthday.

Mary gave me permission to choose from among the more than ten thousand photographs she owned.

Contents

one
1899–1961

October 18
Oak Park, Illin
Christening ro

Ernest Miller Hemingway
Born
July 21, 1899
Oak Park, Illinois

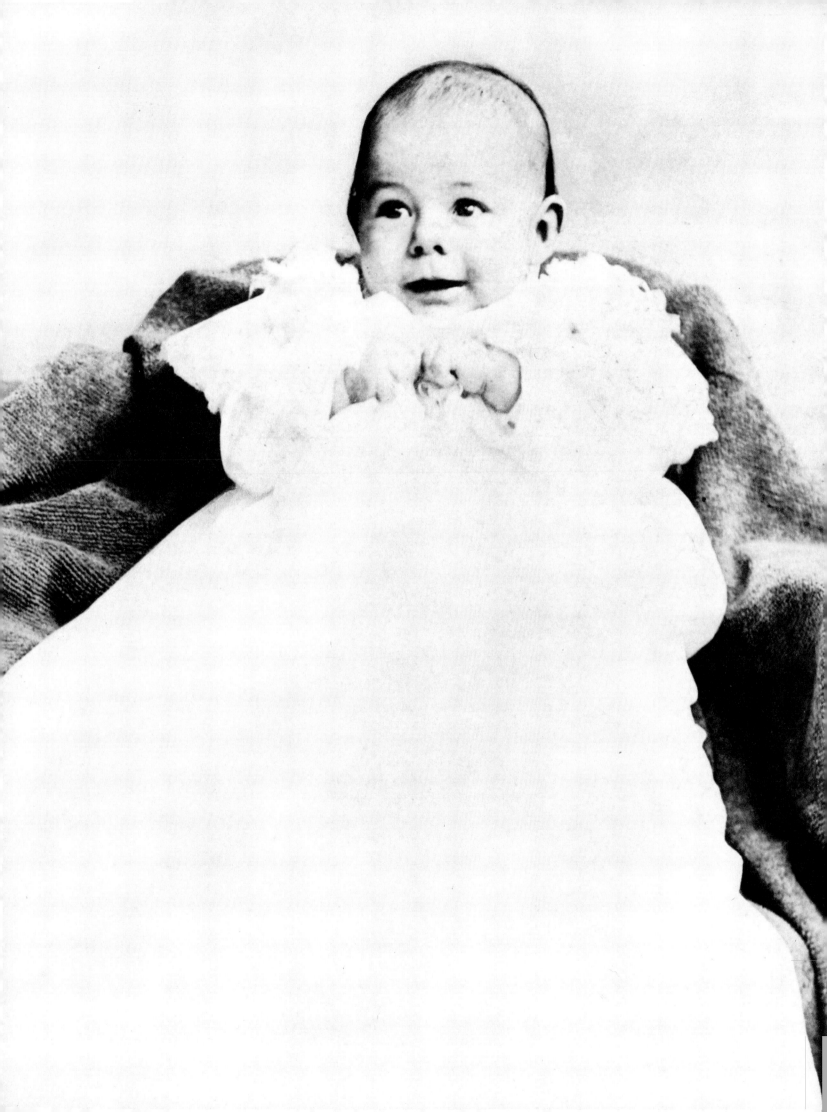

December 1899
Oak Park

July 1900
Oak Park

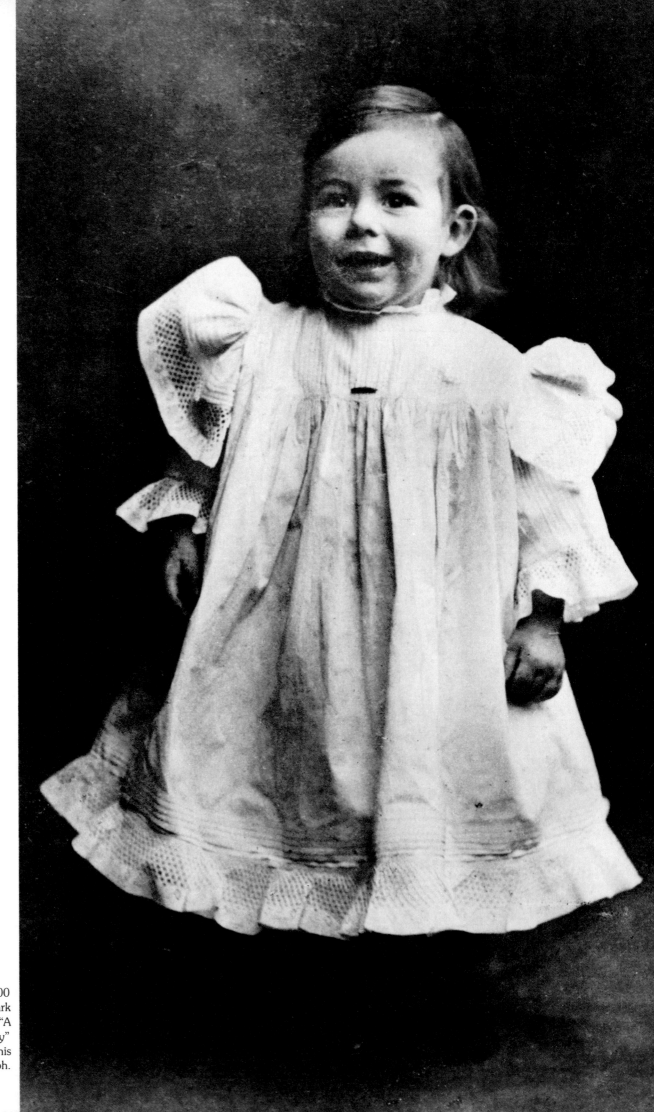

December 1900
Oak Park
Ernest's mother wrote "A
radiant little personality"
on the back of this
photograph.

June 1901
Oak Park
And here she wrote
"summer girl."

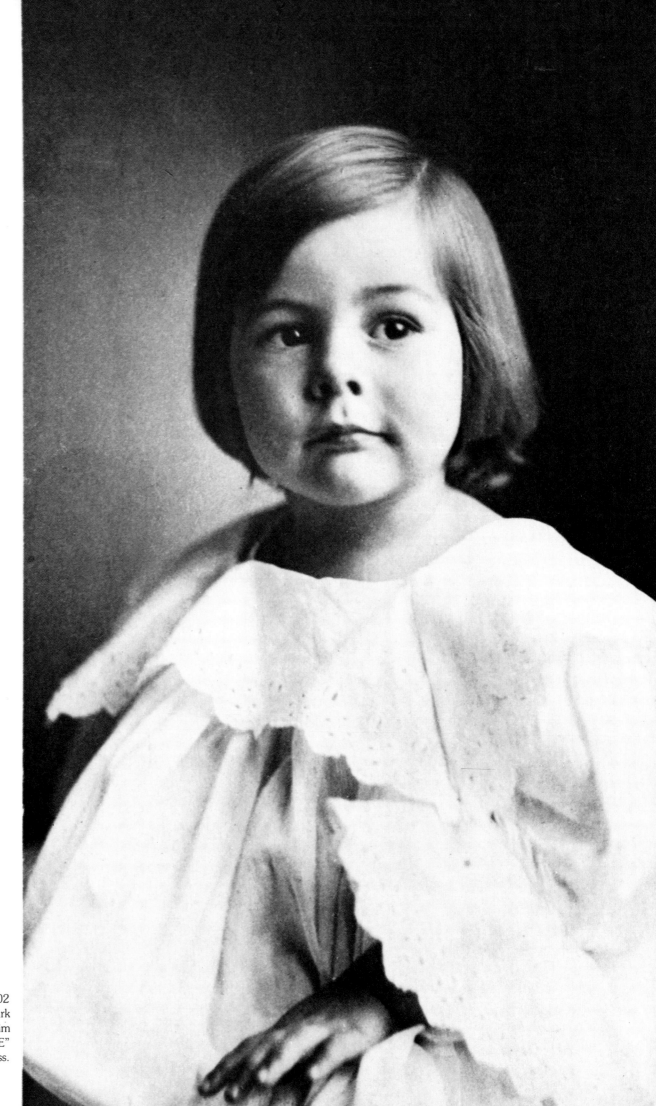

April 1902
Oak Park
His mother called him
"SWEETIE'S DUTCH DOLLIE"
in his pink dress.

July 1903
Lake Walloon, Michigan

July 1904
Oak Park

August 1904
Horton Creek, Michigan

1911
Oak Park
Third Congregational Church
Choir

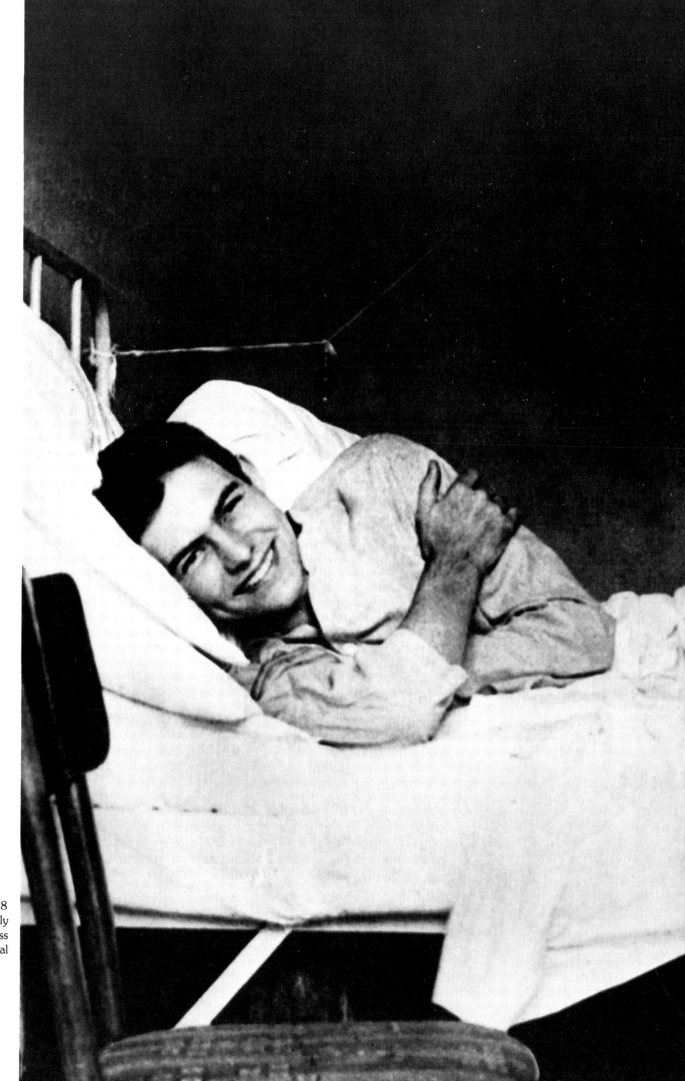

July 1918
Milan, Italy
American Red Cross
Hospital

June 1917
Oak Park
High School

August 1918
Milan
American Red Cross Hospital

September 1918
Milan
American Red Cross Hospital

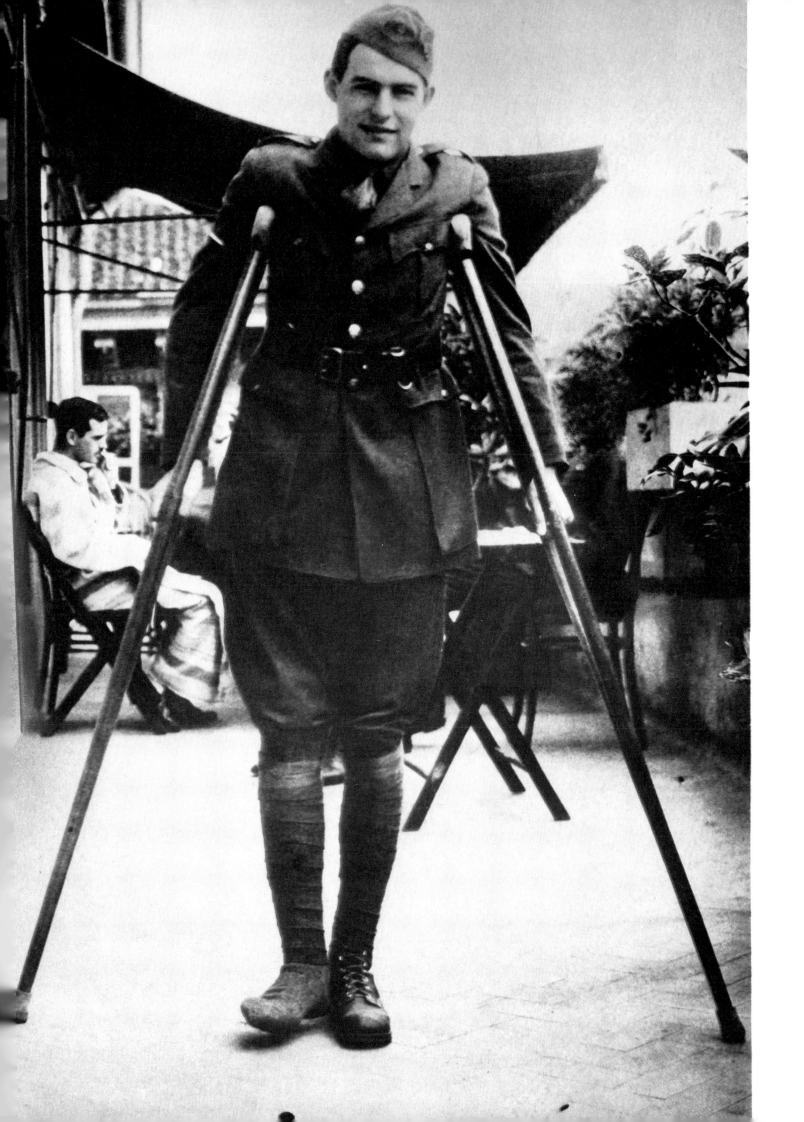

January 1919
Oak Park

October 1918
Milan

1920
Oak Park

1920
Michigan

1921
Oak Park

December 1922
Paris

1923
Paris

1923
Pari

1924
Paris

1924
Paris

1928
Chicago

February 1927
Gstaad, Switzerland

1929
Key West

1931
Atlantic Ocean
On board the *Ile de France*.

1932
Gulf Stream

1933
Paris

1934
New York

January 1934
Tanganyika, East Africa

1937
Guadalajara, Spain
Civil War

1938
Valencia, Spain
Civil War

December 1939
Sun Valley, Idaho

1939
Havana

1940
Idaho

1940
Idaho

1940
daho

March 1941
China

1942
Gulf Stream

1941
Idaho

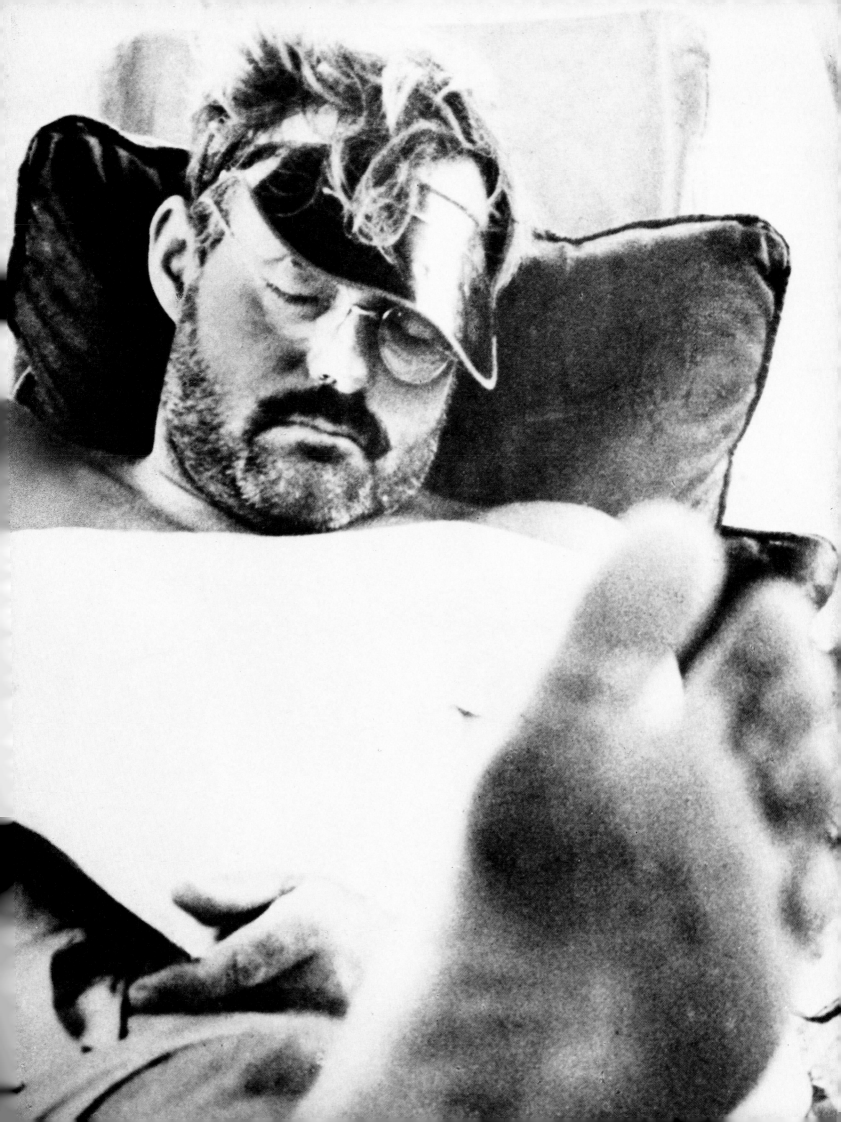

May 1944
London

May 1944
London

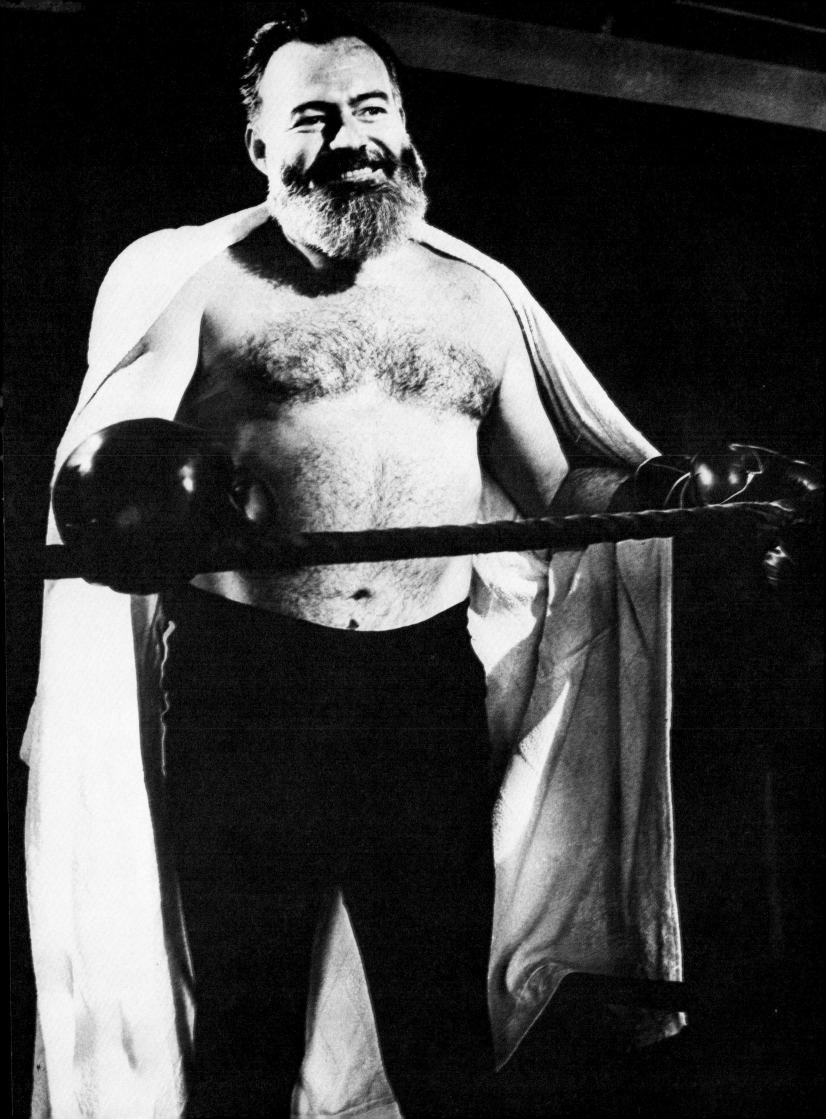

June 1944
England
Bomber base

August 1944
Chartres, France

September 1944
Schweiler, Germany

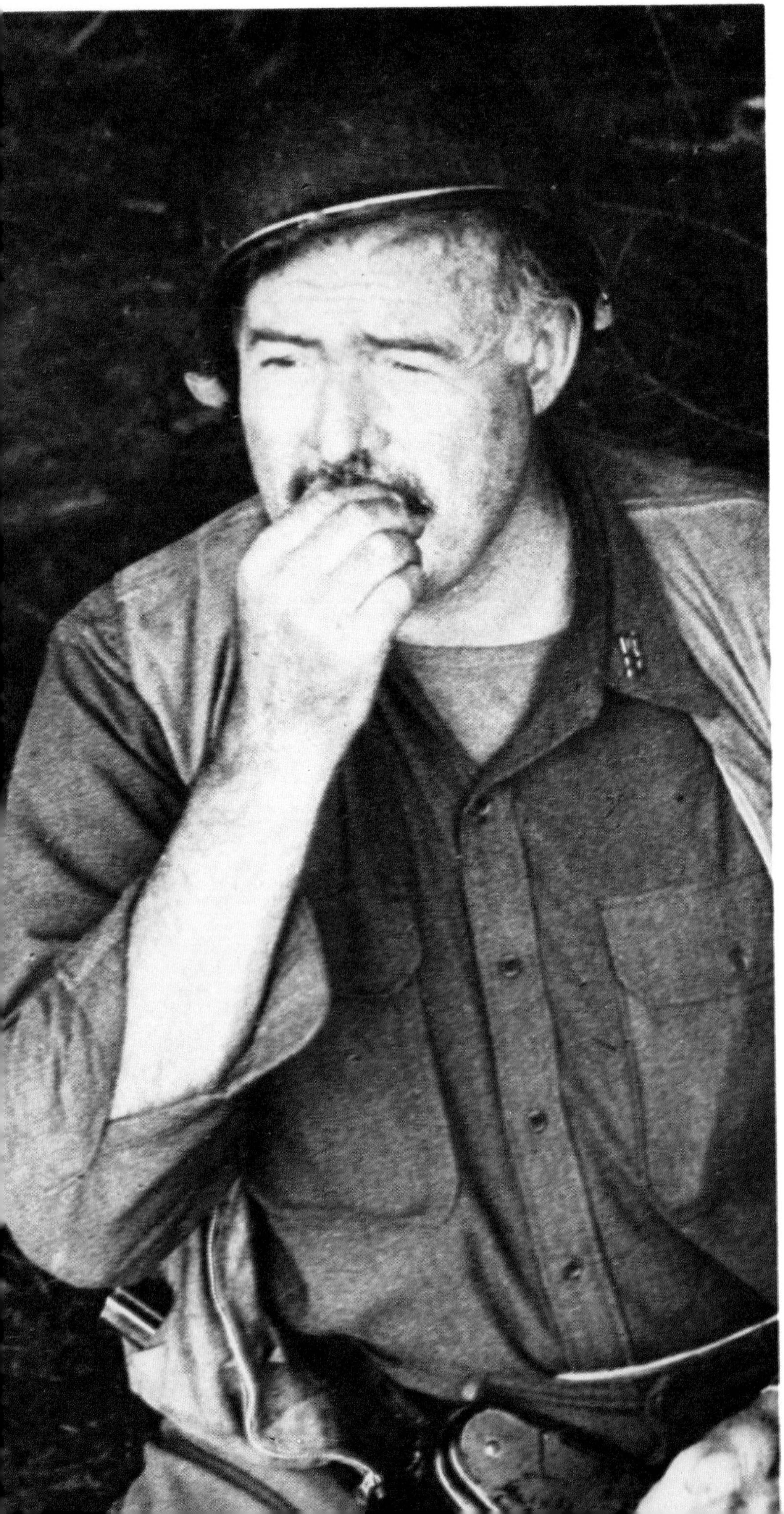

June 1945
Gulf Stream

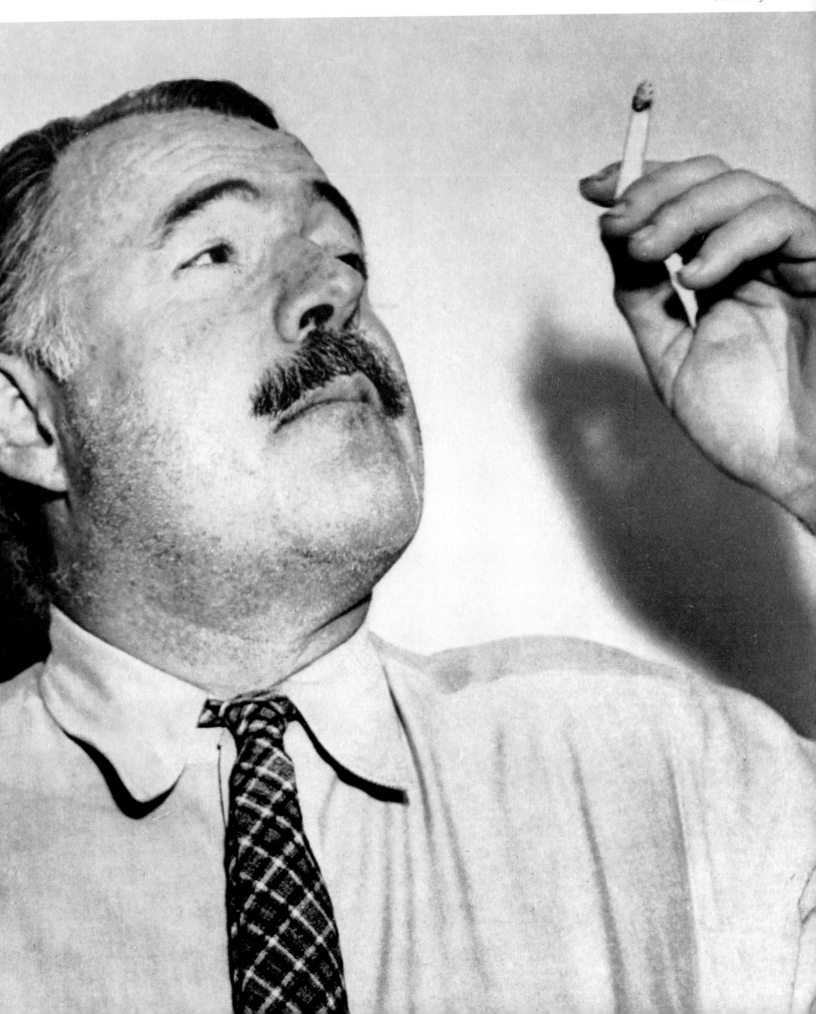

1948
Stresa, Italy

1948
Sun Valley

1949
Gulf Stream

1950
Cortina D'Ampezzo, Italy

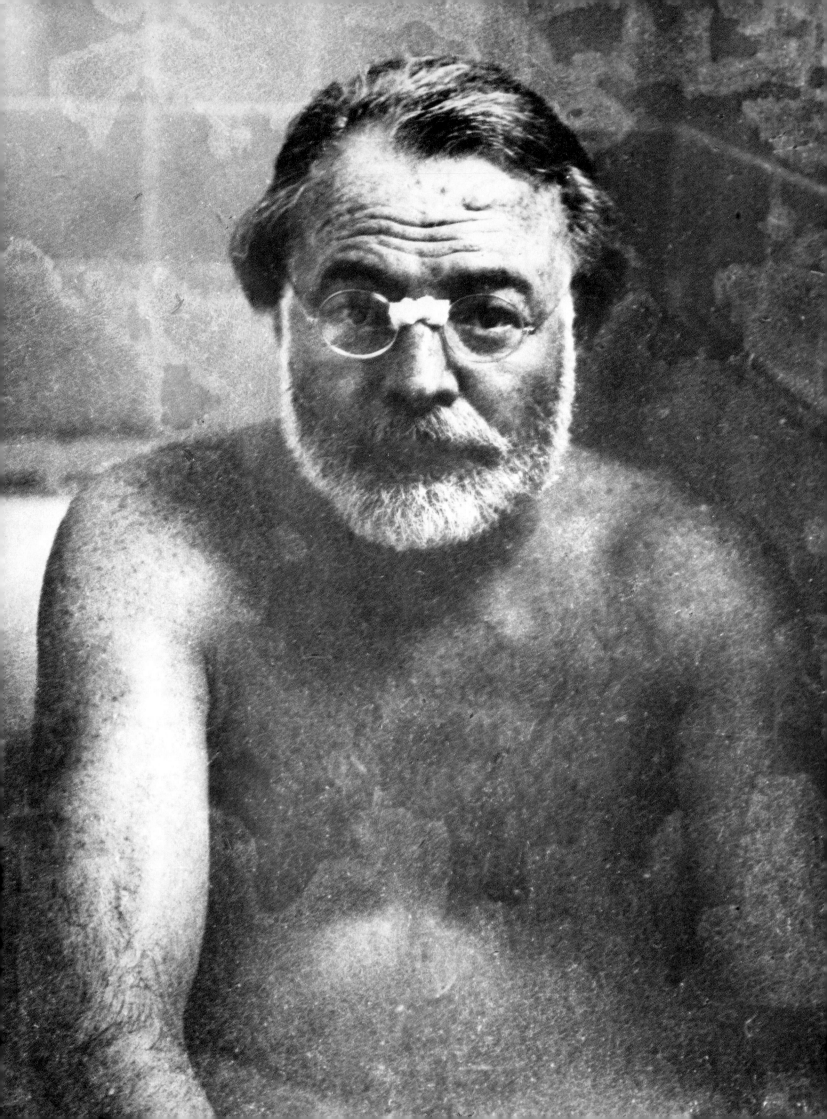

1952
Finca Vigía

1952
Finca Vigía
Cuba

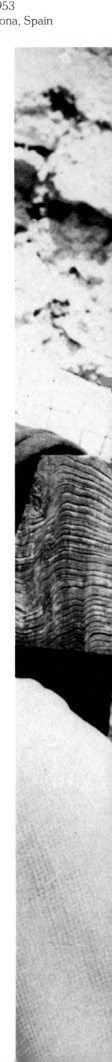

October 1953
Oleibortoto Creek, Kenya

September 1953
Kenya
On safari.

January 25, 1954
Entebbe, Uganda
day after the second
airplane crash.

ember 1953
ana camp,
ya

February 1954
Shimoni, Kenya
The day Ernest fell in a
brush fire.

1954
Mombasa, Kenya

March 1954
Venice, Italy

May 21, 1954
Madrid, Spain

1956
Finca Vigía

1956
El Escorial, Spain

1957
Finca Vigía

1956
Zaragoza, Spain

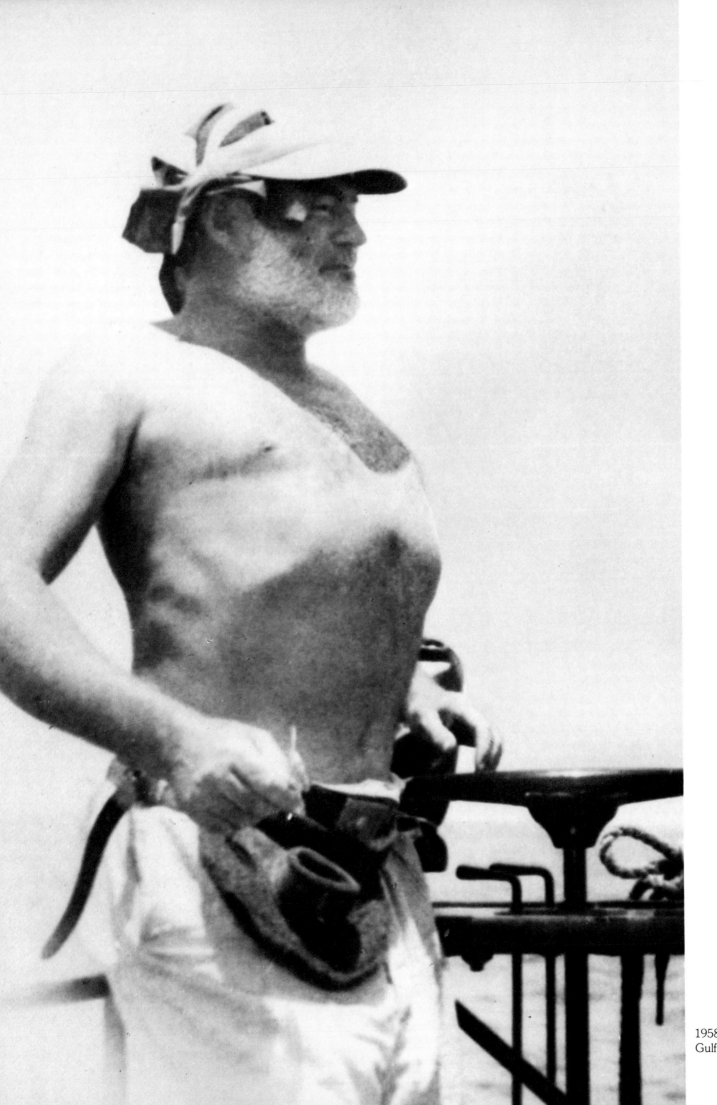

1958
Finca Vigía

1958
Gulf Stream

April 1959
New York

1958
Ketchum, Idaho

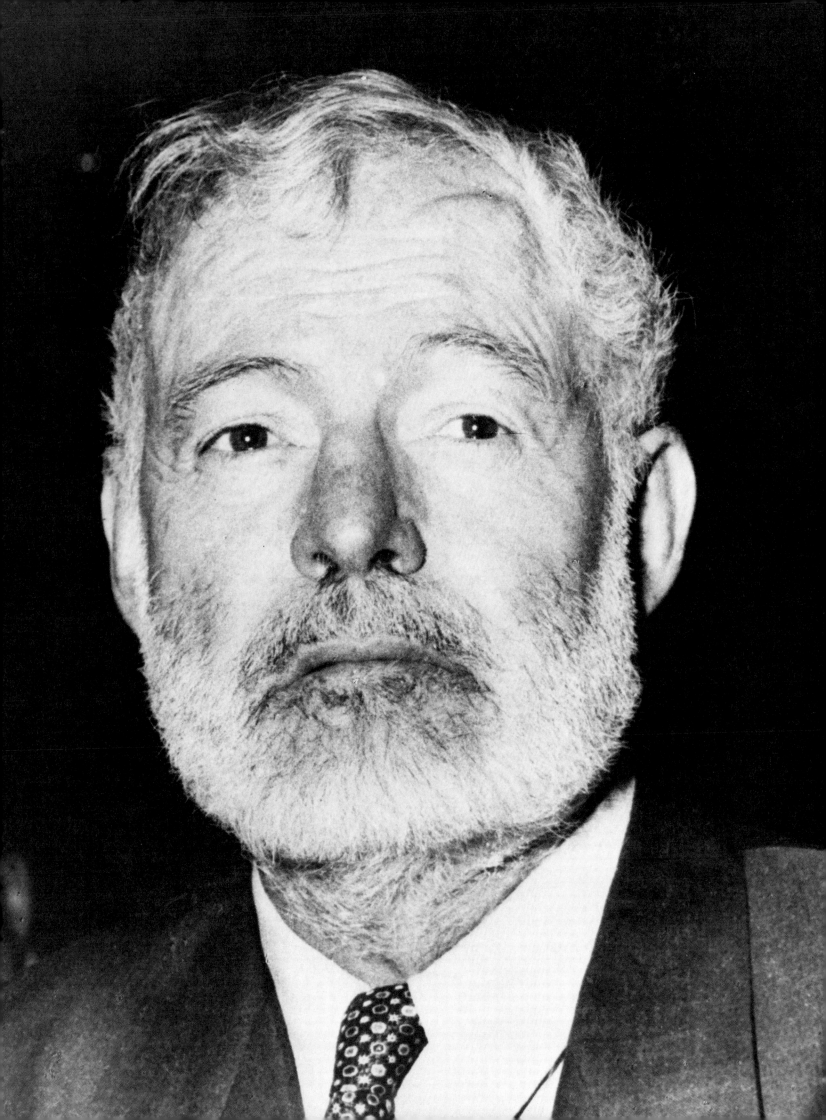

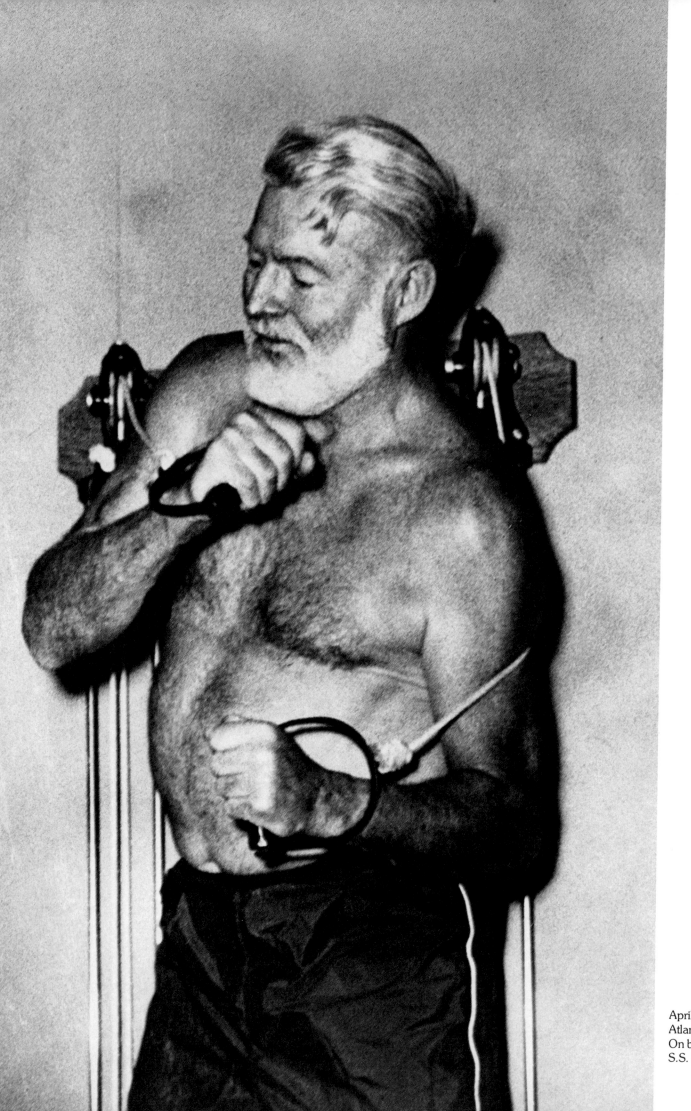

April 1959
Atlantic Ocean
On board the
S.S. *Constitution.*

December 1959
Ketchum

October 1959
Aranjuez, Spain

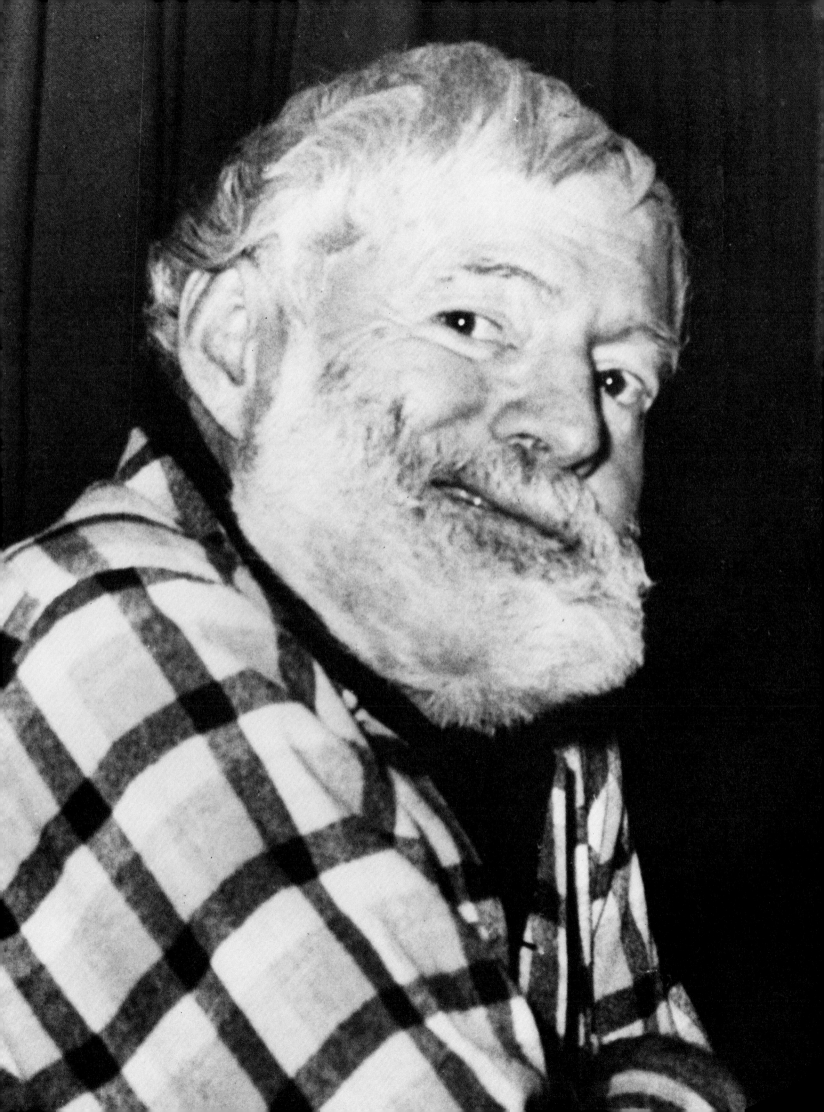

January 1960
Ketchum

February 1960
Havana

January 1961
Ketchum

November 1960
Ketchum

Died
July 2, 1961
Ketchum, Idaho

born in Oak Park. The name suited the place; an oak never bends, and a park is a special place cut off by a fence. The people of Oak Park had strong convictions and they acted as people who knew they were right.

Dr. Hemingway's father was the owner of a prosperous real estate business. He was precise in all the details of his life, both public and private. Sales of land and of houses were transacted according to the most rigid rules. His personal appearance was at all times governed by his sense of what was correct. He dressed carefully, manicured his nails daily, trimmed his neat white beard, kept an eye on his shoes to be certain they were spotless. He stated with pride that the first student at Yale University had been a Hemingway.

Grace Hall's father owned a wholesale cutlery business. His name was Ernest, after whom his grandson was named. Grandfather Ernest Hall had blue eyes and fluffy white sideburns. He wore dark suits made of the very best material, wore pearl-gray gloves and a black derby or high top hat, and often took his white woolly Yorkshire terrier for a walk. When the United States Government offered him a soldier's pension because he had fought in the Civil War, Ernest Hall refused it, saying, "I offered my services. I did not sell them!"

Oak Park was founded by a man who feared God. He built his house on the crest of a ridge, twenty miles west of Lake Michigan. He bought land on both sides of this ridge, but he never sold any without including a clause in the deed prohibiting the new owner from ever selling intoxicating liquor on his new land. Early settlers called this ridge Quality Hill. Their houses were made of the best wood, and they were painted white with dark green shutters. The women took pride in their neat flower gardens and on Sunday a lady brought red roses with her to church to decorate the pulpit. The proper dress for both the women and their husbands on Sunday was black.

Tall black oaks grew everywhere on Quality Hill. These trees had a hard, durable wood and the people thought they were the aristocrats of the entire oak family. Everyone took pleasure in the birds. "The abundance and beauty of them were quite beyond words to tell," a lady born on Quality Hill wrote. ". . . thrashers sang all day long and wood thrushes sang their whispers far away in the hushed twilight, trilling high in the topmost branches, and the orioles sung pouring out carols and madrigals."

In the deep shade of the black oaks, the people built in straight lines. Inside the houses the finest lace curtains imported from Belgium hung in straight lines from ceiling to floor. Patriotic scenes decorated the walls: The Signing of the Declaration of Independence; Washington crossing the Delaware; Thomas Jefferson addressing the Congress. Sofas and chairs were thick and solid, of mahogany or black walnut, built to last for generations. On the tables heavy yellow and brown vases held dainty ferns. Statues, representing the principal characters from the Bible, stood in corners of the rooms. Fragile lace doilies made by the lady of the house and her daughters decorated the rich upholstery. Everything was clean and in its right place.

Oak Park was quiet in 1899. The men wore high stiff collars, and they and their families prayed every day. Oak Park was safe; it was certainly safe from poverty and all the misery which poverty brings with it; it was safe from liquor and gambling, safe from prostitution and public dance halls. There were no flashing lights in Oak Park, no noisy parties at night. Only Protestant gentlemen and their ladies and their children and their servants lived there.

The churches of Oak Park were the greatest pride of the community: the Lutheran, the Evangelical, the Baptist, the Methodist, the Presbyterian, the Episcopalian, the Unitarian, the Congregationalist, the Universalist; each sect built its own church. It was not by chance that at the Oak Park city line the bars stopped and the churches began; it was not by chance that outsiders called the people of Oak Park "The Saints."

Sin was the one thing which Oak Park feared. The churches were built as fortresses in the war against sin. SIN IS LETHAL was the title of a sermon given in Oak Park. To fight the deadly enemy there was but one weapon, obedience; obedience to the laws of God, obedience to the ministers of God. The men of Oak Park thought of themselves as God's soldiers, and they had every intention of carrying out His orders.

Fathers and mothers constantly searched for sin. They laid down the rules to help their children in the daily battle: strict rules of dress, and strict rules of manners. This was the right thing to wear and that one was the wrong. A tea cup was held one way and not another. A child stood when an adult entered the room. A child said "sir" and "ma'am." A child learned what was done and what was not. He was given no chance to make a mistake. Rudeness was never tolerated and vulgarity was unheard of. Virtue was constantly encouraged and sin was forever prohibited. There were no two ways about it, you did what you were told in Oak Park and everybody grew up to be his own policeman!

All contact between individuals was rigidly controlled. People nodded politely when they passed one another. They always said, ''Good morning,'' or ''Good afternoon.'' Social calls were paid at the right time of day. Those paying calls wore the right clothes and the right words were spoken.

Young women were instructed in proper behavior not only at home, at church, and at school, but also in the press. The editor of the Oak Park newspaper, *The Vindicator,* gently warned against any open display of affection:

I may as well be frank at once and say I do not like the girl who woos. She is usurping the privilege of her knight, and if I were he I would turn and flee . . . Like flowers, the ones worth having, sweet of perfume and restful in color, are not the ones that protrude themselves on your vision, and say, as do some flowers, and some maidens, 'Take me!'

Neighbors acted as good neighbors even though they may not have felt like it, and if anyone ever got into trouble it was only talked about in whispers. On the surface life ran smoothly. Sexual words were never spoken; the word ''virgin'' was forbidden to appear in school books. There were some who felt the word ''breast'' should be struck from the Bible, while others would have preferred life if sexual intercourse had not existed. If masturbation was mentioned to a child it was only to inform him that his sin would drive him insane. On that rare occasion when a forbidden word was spoken, the child's sinful mouth was scrubbed with a brush which had been dipped in hot soapy water.

Many things seemed not to exist in Oak Park. A law of silence not only kept such subjects as masochism and frigidity from people's lips but also drove these subjects from their minds. However, there were other subjects to which people could not close their minds even though they would have liked to. Passion was thought to be a direct threat to the family, and under no circumstances did Oak Park intend to allow it the freedom to destroy; if anyone permitted his passion to erupt there was no knowing what might happen. Adultery was known but not talked about, except to damn it. Divorce was almost unknown. It was thought to be unchristian, a tool which the devil used to destroy families. Far worse in most people's minds was the fact that divorce was not respectable. It existed, but it was condemned to silence, as were the bitter feelings which led to divorce.

In Oak Park a father always knew best. His word was law. His wife gracefully submitted to this law; if she did not, she risked troubling the harmony of her family, and this was a risk few wives dared to face. In Oak Park everything was supposed to be as it should be. People did not hope that families would be bound together by love; rather they expected it, and the expectation became the rule. To violate the rule was wrong, and so women learned that it was far better to pretend they were happy than to face shame if it became known that they disobeyed.

Much of life was conducted in silence. To break this silence was itself considered wrong. Life was lived as if there was a real chance that if you didn't see something it did not exist, and if you didn't speak of something it might stay away.

The correct thing, the right thing, was never, never to touch what lay beneath the surface. No one looked in dark corners and no one ever thought that silence was a lie. Above all everyone tried to be respectable. A man's dreams, his tears, his doubts, did not count as much as the way he acted. Respectability was the virtue honored above all others. People were watchful, ever ready to drop a man or a woman from a position of respect to one of low esteem, if he or she failed. A new family in a neighborhood was examined. First their basic Christianity was judged by discovering which church they attended. Next the family's regularity of attendance at religious services was determined, and soon it was learned whether the new neighbors drank, danced, swore, played cards, chewed gum, or made loud noises.

Ernest's parents grew up in a town which approved of entertainment only in the family church. Gentle games were encouraged, games in which the players competed with one another at guessing the exact height of a flagpole, or the exact number of pins in a cup. The players knew they lived in the best of worlds and their church societies sent forth missionaries to the far corners of the globe so that they might instruct the ignorant in the correct way to worship the correct God. The members of these societies, and all those who supported their work, believed strongly in the noblest ideals of mankind; they spoke of self-sacrifice, self-improvement, and self-discipline.

Ernest's father was honest; he admitted he was a thief. He said that as a young man he and his brothers had once caught and milked a cow, without permission of the farmer who owned the cow. As a doctor, years later, he cared for the farmer's children, but he was careful to send no bill. This was his way of atoning for his sin.

Dr. Hemingway invented new surgical forceps, but he refused to accept any money for his invention. He believed that he had no right to profit from something which was created for the benefit of mankind. He was a man who had high ideals and he lived according to them.

Dr. Hemingway led his life by the rules which he had been taught; he was given no choice. He never drank liquor and he never swore. The words, "gosh" and "darn" were forbidden as being too close to blasphemy. His strongest language was "oh, rats" or "hold your horses." As a young man he was taught that card playing and dancing were evil. He not only forbad drinking and smoking in his house, but he looked upon them with disgust. Once he took his children to visit a state prison; not for the pleasure of seeing the thick walls, but to impress them with the fact that by obeying their parents they could avoid prison.

Dr. Hemingway believed in doing the right thing; he didn't talk about good intentions, but he did take care of anyone who needed his help, and if a patient could not pay, Dr. Hemingway did not ask him to. He was a man who never drew the line between an Indian woman living in a shack and a banker living in Oak Park.

He loved his children and he was a generous and a kind father. He was gay and he could laugh, but he could never compromise between right and wrong, never. Ernest sat in his father's lap, giggling and being silly one minute, his father smiling, and the next minute Ernest lay across his father's knee being spanked. Something Ernest had done, something Ernest had said, or something Ernest had forgotten to do and which his father suddenly recalled, triggered the change. Immediately, the punishment over, Ernest was obliged to kneel and implore God to forgive him for his sin; then off to his room without supper.

Dr. Hemingway was a precise man. Once a week Ernest had to show his account book to his father; the book showed that Ernest received an allowance of one penny per year of age per week, out of which it was his religious duty to make a weekly charitable contribution in Sunday school. All other transactions were also carefully entered so that an exact record of how Ernest's allowance was spent each week could be seen at a glance.

During the first years of his life Ernest lived in his mother's father's house. Grandfather Ernest Hall believed firmly in God. In his dining room at every meal there was both a prayer and a blessing, and every day in his living room there were morning prayers. Grandfather Ernest Hall knelt at a table in the center of the large room, his family and his servants surrounding him. In a strong voice he read aloud:

If we expose ourselves to the flaming purity of Jesus we are forced to admit that we are in need of cleansing. We feel the sharp lash of his rebuke. Our conscience is forced to quiver in pain, in humiliation and in shame. We may turn from his fury and flee but there is no escape.

It was made clear to everyone in the household that they were weak, that because of their weakness they needed the strength which only God could give. If, and only if, they made a true effort to gain strength from God, only then might they prove strong enough to fight sin.

Before he went to sleep each night, Ernest knelt by the side of his bed to say his prayers. In the house in which he grew up he learned as a boy that God is everywhere. Whether it was fought by God, by grandfather, or by father, the battle against evil never let up.

Grandfather Hall issued a warning when Ernest was five. If his grandson was not careful to use his energy and his imagination to do the right thing, if instead he chose to do the wrong, he would certainly end in prison.

When Ernest was six his family moved from Grandfather Hall's house into their own. They only moved a few blocks, but in the new house, as in the old, the vigil continued. Any book thought to be vulgar or violent was strictly forbidden; Dr. Hemingway refused to give permission for Ernest's sisters to study ballet, and he stated his belief that dancing schools, which taught boys and girls to dance together, led to "hell and damnation."

Dr. Hemingway was a harsh man when he thought anything was wrong; his rigid sense of right did not allow him to spare even his children whom he loved. But when Dr. Hemingway felt that all was right with the world, his children saw him become a gentle father who enjoyed sharing all that he loved with them.

Ed Hemingway loved the woods of northern Michigan; he loved the animals and the plants he found there; he loved to walk along the streams which ran through the woods and he loved to row across the wide lakes. When Ernest was a baby seven weeks old, his father took him to the lake in the woods for the first time. In 1899 it was a long hard trip from Oak Park to northern Michigan; by train, by carriage, by boat, and again by train.

On his first trip to Lake Walloon, where his father planned to build a house on the water's edge, Ernest did not stay long. He soon came back to spend the first winter of his life in Oak Park. But the next summer Ernest went back to the lake in the woods, and the next summer, and the next, and Ed Hemingway enjoyed each trip with his son.

Ernest grew to love the trip up north and he grew to love his father. Ed taught his son all he knew about the world they explored together. Ed Hemingway was a scientist and when he went to the woods he took with him the same care and precision which he gave to medicine.

He taught Ernest about the weather, about the effect it has on animals, how freezing winter winds drive bears into their dens, and how the spring thaw brings them out again. He taught Ernest about the leaves, and the grass, and the flowers, when they grow and when they die, and about which animal eats which plant. Ernest learned when the doe gives birth to her fawn, when the trout spawns in the stream, when the owl's egg cracks and a bird is born. Ernest learned the rules which govern life in the woods from his father and he remembered them forever.

The people who lived near Lake Walloon were farmers and Indians who knew nothing of the rules which were so strictly obeyed in Oak Park. The farmers planted and harvested their crops according to the seasons of the year. They stored food for the winter in their cellars so that they would have enough to eat when the heavy snows cut them off from the outside world. The trappers who went in search of furs were obliged to lead their lives according to the way the animals lived. The loggers began their work in the spring and stopped in the fall.

Over the years, as he grew from a boy into a young man, Ernest met the people of northern Michigan. He knew the farmers and he worked for them in their fields and on their farms. He knew the Indians and he went hunting in the woods with them.

Ed Hemingway liked to hunt and fish. He taught Ernest how to do both when his son was very young. Ernest was a good pupil from the start; he learned the exacting rules about how to handle a gun and a rod, and he learned to take pride in using them well. In turn Ed was proud of his son's skill. Ed enjoyed eating the game he shot, and the fish he caught; he never killed for the pleasure of the kill.

Wherever they went, Ed told Ernest the name of each thing they saw or touched, not a nursery-rhyme name, but the real name. A hawk in the sky was called a hawk, never a ''birdie,'' and if it was a chicken hawk, the fact that the bird's name came from its habit of eating chickens was made clear to Ernest, and the distinction between a chicken hawk and a fish hawk was also made. No ''bunny'' ever crossed Ed and Ernest Hemingway's path. It may have been a cottontail rabbit or it may have been a hare, but it was not a ''bunny.''

Ed explained things in a way which fascinated Ernest. By the time he was eight, Ernest not only knew the name of every tree and flower, every fish, bird, mammal, and reptile in Illinois and Michigan, but he also understood how plants and animals existed together.

Often in the summer, when he was older, Ed invited Ernest to join him on emergency medical calls. Ed Hemingway was the only doctor on Lake Walloon, and he had to treat dangerous infections, broken bones and sudden accidents. To save a man's life far from a hospital, he had to operate with simple instruments in a cabin or a barn. Ernest watched his father clean a gunshot wound and he helped close a deep cut on a boy's arm. Operations were done without anesthetic. Ernest saw and heard the wounded men's pain. Whether he was walking with his son in the woods or operating on a man's leg which had been split by an ax, Ed Hemingway made the world very real to Ernest.

As a young man Ed Hemingway had dreamed of traveling much farther than the three hundred miles which separated Oak Park from Lake Walloon. His dream took him east, across Canada and the Atlantic to the frozen plains of Greenland, and it took him west, across the United States and the Pacific to the island of Guam. He had the chance to make his dream come true, to go to Greenland or Guam as a medical missionary, but his wife said she did not wish to go. Later Ed Hemingway decided he wanted to practice medicine in Nevada where he could escape city life, but again his wife said, "No."

Grace Hall Hemingway felt she had the right to stand in the way of her husband's dream, for she believed that she had sacrificed a great career in order to marry him. Her sacrifice entitled her not only to demand her way, but to expect that her demands be met. Having paid with her career, it was up to her husband, and later up to her children, to pay her back. No one was ever allowed to default on his debt. She accepted only one form of payment: her wishes had to be obeyed.

Grace Hall never thought of her wishes as demands, but if she was crossed by one of her children, Grace Hall instantly announced that she had a "sick headache." Quickly she withdrew to her room and, as if the sudden crisis was more than she could possibly bear, Mrs. Hemingway pulled the shades and lay down to recover in darkness.

She seemed poisoned by the feeling that she had given up a career in order to have a family, and it seemed as if the only antidote for her loss of the audiences which would have come to applaud her lay in the absolute devotion she expected at home.

As a young woman, Grace Hall dreamed of appearing on great stages, and of seeing the crowds which had come to hear her voice. She trained her voice. She sang. She read the wonderful words of praise written about her. When she was in London, Grace Hall hoped to sing before the Queen and she spoke to a relative of hers, the personal physician to Queen Victoria, about giving a performance at Buckingham Palace. Grace Hall was not unlike Victoria: pious, stern with her children, forever disappointed by her eldest son, demanding, and totally unyielding. For the first eighteen years of his life Ernest was a prisoner of Oak Park; it was a maximum-security prison for those who liked to feel protected, but neither Ed Hemingway nor Grace Hall, nor anyone else in Oak Park, had invented the safe and respectable lives which they led.

Almost every settler in Oak Park was English; the name Hemingway was English; Grace Hall's mother and father were born in England. In Parliament English statesmen spoke proudly. "We happen to be the best people in the world and the more of the world we inhabit the better it is for humanity!" In Oak Park as in England the people took pride in their moral superiority. "The English Race is the greatest governing race history has ever known. We are predestined to spread over the habitable globe!" The first houses in Oak Park were built by an Englishman. The sense of his own excellence led the Victorian to look down on the world, convinced that progress was automatic, if inferior societies would only look up to him for leadership.

In England, as in Oak Park, obedience to God was the greatest virtue. "Trust in the Lord and verily shalt thou be fed." But the poor went hungry. "Fear none of those things which thou shalt suffer." But the poor lived in pain. "To suffer in silence is acceptable to the Lord!" And so silence became a rule. The poor were urged to pray, but were forbidden to strike.

In 1897 Queen Victoria celebrated her Diamond Jubilee; it was "splendid beyond imagination, a pageant, a spectacle. The Queen and all her Lords rode in triumph." But some men felt no triumph; they did not think the world was beautiful. These men broke the rule of silence and they spoke: "The horrid glimpses of a foul current of life, like a pestilential sewer beneath the smooth surface of society, make us doubt our boasts about our moral superiority. The destitute in the great towns live a life more degraded than any savage. The poor know only sickness and hunger."

Grace Hall disliked anything which disturbed her beautiful world. She hated diapers. She disliked upset stomachs, and she did not want to clean house or cook. Even though he was a busy doctor, busy paying house calls and operating at Oak Park Hospital, Dr. Hemingway was forced to telephone home and say, "Time to put the roast in the oven, Gracie," if he wanted his and his family's dinner served when he got home.

Even on vacation at Lake Walloon, Ed Hemingway's days were filled with housework. He was responsible for finding the maid to do the laundry, and seeing that she did her work. He shopped for food. He cooked himself, and he was a good cook, and he saw to it that the children were washed at meal times.

Grace Hall began her day expecting the family breakfast to be correctly served. She wished to see her children properly dressed and wished them to act with decorum at the table. Ernest and his sisters were well aware that it they failed to meet these expectations their mother might feel she had been let down and this in turn might oblige her to withdraw quickly to her room.

Ernest was very young when he found out that diapers and upset stomachs weren't the only things his mother hated. Grace Hall certainly did not want to see or smell the diarrhea and vomit of her children, nor did she wish to see the small spiders which spun their webs in her garden. Ernest watched her turn in disgust from the earthworms which crawled out of the lawn in front of their house. He watched her shy away from any false note she saw or heard, and a false note to Grace Hall was anything from a disobedient child to the fact that sometimes some people tell lies. Grace Hall refused to admit into her world anything she didn't like.

But Grace Hall loved the song of the robins; she remembered how they had sung their sweetest song on July 21st, 1899. And she loved the perfume of flowers and she loved music; above all she loved them in combination. In her mind certain flowers went with certain operas. The smell of roses reminded her of *Romeo and Juliet*. The odor of violets reminded her of *Aida,* and the strong perfume of freesia recalled the great arias of *Faust*. When she spoke of flowers and of operas, Grace Hall was happy. She could wander freely in her imagination from a masked ball given by Juliet's father in Verona, to a triumphal march in ancient Egypt. On the stage everyone wore beautiful costumes and everyone sang beautifully; lovers swore to love each other forever, and if anyone died it was only make-believe. In the end the audience always stood and shouted, "Bravo!"

Grace Hall lived as if the world were her stage. She never walked into a room; she made an entrance. She didn't walk to church; she paraded. And always, Grace Hall wore dresses which reached to the ground, like the dresses worn by the heroines in the operas she so loved, long after fashion dictated that dresses end at the knee. She gave the feeling of being a great lady. Grace Hall would not have been surprised if people had bowed to her as she passed. She would undoubtedly have been pleased if they had, and if she had received a standing ovation every day of her life, Grace Hall would have been a very happy woman.

Mrs. Hemingway wished to be pleased. She therefore expected her children to behave in such a way as to give her pleasure. When Ernest was

"2 years and 6 months old," Grace Hall wrote in her scrapbook: "He is very obedient, asks constantly whether he can do this or that rather than to make a mistake and displease." Ernest learned very young that he had better watch out. His mother wanted no trouble from him and she said so. Ernest "is really no trouble at all; as he is *so* obedient," she wrote, being careful to underline the word, *"so."* By the time he was four Ernest knew how to please his mother. She wrote, "He gives himself a whipping with a stick when he has done wrong so Mama does not have to punish."

Ed Hemingway was a very strict man, but he did not seek anything for himself when he demanded that rules be obeyed. Fingernails had to be clean, hands and face washed, back straight, elbows tucked in, shoulders back, clothes neat when one sat at the table; not because Ed Hemingway liked it, not because he said so, but because that was the right way to act! An honest man neither lied nor cheated. A gentleman neither drank, nor swore, nor raised his voice, and a Christian always honored God. These matters were not questioned. Ed Hemingway felt that it was his moral duty as a father to act in the name of the authority which ruled society.

Grace Hall was willful; she wanted rules obeyed as did her husband, but she wanted them obeyed because she said so, because she liked having her will done.

Ernest felt very differently when he obeyed his father from the way he did when he obeyed his mother. When Ernest did what his father told him to do he felt he was doing the right thing, even if he did not want to do it. When he obeyed his mother, he felt he was pleasing her. Ernest often frowned at his father, but he smiled when he looked at his mother.

His son's frown was honest because Dr. Hemingway was a hard man, hard on himself, and hard on Ernest. The smile was different because Ernest knew how much his mother wanted him to smile at her. His smile told her that everything was all right; a frown was, after all, only meant for something ugly, a diaper, a spider, or a feeling of hatred, but a smile, a smile meant that her son loved her and that her world was beautiful.

When her father died, Grace Hall used her legacy to plan a house for her family. She had been impatient to have her new home built, and she had hurried both the architect and the workers. The most important room of the new house, the one she eagerly looked forward to, was the music room which she had designed to be large enough for her to use as her private theater in which to stage her private concerts. Thirty feet wide, thirty feet long, two stories high, this music room had a balcony for the audience.

For many years this room gave great joy to Grace Hall. In it Ernest was obliged to play the cello in order to please his mother. It didn't matter that he didn't want to. He had no choice. It took a long time for her to realize that Ernest refused to become a musician; by then he had come to hate the beautiful music room.

There was a difference between the way Grace Hall felt toward the young man with thoughts and feelings of his own and Ernest, her baby. She took delight in singing lullabies to her newborn at all hours of the day and night, and she took great pleasure in keeping her baby close to her breast for hours at a time. Her baby was hers, to do with as she pleased.

When he was three and a half months old she took him with her to the Benevolent Society lunch and was overjoyed to find that "Ernest Miller . . . behaved beautifully, At 5½ months Ernest Miller shows an easy disposition." Grace Hall wrote. "He is as little trouble as a baby could be. He sleeps with Mama and lunches all night . . . He is so strong and loves his Mama so tenderly. He feels my face in the night and squeezes me so close." As a baby Ernest was not only able to please his mother when she took him to lunch with the ladies, but as a baby he was able to love her in a way which made her very happy.

Grace Hall called her baby her "Dutch Dollie" and, just as little girls love to dress up their dolls, Grace Hall loved to dress up Ernest, "in pink gingham dresses and white battenburg lace hoods." She said they "had a lovely visit" and described Ernest on the day she took him to see his aunt. He "wore his scarlet coat embroydered in black braid and a scarlet silk Brownie Bonnet trimmed in black astrachan" fur. "He looked like a little tanager," she happily wrote. Ernest easily fit into Grace Hall's beautiful world, as long as he was a baby.

It was soon apparent that Ernest wanted to be Ernest rather than a doll: "He grows indignant when I call him 'Dutch Dollie.'" Grace Hall describes an angry boy who stamps his foot and says he does "not" want to be a "Dutch Dollie" because he is Pawnee Bill and "Bang" he shoots his mother.

Until the day Ernest decided to change into gun-toting Pawnee Bill, he was a delight to Grace Hall. Her baby willingly, happily lived from breast to lullaby and back to breast again, in a dream world where everything was beautiful just the way Grace Hall wished it, a world in which "Robins sang their sweetest song," and "Ernest Miller behaved," and was "as little trouble as a baby could be."

Grace Hall's dream was like every other dream; it wasn't real; it did not include the fact that her dollie would grow up into a man, nor that this man might not always want to please her. Trouble began when Ernest stopped sharing her dream; from that time on she felt differently about her son. She never forgave him for breaking away and she never stopped trying to force him back.

Ed Hemingway and his wife were different; the most important difference was that he thought about what he could do to help people. He tried his best to cure rich and poor alike; he tried his best to teach and to live up to his own teachings. He gave Ernest his love of the earth and the sky. He hurt his son, but he loved him.

Grace Hall focused on how others could serve her. She was willing to charm people so that they would in turn be charming to her; she sang so that her audience might applaud. Grace Hall never did anything without demanding a price. A child with a will of his own was a thing she would have none of. A will opposed to her will was an unbearable reality. And, just as she quickly withdrew from any family crisis which disturbed her, Grace Hall withdrew from Ernest when she felt him move against her.

Ernest felt as if he had been told a lie. He had believed his mother loved him only to discover that she loved a dollie instead. He never forgave her.

Ernest learned what the real world is like from his father, and he learned how unreal it can be from his mother; not just how false it is, but how it tries to make others false. Each liar was busy making more liars; each person who said, "I love you," when it was not true, was forcing another to say, "I love you" when it was not true.

Ernest watched this happen to him. As he grew older his mother urged him to follow the rule that every child must say he loves his mother. Ernest resisted, but it was hard when his mother made him feel how much he hurt her by not obeying it. Her pain was her weapon and she used it. Ernest smiled and said, "I love you."

Ernest escaped from Oak Park on long hikes across the prairie down to the banks of a wild river where he fished. In Michigan it was easier to escape; he could take a canoe far out on to the lake or disappear deep into the woods; wherever he went away from home, Ernest found a world he loved. He explored this world until he knew it as well as he loved it. There was no one to make him feel that he was bad and no maple tree or hawk or trout ever lied to him. In this world Ernest was free from sin.

If he didn't escape out of the house, Ernest escaped to his room with a book. He learned from a book just as he learned in the woods, if the book told the truth, that is. Ernest was hard to fool; he was very good at discovering an author who only pretended to know. He had seen dead birds in the woods and knew that they don't always sing sweet songs. He quickly spotted any book which tried to make him think they did.

In school Ernest liked to tell stories, and he often got a friend in a corner and insisted on holding his attention while he told him one. He played football at Oak Park High, and he earned a school letter. If there was a dance at school, Ernest helped to decorate the gym, but he didn't want to go to the dance.

In English class he studied grammar, grammar, grammar. Each sentence was analyzed, word by word. Which word was the verb and was the verb a simple or a compound verb, and was this word the subject of the sentence, and was this one the object, and which word or phrase was the predicate, and was this a gerund or a past participle? These questions were asked, and answered, over and over again, until Ernest learned to know the pieces of his language.

Ernest's English class was taught in the Oxford Room at Oak Park High. The room looked like a classroom at Oxford University: tall windows made of stained glass, a ceiling crossed by sculptured beams, high-backed chairs of heavy black oak, brass sconces affixed to the walls, and directly in front of a huge oaken bench, a great fireplace gave heat to the room in winter.

A word was written on the wall, TAGARISTA, the Greek word ''best.'' The word came from the school's motto: THE BEST IS NONE TOO GOOD FOR US. At school, as at home and at church in Oak Park, the best was demanded of children; every student was expected to be proper, well dressed, neat, clean, prompt, always courteous, and respectful of his teachers. All work was to be handed in on time, and it too was expected to be neat and clean. Disciplinary problems were unheard of, but a watchful eye was kept.

Ernest wrote stories which were often read in class. He also wrote for the weekly school paper, but the principal of the school did not like what Ernest wrote. Every week Ernest wrote, and every week the principal complained. He said that what Ernest had written was offensive: too slangy, too colloquial. Every week his teacher stood up for Ernest and told the principal that he thought the boy should be allowed to write as he chose, not because he found what Ernest said to be wonderful, but because he felt Ernest had a right to say it in his own way. Then the teacher added the fact that the children very much enjoyed what Ernest wrote. He said they thought it was real, which only annoyed the principal further.

The principal was afraid of what people would say if they read something distasteful in the school paper. He combed the weekly ''Joke Column'' in the paper to make certain that no joke had a double meaning. And sometimes he found one where none was intended. And he worried about Ernest's stories.

Parents watched the school carefully to make certain that their children were taught by men and women of high moral character. The teacher who stood up for Ernest every week came under suspicion in 1916 when it was discovered that he enjoyed Charlie Chaplin; one mother wondered what kind of an influence such a man might have on her children.

Ernest liked action. He never just sat around; he wanted things to happen. If nothing much was happening he would stir something up, to see what people would do. Ernest sometimes said a forbidden word and then waited to find out what would be done about it. Usually his mouth was washed out, but sometimes he was lucky. Once, during a school concert, he deliberately snapped a string on his cello in the middle of a sonata just to see the reaction it would get.

And Ernest loved the Greek myths in which gods and goddesses leaped back and forth from one mountain top to another, and from the sky to the earth and back to the sky again, in which islands floated across the waves only to be anchored to the bottom of the sea by pillars made of diamonds, in which Zeus threw thunderbolts and in which heroes were always heroic, stories of ancient Greek battles which told of clashing swords on land and sea.

In the crowd at a football game on a cold November afternoon, Ernest stood with his friends and shouted his school song:

OAK PARK RAH
OAK PARK HAIL
RAH, RAH, RAH,
ORANGE AND BLUE, WE'RE LOYAL TO YOU.
WE'RE STRONG AND BRAVE AND TRUE.
WE NEVER FAIL.
OAK PARK HAIL
TAGARISTA RAH
TAGARISTA

The best, only the best was good enough for Oak Park. They not only fought for the best, they thought they were the best; in their opinion no higher social class existed than their own. They did not measure their rank by anything so vulgar as money, nor anything as accidental as birth; instead they chose their moral respectability as the supreme good. According to this rule, they judged all men. Sometimes they were criticized. There were those who said that Oak Park was a place of broad lawns and narrow minds. Such criticism was quickly rejected by saying, "Even if narrow-minded, we are respectable."

Grace Hall believed very much in the best. The motto of her ladies' club was, WHY STAY WE ON EARTH UNLESS TO GROW. Together the ladies agreed that they would strive for "the promotion of higher social and moral conditions," and united their efforts "toward the higher development of all humanity."

Grace Hall never let a day go by without making certain that Ernest knew how devoted she was to these ideals. She never forgot to reprimand him for a lack of self-control, often saying, "Remember, that he who ruleth his spirit is greater than he who taketh a city." Or, if she found him doing nothing, she would say, "There can be no idle hands in God's Kingdom." Ernest's life was filled with his mother's urgent hopes and instructions. "I hope you make your life count for the best things," and "I hope you are growing every day in Strength of Character." Ernest was given no rest. "I trust you won't disappoint me or the grandparents in Heaven who are watching you," and "I am counting on you in this wonderful day of opportunity."

Improvement was not only on Grace Hall's lips, it was everywhere. Since the founding of Oak Park, the need to improve had been the one theme of life; the need to improve the drainage ditches, the police department, the schools, the streets, the gardens, and the need to improve the self in a Christian way. Oak Park was concerned with ridding the town of garbage and ridding the soul of sin.

No one ever tried to improve the prairie or the woods where Ernest loved to go. Every fall when the hunting season opened, he and his father loved to go away together. They tramped through the woods and Ernest continued to learn everything he could from Ed Hemingway. What his father knew and believed in were very real to Ernest. He often disagreed with his father and he was often hurt by him, but Ernest loved him and respected him.

Ed Hemingway didn't deceive himself and he certainly didn't try to deceive Ernest; it was often obvious that he and his wife did not get along well. Grace Hall expected her husband to bow to her wishes just as she expected Ernest to; it seemed as if neither husband nor son could ever do anything to please her. Grace Hall, however, did not allow anyone to find fault with her.

It made Ernest sad that his father did not stand up to his mother, but there was nothing he could do to help. It was easier for him to escape than for Ed Hemingway. Ernest could read for hours at a time in his room on the third floor in Oak Park; in Michigan he could sleep in a shack instead of in the family house.

As a boy Ernest had hated being toyed with; as a young man he hated being told to improve himself every day. Above all he hated the fact that his mother demanded from others what she refused to give them. She constantly spoke of spreading "universal love" when she was not a mother to her own children. If her husband could not find the time to be both a father and a mother when they were on vacation in Michigan, she expected him to hire a girl because her children were too difficult for her to handle. And she expected her husband to be not merely a father and a mother and a doctor, but a cook and a housewife too, for Grace Hall could not trouble herself to do anything she did not like to do. She often spoke of "harmony," but the only harmony she understood was the pleasure she felt when others did as she told them. She talked of happiness, but she didn't try to make anyone happy; she wished to be pleased, but she gave no pleasure.

Grace Hall smiled as she walked slowly to church on Sunday morning and there was no more obviously devout member of the First Congregational Church in Oak Park. At home, a gracious hostess, it pleased her greatly to think that guests spoke well of her, and that they were delighted to attend the recitals which she gave in her lovely music room.

Grace Hall believed "the Robins sang their sweetest song"; she believed humanity could be more highly developed; she believed that she lived in a beautiful world and she believed that hers was a day of wonderful opportunity. She dreamed only of victory and joy.

When she wrote, "October 1st 1899, Doctor and Mama walked up the aisle and carried Little Ernest Miller as an offering unto the Lord to receive his name and be counted as one of God's little lambs," Grace Hall didn't dream that one day over two hundred pieces of metal junk would be driven into her son's flesh. She didn't dream that machine-gun bullets would smash him, and she never thought that seeing so many men die, her son would feel that it made more sense to die than to live.

Grace Hall was happy on the day she sat in her father's big house on Oak Park Avenue writing about the birth of her baby. It was hot in late July, and the windows of the room were open; outside, the leaves and the branches of the oak trees covered the lawn in shade. Only the sound of a carriage passing on the avenue, or a fly, or some children playing next door, could be heard. Ernest lay asleep in his crib; a light blue comforter hung over the side. Before he had gone to sleep, his mother had sung him a lullaby; now she listened, as she sat writing about the first days of his life, to hear his cry if he should awake and want her breast. "Ernest Miller slept for 48 hours after he was born," she wrote. "One week old he took a liking to a nursery rhyme, 'Robin the bobbin.'"

Then Grace Hall listed the names of family friends who had sent presents to her baby. First the names of those who had sent him flowers, among them Miss Jennie Dupuis who sent "a basket of sweetpeas." Next, Maude Wilson who "sent a dainty lace bib," and Mrs. French who "sent a gold bib pin."

Aunt Hattie Hemingway brought pink socks to go with the pink kid shoes which another lady sent. And "Grandma Cherrie sent Ernest Miller his 1st silver spoon marked E.M.H. in the bowl. Grandpa brought a silver mug lined with gold."

As she wrote, Grace Hall never dreamed that Ernest Hemingway would one day write, "The worst . . . were the women with dead babies. You couldn't get the women to give up their dead babies. They'd have babies dead for six days. Wouldn't give them up."

I find it hard to make Ernest live, even with all the words and the thousands of pictures to choose from, and even though I feel sure about what I think and feel.

I knew him. This is what makes it hard. I am too aware of the difference between words and pictures on a page and Ernest eating an onion sandwich on a picnic in the mountains near Madrid.

High above us the wind was steady and the pine trees bent in the same direction. We made our sandwiches as we ate, slicing the hard onions into thick slabs, wrapping the bread around the slabs, eating the sandwiches with black olives and red ham and cold wine. We hoped that the weather in Zaragoza would be better for the bullfights than it had been in Logroño where it had rained almost every afternoon.

"You need the sun," Ernest kept saying between mouthfuls.

I want to pick him up, all six feet, 210 pounds, and put him here. You could shake hands with him then. Ernest would look at you carefully and he would listen to you carefully. The two of you could work things out.

You could eat onions together, get mad at each other, drink, fight, fish, argue, go to the races, decide to live in Paris, wonder about the Gulf Stream, hope you wouldn't get hurt if you got into trouble. Or you could look at a painting and say nothing.

You would learn, if you got to know him well, that Ernest wanted to write the truth more than he wanted to do anything else. And you would find that he hated anything phony.

If only I could put him here, but I can't and I have to be your witness, and my words and my pictures—my choices—must stand in place of Ernest.

I liked him and I hope you will, but even more I hope you will understand him. The danger exists that you see Ernest as the famous Ernest Hemingway. It is unfair to see him that way because fame makes you blind. Of all the people who seemed to like Ernest, many liked his fame more than they liked him. The fame exists; I don't deny it. I just want it kept in its place. Though it is real and important, his fame should not be allowed to hide Ernest.

Ernest Hemingway wrote stories which are read by millions, but so have others who are not famous. He won the Nobel Prize, but so have other men whose names mean nothing. His name made the headlines; so do others. He shot lions and buffalo and he caught marlin and tuna, but so can anyone if they can pay the bills. He went to many bullfights and he saw five wars, but think how many people go to bullfights and how many more go to war. Yet he is a famous man.

"What was he like?" I don't like the question because I can't say what anybody is like in a couple of words. I feel that I am expected to unlock the mystery of the great writer or expose his intimate life. I am not polite. I don't answer. The idea that there is a quick and easy way to explain a man makes me angry and I find the idea of exposing a man rude.

A few never ask and sometimes I say to them, "Ernest was the most enjoyable man to be with I have ever known, and he could be the exact opposite."

Ernest liked to wear the same old tweed jacket for years, and he once decided to harpoon a whale. After killing the whale Ernest planned to inflate it, to keep it from sinking, by using the pump he kept aboard his boat for his air mattress, and, having done the impossible, Ernest planned to enter Havana harbor in triumph.

Ernest asked the name of any stranger who came up to him with a request that Ernest sign a copy of one of his books, because he felt the stranger deserved a personal dedication, not a hurried autograph, and Ernest took care to spell the name correctly and write it legibly.

He let the fat from the bear meat he was eating drip into his beard when he was on a hunting trip in Wyoming. And he spent more than two hundred days in one year fishing in the Gulf Stream, and once he bought ten thousand shotgun shells before going to shoot in Idaho.

And Ernest cried when he drove into Paris on the day the city he loved more than any other was freed from the Germans.

And he saved his wife from death by dictating the exact emergency procedures to be followed by the doctor who gave up all medical treatment, and told Ernest his wife was about to die.

Once, when he was a little boy, Ernest had said he was "afraid of nothing," and as a young man he wrote "my breath would not come" in a letter describing to his parents how he had almost died when he had been wounded by the explosion of a shell in the First World War.

And later, years later, Ernest made jokes about his reading his own obituaries, which he said was a "new and attractive vice." Ernest had the chance to know what the world would say about him after he was dead, because he was thought to be dead after he had been in two plane crashes in one day. He said that many of the obituaries stressed the fact that he had sought death most of his life and he asked whether anyone thought that if a man was looking for death he could not have found it long before reaching the age of fifty-four.

Ernest explained that though he had been near death and had often seen death, this did not mean he had ever wanted it. Ernest said, however, that he had studied death. If he had not, he would have broken his own rule which said that he must only write about what he knew, truly knew from his own experience. Ernest said that all stories, if carried to their conclusion, end in death; he was therefore obliged to study the way in which all stories end.

And he used to say that studying a Cézanne still life of pears and apples taught him as much about how to write as any poem, and he used to organize a day of fun in Paris, a day of eating and drinking and betting at the racetrack with the precision of a general planning an attack, and at the racetrack Ernest wanted to win.

Ernest made very clear what he wanted to do. First, he wanted to make his readers see and feel what he had seen and felt, and secondly, he wanted to enjoy himself. He concentrated on both.

Ernest loved to read. When he was a boy his mother listed the books he read and liked. As a man Ernest traveled with a special suitcase for books, and he constantly ordered books sent to him wherever he was, and he looked forward to reading them the way some men look forward to a special bottle of wine. He was sad after he had read a book he loved very much, for it meant he could never again read it for the first time.

And Ernest loved the sea and how he felt when he was on it. He loved the waves and the fact that they are never the same, and he loved the glass calm, knowing that soon the glass would break into new waves. Ernest studied the waves which would carry him to harbor or drown him, depending on the skill of the captain. He knew the colors, the blue-black of the deep ocean, and the blue-white of the shallow, sandy bottom. The straight white line told him there was a reef; the dark patch warned him of rocks. Different colors also meant different fish and Ernest could tell you where the fish lived and he could tell you the colors of the fish and their habits, and he could tell you about the clouds which drifted above the sea.

Ernest loved the mountains, the feel of the wind blowing down a valley. During the day he studied the earth and he learned to read it. The hills in a landscape told him where water flowed, from where it came, and where it went, and even how fast it flowed, and the trees told him where certain birds nested, and the ponds told him where other birds landed. He knew which rocks gave shade to animals seeking to escape the sun, and he could tell which holes sheltered animals. During the night Ernest watched the stars stretch across the sky and he listened to the animals moving in the dark.

Ernest hated. He hated people who pretend, those who try to seem what they are not. Ernest called them phonys and his contempt for them lasted his lifetime.

In his twenties in Paris, Ernest worked very hard. He knew he would never be able to write well, write stories which would last a long time, unless he spent hours alone every day working at a job which demanded more than he could give because the job was so hard. He was a young man when he found out that he had to go way beyond himself if he hoped to do what he wanted.

Ernest almost never spoke about the art of writing; instead he wrote, but there were others in Paris who only spoke of their art and of themselves and of the great pains and the great joys which they associated with the process of creating.

Ernest said the most difficult and the most complicated subject to write about was a man's life; he knew this, he said, because he was a man. I wish I did not agree with him.

How did people see Ernest? If I tell you that some saw him as a bear, and others as a rabbit, you will realize how hard it is to know what he was like; no harder, of course, than knowing what you and I are like. Some said "genius," others said "ox," some said "gentle," others said "bully." Am I to decide for you what he was like, or am I to give you the facts and let you decide? But then I can pick facts, good or bad facts, and only pretend to let you decide.

I can also choose the words in which I dress the facts. If I say, "Ernest invented stories about himself," you won't think too badly of him, but if I say, "Ernest exaggerated stories about himself," you'll begin to think less well of him, and if I say, "Ernest lied about himself," you'll condemn him.

Ernest called himself "Ernie Hemorrhoid" and "Dr. Hemingstein," and once he told an army psychiatrist that his most serious problem was the fact that he could not stop himself from having intercourse with his cats.

Ernest was a man. Was he a genius? Ernest was intelligent; he concentrated very hard, really very hard, he had some luck and a lot of imagination and he was not afraid to go where no one had ever gone.

Ernest never displayed his intelligence; he displayed very little of what he was; he was not a showman; he did not want his private virtue and his private sin to be seen by the world. Ernest was generous, a helpful man, but he didn't want to talk about it. He was envious and greedy and he wished he was not; he was afraid and he didn't like it; he wanted to do the right thing but he found it was very hard. Was Ernest kind or was he mean? He was both, if kind is delicate and sensitive; if mean is hurtful and brutal.

Ernest made big muscles and he punched hard, but a few punches tell you nothing about him. Ernest was a man who had to win, and when you know why he had to, you will know a lot about him. He was also a man who had to watch his weight, a man who had a favorite belt, who liked whiskey mixed with lots of fresh lime juice, who was happy in Venice, unhappy in New York, a man who was a strong swimmer, who suffered many concussions, a man who lived from 1899 to 1961.

None of us can fit into a frame and Ernest was a man who very much disliked being made to fit. But of this you can be certain, Ernest never missed a thing; he was always aware. He never stopped looking at the world around him. He wanted to see.

On the eastern coast of Spain, downtown in Valencia, behind the bullring, exactly a week after his birthday in 1953, Ernest and I went to the *apartado* at noon. At the *apartado* it is decided which bulls will be killed by which matadors later in the afternoon. Ernest had seen many *apartados* before. Nothing had changed in the thirty years since he had first gone to Spain. Ernest knew the exact ritual. He had been the first to describe it accurately in English, and yet he watched and listened as if he had never seen an *apartado*. He didn't speak unless he was spoken to, and when he did he spoke softly. He stood still, only moving when others moved. He concentrated on the *apartado*.

He felt the rough bark of a tree. He flicked some peeling white paint off the walls which formed the corral where the bulls were kept. He watched the representatives of the matadors when they examined the bulls, and he stepped into the corral and studied the bulls himself. He watched the men speaking to each other and smiled when one of them made a joke. It was hot in the sun and not much cooler in the shade. Now and then Ernest wiped his glasses. The *apartado* lasted a half hour.

Before leaving the bullring, we stopped in the patio where the horses are made ready for the bullfight. Ernest knew the broad, heavy, tough mattresses which have been hung on the picadors' horses ever since they were first used in 1928. Long ago he had described them in detail in his book on bullfighting. He nevertheless ran his fingers slowly over the surface of a mattress, tested the material to see how strong it was, measured its thickness, asked the stable men questions which demanded precise answers, and listened carefully to their words.

Later, in a café on the main square, we talked about the bulls; their weight and how their weight was distributed, whether it was in bone or muscle or fat, whether it was mostly up front or in the hindquarters, and what the results of this distribution would mean to the bullfight. We agreed that the one gray bull was the biggest.

We discussed the size and the shape of the horns of each bull, speaking of the bulls according to the numbers branded on them. We talked for a long time about the *apartado*.

Ernest never spoke of anything other than all the things he had just seen.

He said that he had never before smelled jasmine flowers in the corrals of a bullring, and I remembered the moment he had taken his eyes off the bulls to look at the small white flowers on the vine which climbed over the wall next to him.

We bet a thousand pesetas on whether or not the gray bull would weigh over six hundred kilos. I said yes. Ernest said no.

Ernest wanted to see everything. He wanted to see the animals and plants, the earth, the ocean, and the sky, and he wanted to see people, and all the wonderful and terrible things which people do.

Ernest wanted to know, needed to know so badly that he never stopped looking, and he never looked with another man's eyes. He had to know with certainty, and there was no greater certainty than seeing with his own eyes. Why did he need to know, to know with such certainty what the world was like, and once he knew, why did he have to write about it?

Ernest believed there is a great difference between the way life is and the way we are told it is. He believed this because he spent his first eighteen years in a make-believe world which tried to make him think that life was one way, when life wasn't that way at all. And so, Ernest felt that he was being lied to.

Too many people spent too much time telling Ernest how he should live; they complained about his language; told him he should not enjoy boxing and hunting; they insisted he keep away from wars and bullfighting, and they said that he had the wrong kind of friends. A literary man, it seemed, must not have bartenders, boxers, and bullfighters as friends. The trouble was, Ernest did not think of himself as a literary figure, but rather as a man doing a hard job who saw no reason to restrict his friends to the higher professional classes in order to please people who had no decent business of their own to mind.

Not only did Ernest have the wrong friends but he wrote about the wrong people. Indians and soldiers, whores and waiters, it seemed, did not merit the attention of an artist.

Ernest was called names. He was a brute if he shoved, as if anybody who ever shoved was a brute. He was a drunk if he drank too much and made noise, as if anybody who ever drank too much was a drunk. And if he was ever rude it was called inexcusable.

Ernest was also a quiet, a polite, and a shy man, who tried to obey rules. You never shot an animal from a car. You did not pay a dishonest hunting outfit to guarantee you an easy shot at a drugged animal. You tried to kill an animal quickly. If you wounded him, you followed him until you found him and killed him, even though you exposed yourself to danger. You did not call a fish your own unless you caught it without help. You did not cheat, tiring out the fish on your line by using the engines of your boat to drag the fish through the water.

And there were rules about dress. You dressed in a manner so as not to offend those around you. In Havana, Ernest went downtown in loafers with no socks because it was all right, but in a small provincial town in Spain, Ernest wore a jacket and a tie to the dining room of a third-rate hotel, because he felt the people of the town preferred it.

And rules about life, about accepting bad luck without complaint, about keeping promises and honoring obligations, about saying you were sorry, if you really were, whenever you could bring yourself to say it, and, if you couldn't, being sorry inside yourself.

When it came to the fight for survival, Ernest felt strongly for the wounded. A wound was worth a thousand medals to Ernest; he knew what a wound felt like. He could not forget his own when he had felt his life go out of him; and he could not forget the shrieks of all the wounded he had heard on all the battlefields he had seen. To Ernest a wound was proof that a man had fought. There was no such thing as a make-believe wound. A wound was real and reality was what Ernest was looking for. To see it, to know it, to write it as he saw it, so we could see it too.

"Why fight to see reality?" you ask. "It was easy for Ernest to remember what six bulls looked like five minutes after he'd seen them," you say. You are right. It was easy. If you can concentrate, if you know on what to concentrate, if you are free to see what there is to be seen, to hear what is said and how it is said, free to know what there is to be known instead of what you have been told you must know, and free to feel what you do feel as opposed to what you have been made to feel, then it is easy.

Whether it was six bulls on a hot day in Valencia, or a blue marlin on another day in the Gulf Stream off Havana, or an avalanche in the Alps, or a woman in Michigan giving birth in pain, Ernest tried to know what he saw. Reality was good, even if it hurt; only a lie was bad.

The first step was to see; the next was to tell you and me what he had seen, to make us feel it so that we would know what Ernest knew.

If that does not sound like an ideal goal for a great writer, it is because Ernest did not pick an ideal goal. Instead, he chose to see clearly and

write clearly. That was the job he gave himself, and he thought it was the hardest job in the world.

Once we spoke about ideals and Ernest said what he thought:

"People talk a lot about them; that way they don't have to do anything."

Ernest left us his words, written words, plain words, put together with care. They tell us what he saw during his life.

"Obey my voice," Grandfather Ernest Hall read. Ernest was kneeling beside his mother. "I will be your Lord. Walk ye in all the ways I have commanded you." Ernest had knelt on the same floor and heard the same voice almost every day of his life. "Obey that ye may be free of sin!" The words changed from one day to the next but the message did not. "Say a continual 'yes' to your Father's will." These same words were read aloud on Oak Park Avenue and in England.

Ernest was taught, "To be silent is acceptable to the Lord," and he was urged to "consider the lilies of the field." It was pointed out to him that "the little white flowers grow and smile" and never ask for anything. But Ernest didn't want to watch lilies, and he didn't want to be silent. He wanted to see what was going on around him and say what he felt about it. It was not easy.

As long as she could remember, Grace Hall had heard her father reading aloud of "the little white flowers we see in the spring opening their bosoms to drink in the sun's glory." Grace Hall thought the words were beautiful; it made her happy to think of the flowers "rejoicing in a calm rapture, diffusing around a sweet fragrancy, standing peacefully and lovingly." If it wasn't flowers, Grace Hall listened to her father read about the "thrush that built his nest to feel God's love," or about "the inexpressible joy to look through apple blossoms, to look beyond to the bright blue depths of the sky, and to feel they are a canopy of blessing."

Grace Hall dreamed of flowers and thrushes and joys. She dressed Ernest up like her doll, but he wanted to go fishing.

Grace Hall shared the Victorian dream of happiness for all mankind, but it was only a dream in Oak Park, just as it was in England. In Chicago, right across the street from Oak Park, poor immigrants from Eastern Europe worked for eighteen

110

hours a day, at four cents an hour. Three-year-old children helped their families earn enough money to keep from starving.

In England the poor "huddled together like whipped beasts"; in the United States the poor were "wretched, overcome with exhaustion, hunger and disease, many lives were broken, many rubbed out like dust."

An American nurse who saw life as it is, and not as it is supposed to be, who made the lives of the poor immigrants better, who worked very hard in the slums, with no hope of reward beyond the reward of knowing she had helped someone in pain, a woman with no theories, who never shrank from a wound, this nurse wrote about her work.

She began her story with a question. "Have you ever seen a hungry child cry?" In eight words she did what all the Victorian ladies in London and Oak Park never did; she touched something real! She asked, because to her the most important thing of all was to see; the first step toward helping was to see.

Ernest would have liked the question; he would have liked it very much. He spent his life seeing. If it had not been for Ed Hemingway, Ernest might never have seen the world.

By the time Ernest graduated from Oak Park High in June 1917, he was a strong young man, six feet tall. He had begun to write because he enjoyed telling stories; he wanted to write down what he had seen and how he felt about it, but even though it sounded easy, he found this was hard to do.

In Oak Park, Ernest had learned to be careful not to say what he felt or thought; the rules said he should behave this way, and though he disliked the rules, he found that often it was best to obey them even if he disliked them. He found table manner rules, and how to dress for church rules easy to follow; they didn't really matter, because they had nothing to do with him; he obeyed. But rules about how he was supposed to feel and think, rules which no one ever really said were rules, but which he knew were rules, these were hard to obey, and hard to fight; hard because they involved him in ways he didn't want to be involved, and hard because it made it difficult to know things about himself which he very much wanted to know.

What should he do if he hated somebody but knew he shouldn't hate? What was he supposed to say if he felt someone was lying to him and he knew that if he said they were lying it would hurt them and he had been taught never to hurt anybody?

How did he tell somebody he loved a lot that they were hurting him when they didn't really mean to hurt him? How did he know if he loved anybody or if he hated them?

And he didn't know what to think of people who always tried to make him think their way. And he didn't know how to know what was true and what wasn't. Was the world always beautiful? Did everybody really love each other? Could all mankind be improved? Ernest was caught and he wanted to get out.

What was real and what wasn't? It wasn't true that Ernest and his older sister were twins, but his mother pretended they were. It wasn't true that Ernest was a girl, but his mother wrote that he was. It wasn't true that it was Ed Hemingway's fault that his wife did not enjoy the applause of the crowds, but she blamed him for it. It wasn't true that Ernest's mother was better than other people, but she acted as if she were, and it wasn't true that she spoke the truth, though she thought she did. Grace Hall was born into a make-believe world.

When a magician saws a pretty girl in half, the girl smiles because she knows how to twist her body to avoid the saw, but the boy whose mother insists her son is something to play with doesn't know the game, and he can get hurt. Make-believe is fun when everybody knows that's what it is. Ernest didn't start out knowing; it took him time and he got hurt before he learned.

Ernest was very young when he found out he had to hide his emotions. Grace Hall did not wish to see her son's pain, nor did she wish to see the far greater pain which this gave him. Grace Hall enjoyed seeing Ernest smile.

If it hadn't been for his father, Ernest might have been caught forever in make-believe. Ed Hemingway lived in a way opposite to the way his wife lived. While Grace Hall sat discussing the improvement of mankind at her ladies' club, Ed Hemingway stood at the foot of the delivery table in the hospital trying to save the life of a woman and her baby. While Grace Hall sang in her beautiful music room, Ed Hemingway fed the rabbits and the chickens in his backyard, and when, late in the afternoon, Grace Hall was walking slowly down Oak Park Avenue wearing her new ostrich-feather hat, her husband was busy canning fruits and vegetables in the kitchen.

Ed Hemingway taught Ernest exactly how to use an ax; exactly how to build a fire; exactly how to tie fishing flies, and he showed him how to build a shelter to protect himself from a storm. Ed Hemingway taught Ernest with precision; he left no room for error. Neither forceps nor fishing rods were toys in his hands.

By the summer of 1917 Ernest had made a choice; he spent as much of his time as possible fishing and hunting and camping with his friends, far from Oak Park.

Ernest had to make another choice after high school; he could join the army or he could go to college, or he could get a job. Ernest decided not to go to college, and his father decided he should not go to war right away. Ed Hemingway turned to his brother Tyler who lived in Kansas City; he asked him if he could find a job for Ernest on a newspaper.

When Ernest was told he would have to wait till fall before going to work, he was glad. It meant he could spend one more summer in the northern woods, canoeing slowly down quiet rivers, fishing in the wide lakes, cutting hay, planting vegetables. As he lay in the grass by the edge of a stream after a quick dip in the cool water, watching the leaves and clouds moving in the wind, it was impossible for Ernest to imagine the war in Europe which was turning men into mud.

By October 1917 Ernest was glad to leave for Kansas City; he wanted to be on his own. His father cried and said a prayer when he kissed Ernest good-bye at the railroad station.

Uncle Tyler met Ernest, and the next day Ernest was offered a job as a reporter on the *Kansas City Star* at $15.00 a week. His uncle's house and the neighborhood in which it stood resembled Oak Park. After only a few weeks Ernest moved out and into the small apartment of a friend and, for the first time in his life, except for the days he had spent camping, Ernest was free from his family.

He was a happy young man. He talked a lot; he wanted to please people, and he was liked. At work on the *Star,* Ernest asked questions. He wanted to know: how reporters found their stories, how they interviewed witnesses, how they chose the most important facts, how to keep out of trouble, how to be certain you were right or wrong and, of course, how to write a story. Ernest had always been shown how to do things by his

father, and he carried his need to know how, exactly how, into his job.

He learned on the *Star* that professional reporters stated the way things are. They did not ramble on about how things might be if this or that were true; they declared what was. The idea was to tell the readers what had happened, but first a man had to go out and find what was happening.

Ernest liked his work. He wanted to be where there was action. He covered a police station and a general hospital. Up to now, escape had always been in the direction of the prairie and the woods; now it was toward the streets of a big city.

There was a lot to see in Kansas City, and every day Ernest went out to find it. He wrote about smallpox victims, accidents, and violent crimes. He talked to butchers and bartenders, truck drivers and cops, drunks, boxers, con men, whores, railroad porters, trolley car conductors, and cowboys, and he listened to what they said and he remembered what they told him. Ernest knew he wanted to write and he knew he only wanted to write about what he had seen and heard. The more the better, in his mind.

The biggest action in the world in 1917 was the World War in Europe, and Ernest wanted to join it. He was rejected by the army because the vision in his left eye was poor, but by Christmas he had decided to drive a Red Cross ambulance at the front. At the end of April 1918, Ernest left the *Star,* took the train to Chicago, spent one night in Oak Park, traveled to Michigan where he wanted to fish once more before going to war, rushed home, said good-bye, and went to New York.

In New York he passed the Red Cross physical exam, bought himself an expensive pair of leather boots, paraded down Fifth Avenue in front of the President of the United States, and, on the morning of May 23rd, sailed for Europe on a French ship. In Ernest's mind he was sailing to see a great game being played by two great teams.

At night Ernest looked up at the stars and down at the sparks of phosphorescence which shone on every wave. During the day he watched the flying fish and the fast porpoises. He loved the calm water and the fact that he could see forever in every direction, and he loved a storm at sea. Ernest knew there were German submarines under the waves waiting to torpedo his ship, and he asked if they would see one. Ernest was in a hurry to go to war.

He landed at Bordeaux, took a night train to

Paris, hoped to see the city being shelled, heard one shell land near him, and within a few days took another train south. Crossing the border into Italy, Ernest and the other Red Cross drivers joked and sang and enjoyed the lovely ride through the beautiful country on their way to war.

Ernest arrived in Milan ready to rescue wounded soldiers at the front, but within a day of his arrival, what looked like a battle front lay at the edge of the city. A large munitions factory had exploded, scattering the workers into ten thousand pieces. Ernest was sent to help clean up. In a field in northern Italy he was obliged to pick the bloody remains of Italian workers off the strands of the barbed wire fence which surrounded their factory.

Two days after the explosion Ernest took a train to Vicenza. From there he drove in a Red Cross ambulance to Schio in the foothills of the southern Alps. Ernest waited for the action he had come to see, but the front was quiet near Schio, and the beautiful scenery didn't interest him. Ernest drank more wine than he ever had and forgot that he was committing a "lethal sin" every time he did, but Italy was different; it was harder to sin in Italy than in Oak Park.

In Italy those rules which forced people to hide their feelings in Oak Park did not exist. No one was ashamed of his feelings; in the streets men even followed women and spoke their feelings, and if the woman didn't like the man she ignored him, and if she did like him she smiled. There were few rules to keep people from doing what they felt like doing. When they wanted to, mothers and fathers hugged and kissed their children a hundred times, and when they were angry they smacked them. In an argument the person who yelled loudest felt certain he had won, and almost nobody ever thought he was wrong.

If a poor man faked his feelings for a rich man, everybody knew he was faking, and they knew the reason why. If the customer said, "These shoes are no good," the shoe salesman knew the customer was only trying to get the price down. Nobody pretended that people didn't do what they weren't supposed to do; a bribe in Italy was often necessary if you wanted to get something done.

The enemy increased the attack along the Piave River, east of Schio. Ernest asked to go to the Piave. He was assigned to a Red Cross canteen in the town of Fossalta on the banks of the river.

Nothing happened for a week, even though now Ernest could hear the guns. He talked to the men who fought in the front line at Fossalta and he grew restless. It was July, and in a few weeks he was going to be nineteen. Ernest wondered if he would ever see action.

The 8th of July was a hot day. Late at night it was still hot when Ernest took postcards, cigarettes and candy to the soldiers in the trenches. He said he had come to be with them.

Across the Piave an enemy mortar crew fired a shell in a high arc over the river. Ernest was hit. Hot metal cut into his legs and he fell. His boots filled with blood. Next to him a man was killed. A few feet away another man cried. Ernest stood. He carried the wounded man back, but he fell again when bullets from a machine gun hit him in the right knee and foot. Again Ernest stood, and again he carried the wounded man. His own blood mixed with the blood which poured from the man on his shoulder, until Ernest was covered in red. He was close to death.

He prayed. He saw the dead. He heard the dying. He was given morphine to stop the pain. He spoke to the wounded and he was blessed by a priest. The doctors took some of the metal out of his legs, but they left a lot which they couldn't quickly cut out. A week later Ernest was sent to a hospital in Milan.

Ernest liked the hospital. There were lots of nurses and they took good care of him. Two machine gun bullets were removed from his right leg, one from his knee, the other from his foot. He wrote home to say he was fine and not to worry, and that he was glad to find out he might win a medal; the Italian Army wanted to honor him for having carried a wounded man when he himself had been badly wounded.

In Chicago, Ernest was a hero; the newspapers described his courageous act. Ernest was very glad to know that he was being taken so seriously. He even told his family that being wounded was "the next best thing to getting killed and reading your own obituary."

Ernest described how he felt when he was hit: "I tried to breathe, but my breath would not come." The fact that he had come so near death at Fossalta seemed to make Ernest stronger, as if he had won a fight he had never expected to win. To die, yet not really die, was a dream that Ernest would always have.

113

In August, Ernest fell in love with one of the nurses. Agnes von Kurowsky was a tall American girl from Washington, D.C. Agnes loved Ernest in return, but she was not as sure of herself as he was; Ernest said that Agnes was meant for him, and that he was meant for her. He spoke of marriage, but she backed away. They went to the races together when Ernest's legs were better, and Agnes carried a picture of Ernest. They kissed and every day Ernest grew more confident.

Ernest had seen the horrors of war; he had found the action he wanted at Fossalta; he was a wounded hero, and he was in love. He was proud of having behaved correctly when he was hit, proud of Agnes, proud of his courage in the face of constant pain. In the fall of 1918 nothing seemed impossible to him. When Agnes was sent to another hospital, she and Ernest wrote each other every day, sending all their love back and forth between Milan and Florence.

There also were letters from Oak Park wanting to know when Ernest was going to come home. These were difficult to answer, because Ernest did not want to go home. Instead of saying it, he wrote about death, and about his wounds. He had, Ernest told his parents, faced death and not been found wanting, and now he was a First Lieutenant about to be awarded not one, but two medals. Ernest made it clear to his family that he was not the same young man who had left them only a few months ago. He felt differently about himself now, and he expected them to behave differently toward him as a result. The metal pieces which the enemy mortar had driven into him at Fossalta were real, and as if to nail this down, Ernest made certain that in Oak Park they understood just how important his wounds were to him, as if his wounds were the supreme decoration which could be given to a man.

He described the distinguished officer's uniform which had been cut to his exact measure by the finest military tailor in Milan, and he spoke of the wound stripes which were sewn onto this uniform. Ernest was proud of the stripes; they proved he was a man, not just a man who wore a uniform, but a man who had been to war. Ernest felt that a wounded man could never be doubted.

In October, Ernest put away his crutches and began to use a cane. Milan was too quiet; he wanted to go back to war, and so he went to Schio, but Schio too was quiet. Ernest went east to Bassano to join his friends who were carrying the wounded from the battle on Mount Grappa. He was not allowed to drive an ambulance, but Ernest could watch and he could listen to the war. He stayed up at night to see the artillery barrage. He limped during the day to watch the troops advance in the morning, and he watched them retreat in the evening, and everywhere he went Ernest saw the dead and the dying and the wounded. In November the war ended and the killing stopped.

Ernest and Agnes met now and then, depending on the city where Agnes was sent. They loved each other, but they were apart for Christmas and in January Ernest sailed home from Genoa.

He arrived in New York a war hero to be interviewed by the press, and the next day he took the train to Chicago. Ed Hemingway met Ernest at the station with tears. It was cold and the ground was covered with snow. The heavy front door of his house closed behind Ernest; Grace Hall was waiting.

Ernest was back in Oak Park, but he was homesick for Italy. He wanted Agnes; he did not want to lie on his bed and read letters from her. He did not want to live in a house where he was forbidden to drink, to smoke, forbidden to say what he wanted. Ernest hated hearing the word "no." He had grown used to sitting around a table for as long as he wanted at the end of a meal talking to his friends about whatever he chose, his legs crossed, the waiter ready to serve him another brandy if Ernest raised his empty glass, ready to light his next cigarette, ready to bring him a newspaper or call a shoeshine man. Ernest had become accustomed to men and women enjoying his company, and to enjoying theirs. He couldn't stand sitting at the table at home being watched; he couldn't stand feeling locked up by the rules. Just as before, Ernest escaped up the stairs to his room on the third floor, but the room was too small for a wounded man.

He lay on his bed and remembered: the Atlantic, Paris, the Alps, Italy. He thought of flying fish, and French food, and red wine, and all his friends, and kissing Agnes, and he thought about how proud he had been to wear the wound stripes on his new uniform when he went to the racetrack in Milan with Agnes, and how much fun they had had, even though the horses they picked didn't win. It had been a beautiful day. From the track they had seen snow on the mountains in the north, and after the races they had driven slowly back to Milan in an open carriage.

And Ernest thought of Fossalta, of the explosion which had killed the man next to him. Ernest didn't know what to do in Oak Park. He had brought home some Italian flares among his souvenirs and he exploded them in back of his house. They burst high in the sky, but they didn't help. At Fossalta, Ernest had gone to the edge and come back; now he had nowhere to go.

Ernest lived in the past. He wore a ring in which a piece of the metal which had been driven into his legs at Fossalta was set like a jewel. He wore his uniform, his Italian Army cape, his army boots. He limped because his legs still hurt. He wrote to Agnes. He dreamed. It was true that he had been wounded at Fossalta, but it was also true that he was back in Oak Park.

Ernest was invited to speak about the war at Oak Park High. He spoke, and he showed the uniform he had worn at Fossalta on the night he was hit, as if the holes torn in the cloth by hot metal might make forty high school boys believe that war was real. At a local pool where they all went swimming after his speech, Ernest showed the boys his legs. They boys were even more impressed by his scars than they had been by the uniform which Ernest had so carefully brought all the way from Fossalta to Oak Park.

Ernest said he was not a hero; he said that all the heroes in the war were dead. He had only done his duty, nothing more, but he did want it known that he had done that. His sister Marcelline talked to Ernest about the war, about their mother who said she had known Ernest would not be hurt in the war, and about their father who had worried about his son.

Marcelline said that in Oak Park she felt protected from the real world where people get hurt; not until Ernest had been wounded did she realize what war meant. Together they remembered the stories which Grandfather Hemingway had told about the Civil War. His stories had made them believe that war was an exciting adventure; he had always spoken of "our glorious army," and "our brave boys in blue," as if everybody had been a hero, as if war itself was wonderful. Marcelline thought that Ernest's wounds made war sound disgusting.

Ernest was happy when new Italian friends from Chicago said they wanted to come to his house in Oak Park. They knew, his friends said, that he had been decorated for his bravery by the Italian Army, and they too wanted to honor him. A party, they announced, was the best way to express their feelings; a party which they would give in Ernest's home.

They came, and they brought too much of everything with them, but too much was just what Ernest wanted: lots of red wine, lots of loud talk, lots of spaghetti, picnic baskets which were too full, violins, guitars, mandolins, and a pianist who was overjoyed to find Grace Hall's Steinway piano. First, the friends hung a large Italian flag from the balcony in Grace Hall's music room, then they unpacked everything.

The Italian chefs immediately moved into the Hemingway kitchen where they began to cook. The members of the Italian Opera Compay sang arias as loudly as if they were on a real stage instead of in a house in Oak Park.

Wine glasses were raised. "VIVA ERNESTO!" they shouted, "VIVA! VIVA! VIVA!" They drank a toast to Ernest. "VIVA ERNESTO!"

They said they were happy to be in Ernest's home, proud to be able to celebrate his return from their country. Everybody danced, everybody sang, and for blocks around everyone knew there was a big party at the Hemingways. Ernest was reminded of the good times he had had at Schio, but no one in Oak Park was reminded of anything they knew or liked. Ernest had never before spoken Italian in Oak Park, and never before had Oak Park seen or heard such a party. Military songs, punctuated with a chorus line which imitated the sound of an artillery barrage, boomed through the house.

Ernest was happy. His friends were happy. They said they were disappointed by only one thing—the Hemingways had not invited enough of their own friends. This was too bad, they felt, because they had brought enough food for twice as many people.

Ernest's friends were generous. After the singing, and the mock artillery fire, and the dancing, they served a large meal: great bowls of spaghetti, a mountain of meatballs, great platters of sliced ham, a huge fish salad, a dozen cheeses and many cakes, and there was more than enough red wine for everybody.

The first party was such a success, Ernest's friends promised that they would soon return to give a second party in the lovely big house of their friend Ernesto. VIVA! VIVA!

They kept their word. At noon a few Sundays

later they all arrived. The second party was an even greater success than the first. The friends filled the house. The neighborhood was once more aware that the Hemingways were entertaining.

This time Ernesto's friends stayed all afternoon, all evening, and on through the night into the early hours of the following morning. They were as generous, as friendly, and as happy as before. A few fell asleep in odd corners of the house.

It was all too much for Ed Hemingway and Grace Hall. They was outraged. The Italians had proven themselves to be a public nuisance. They had offended. Ernest was told, "No more parties!" and that was the end.

VIVA ERNESTO!
VIVA!

Ernest felt alone, cut off from everything he wanted. He had really enjoyed the parties. If he ever thought it was possible for his family and neighbors to enjoy his Italian friends, he had quickly found out he was wrong. His friends hoped to come back; they didn't know how Oak Park felt about them. Ernest never invited them again.

"Don't be afraid, Sis," Ernest said to Marcelline. "Don't be afraid," he warned her one day in his room. "Taste this," he said offering her a drink of a liqueur. Marcelline hesitated. "Taste everything, Sis." She drank a little. "Taste it!"

"And don't be afraid to taste all the other things in life," he urged her, "all the other things that aren't in Oak Park." Ernest had never spoken to his sister like this before. "There's a whole big world out there full of people who really feel things." Ernest wanted her to believe him. "They live and love and die with all their feelings."

Marcelline remembered telling Ernest how safe she felt in Oak Park, how she had shared her mother's conviction during the war that Ernest would never be hurt. Listening to Ernest talk about "people who really feel things," she understood why her pain had been so sharp on the day she learned that he had been wounded. It was as if he suddenly became real to her, as if his wounds, which might have killed him, had made him come alive. And she thought about how war had once seemed wonderful, but how she knew now that it was terrible.

"Sometimes I think we only half live over here," she heard Ernest say. "The Italians live all the way, Sis, don't be afraid. There's a big world

out there, people really feel, they live, they love, they die. Live all the way, Sis."

Marcelline remembered Ernest's words; she wondered at night if he could ever again live in Oak Park.

In March 1919 a letter came from Agnes telling Ernest that she had fallen in love with an Italian Army officer. Ernest was hurt by the news; he went to bed sick with a fever and a feeling of being empty. A few days later, when his fever went down, he was in a rage. He hoped Agnes would hurt herself, but there was nothing he could do. In every way the war was over now, except for the fact that Ernest often thought about it.

He told Marcelline he could tell her stories about "what some of those guys I got to know in the hospital had been through," but Ernest neither told stories nor did anything else. He slept late every day, took long walks, read everything there was to read, and then he went back to the river which ran across the prairie. He canoed slowly, trying to forget everything that hurt.

In the spring Ernest began to write stories again. He piled them up; he read them to his friends, and he took them all with him when he went back to Michigan for the first time after the war.

In July, Ernest was twenty. A year ago he was lying in the hospital in Milan; a year ago he was kissing Agnes. Now his legs were almost healed and he was back fishing in the north woods. All summer Ernest kept away from Oak Park. In the fall he went back for only a few days, and then only to tell his family that he was leaving to go north again to write during the winter. At Christmas he came home, but early in January he left for Toronto.

A Canadian family had invited Ernest to be a companion to their lame son. Ernest enjoyed their billiard room, their private skating rink, and he liked their large comfortable mansion, but Ernest needed action. Sitting around having a good time was not enough. Ernest got in touch with the *Toronto Star,* and within a month his first article appeared. Between February and June 1920, ten more articles were printed under his name, for which he was paid a penny a word.

Ernest tried to sell the short stories he had written the year before in Michigan, but he had no luck; he could sell articles to a newspaper, but he couldn't sell the stories to magazines.

Ed Hemingway wrote his son to say that Grace

Hall was suffering emotionally, and that he very much hoped Ernest would want to come home to visit his mother and stay for a while before returning to Michigan for another summer. Ernest went to Oak Park, but only for a couple of days, and only to get himself ready to leave again. Driving north with a friend, Ernest dreamed of sailing across the Pacific in the fall, to India and China.

On camping trips that summer Ernest was happy; friends, a campfire, a tent, fishing rods, a river, a moon, cigarettes, whiskey and loud songs; happiness was easy in the woods; at home it was impossible. When Grace Hall came to Michigan to spend her summer, she expected Ernest to stay with her and do her chores around her house. Ernest had no intention of doing this. He wanted to do what he wanted to do, with his friends, on his time, and in the place he chose. He was also willing to help his mother now and then.

But Grace Hall said that Ernest was "not a constant comfort to his mother" and this angered her. She withdrew to the complete isolation of Grace Cottage, which she had built so she could be alone on a hilltop; a cottage to which she could escape to avoid a husband "who got on her nerves," and children who were "always noisy and troublesome."

Twenty-one years of pain came out in the summer of 1920. Grace Hall insisted she was right; she insisted her husband agree with her, and she insisted Ernest do exactly as she told him; nothing else would satisfy her. Ernest had hoped to enjoy his summer. The fight was between Ernest and his mother. Ed Hemingway was torn between his wife and his son, and his sense of justice.

Because Ernest was in Michigan, and unemployed, he was supposed to paint, dig, sweep, carry, wash, repair, cook, clean, saw, drag; whatever might be demanded of a servant around a summer house. Grace Hall said she had a right to all this and Ernest said he had a right to fish and swim, and live with his friends instead of with his mother.

Grace Hall said she did not think that Ernest's ambition to write was worth being called an ambition. Ernest was, in her opinion, "failing to show the proper attitude, failing in courtesy, failing in life!" Writing stories in the vain hope of selling them was nothing but self-indulgence; Grace Hall was certain it was in vain. Between visits to her private cottage on the hilltop, where she could be "free of her family," Grace Hall wrote to her husband complaining about Ernest. In criticizing Ernest she used her ability to play on her husband's rigid Victorian sense of right and wrong. Grace Hall wanted her will done, and her husband backed her up. Though he would have far preferred to be in Michigan, Ed Hemingway had to spend his summer working in Oak Park.

The rule said a child must obey his parents, but Ernest did not feel like a child. He felt like a wounded man. Up to a point he was willing to help his mother, and it was just this which enraged Grace Hall. To think that Ernest dared to decide which of her wishes he would grant, and which he would deny, was unbearable. She kept reminding Ernest that he had once been "her dear little boy," and when she spoke of "that beautiful time long ago," when the man who had been covered with blood at Fossalta had been "her dear little boy," she spoke with longing. And when she reminded Ernest that ever since "that beautiful time" he had constantly displeased her, she spoke in pain. Grace Hall accused Ernest of having changed.

Ernest was no longer a stranger. He was intelligent and brave; he shot well; he fished like an expert; he ate a lot, and he liked wine and whiskey. Ernest had been a reporter; he had been wounded; he had almost died; he had been in love; he'd been called a hero; he swore; sometimes he made a lot of noise; he lied and he told the truth, and he wrote stories and wanted to write many more.

Ernest did not, however, live up to his mother's hopes. She felt he failed to grow "every day in Strength of Character and Purpose"; failed to make his "life count for the best things." Grace Hall aimed her hopes at the stars; Ernest brought them back to earth. Grace Hall resented this, and in her resentment she exaggerated everything Ernest did and did not do.

To make one's "life count for the best things" meant settling down to a respectable life, doing what Grace Hall and the world she had grown up in expected Ernest to do; above all, it meant being obedient.

Ernest was guilty not just of disobedience, of allowing his hands to be idle "in God's kingdom" when he should have been doing chores to please his mother, but he was guilty of something far worse. Ernest was guilty of hurting his mother. This was Ernest's sin; in her mind this had always been his sin.

The punishment Grace Hall decided upon was to tell Ernest he must leave, until that time when it might please her to ask him back. The day she chose to do this was Ernest's twenty-first birthday, July 21, 1920, in the summer house on Lake Walloon. Ed Hemingway was kept in Oak Park by his patients, but Grace Hall found she was able to give the party without his help, and at the same time ask Ernest to go. Ernest went to live with friends.

One night, soon after he had gone, Ernest's sisters and some other girls and young men planned a secret midnight party by the edge of the lake in the woods far from their parents' homes. They invited Ernest. At the party they sang and ate, swam and watched the bonfire, and kissed. At home, the girls' empty beds gave them away; their mothers were waiting up in the early morning hours when they came back. Grace Hall blamed Ernest because he was the oldest. None of the girls were allowed to have dates for a long time.

Ernest received a letter from his mother as a result of the secret party, a letter in which she accused him of being lazy, as he loafed around; vain, because according to her, he used his good looks to deceive innocent girls; dishonest, he borrowed money without intending to return it. She went on to say that Ernest seriously neglected his duty to his Savior, Jesus Christ, that he selfishly indulged himself in luxury, and that he was a parasite with no other thought than to live off his friends and family.

Grace Hall also wrote about love. Her letter was explicit when it came to love. Love was like money, she said. As his mother, Grace Hall explained, she had deposited a certain sum of love in Ernest, but now, she said, Ernest was bankrupt.

During the months after Ernest left, Ed Hemingway often wrote his wife to tell her that Ernest felt a great injustice had been done to him. He wrote of his love for Ernest, and he urged his wife to join him in loving their son; he urged her to forgive, and he sternly warned her to beg Ernest's pardon if she had falsely accused him. Ernest may have made mistakes, Ed Hemingway granted in his letters; however, none could be compared to the sin of false accusation. He made it clear that he thought this might be true, but it was hard for him to judge from Oak Park where he was busy all day with his patients, and busy every evening making pickles for his friends. Ernest had written to his father, carefully explaining that he did not feel his mother had been justified in her action; Ed Hemingway was certain of only one thing; he wanted

justice, and he did his best to see that it was done.

In the fall Grace Hall returned to spend the winter in Oak Park. When Ernest returned he did not climb the stairs to his room on the third floor of his parents' house, the room to which he had so often escaped; instead he went to live with a friend in Chicago. He looked for a job. He found one, a good one on a monthly business magazine, paying a good salary. Soon he moved into the apartment of other friends.

Hadley Richardson was twenty-nine when she came to Chicago from St. Louis in November. She met Ernest at the apartment where he was living. They liked each other and, when Hadley went back to St. Louis after a few weeks, they started to write one another. Hadley hoped Ernest could come down to visit, but he was too broke to pay for a train ticket.

Not until March the next year did he go, and then he wore a new suit, and took along copies of his *Toronto Star* articles and copies of his short stories. Ernest courted Hadley. A few weeks later Hadley came to Chicago for the second time. They loved one another, planned to marry, talked about Hadley's small income and decided they would live on it in Italy while Ernest wrote.

Hadley loved Ernest. She found his love of fishing, of eating, of drinking, of writing, laughing and talking, and of everything else he did, the most wonderful love she had ever seen. When Ernest was with her the world seemed more important to Hadley. She thanked God they lived at the same time and knew one another.

By May it was decided. Ernest and Hadley would be married. Ernest got the blues now and then at the idea that he might soon have to give up some of his favorite streams in favor of a wife, and he fished as often as he could to make up for any possible future loss of streams.

For his twenty-second birthday Hadley gave Ernest a typewriter. She loved the stories and poems which he wrote.

September 3rd was set to be the day of their wedding in a country church in Michigan. Four hundred and fifty people were invited, but before making his appearance in front of this crowd, Ernest disappeared into the woods for days. He fished and he sang and he looked up at the moon and wondered what was going to happen.

The wedding day was lovely. Before they were married the groom and the bride went swimming separately. At the church Hadley's hair was still a little damp, Ernest's wounded legs hurt when he knelt. The day ended when they rowed together to the Hemingway summer house on the edge of the lake, where they spent their honeymoon.

Plans were changed; instead of Italy they decided to go to Paris; it seemed Paris was a better place to live for a serious writer.

Ever since he'd left Toronto, Ernest had sent articles to the *Toronto Star*. Now and then some of them were published. His own pile of manuscripts was growing slowly, but no one was buying. Soon, however, soon he hoped to be able to write about what he knew, sell what he wrote, do what he wanted, live his way. In December 1921 Ernest and Hadley sailed to Europe.

On the North Atlantic in winter the heavy waves are gray and the wind blows their tops off in a white spray. The sky too is gray with few white clouds. On the open deck the wind is dangerous and very few passengers go outside. They prefer to listen to the violins in the main lounge and ask the stewards to serve them tea. The ship rolls and pitches constantly.

Some days, when the wind blows the sky clean and the sea is a bright dark blue, the edge of the world looks near. It is easy to think a long way on a ship, about all the things that have happened and all those that are going to happen.

At twenty-two, Ernest was the man he was going to be; the love which he felt for the world was in him, and the hate and the fear, and the idea that he had to write about how he felt. In the middle of the ocean at twenty-two, Ernest felt he was free to go anywhere. He saw no flying fish, as he had on his first trip when it had been warm, but he felt he was flying away himself this time. There was no one to tell him what to do, and he felt as he had when he first went to Europe, except that now he was stronger; now he had a wife who loved him. He never had to go back to Oak Park. He was no more free than he had ever been, it just felt like it.

After the ship docked in France, Ernest was going to do a lot of things he'd never done before, and he was going to do them for many years, and he would often feel he could do anything at all. His love of mountains and river valleys, of trees, and of the sky and of every quiet and open place where nobody could get at him, would always lead Ernest back to these places. He never forgot his love; it would lead him on to the great plains of East Africa and it would lead him out into the Gulf Stream where he would be happier than anywhere else in the world.

Ernest wanted to know the laws which rule the world he loved, which decide when the fox leaps, when the snow falls, the natural laws which describe the real world. He knew the other laws, those which men make in the hope of turning the world into what they think it should be.

At twenty-two Ernest knew that silence was a lie, that it only covered pain and made it worse. Silence was magic; it made things disappear but it also made things seem true when they weren't. Silence pretended that every mother loved her child. Ernest decided to be a witness to what he saw. He knew that Grace Hall was a magician; she only had to run away to her cottage on the hill or shut herself up in the dark to make her family vanish; she only had to turn away not to see that Ernest was hurt.

Grace Hall wanted no competition. If Ernest had a wish of his own he was in danger of hurting his mother; when he was a boy this meant that she went away from him; when he was a man it meant she sent him away. Like the rabbit in the magic trick—now you see it, now you don't—Ernest came and went according to his mother's wishes and it made him feel as if he was nothing.

It was a never-ending pain to grow up and feel like nothing. Having done nothing to hurt, Ernest couldn't understand why he was hurt, and confused. He hated the confusion—now you see me, now you don't—and he found the best way not to disappear was to fight back. Going to war and coming home had helped Ernest to feel he wasn't going to die right away.

At five Ernest told a story of how he had once stopped a runaway horse all by himself, a story in which he was the hero. He told "tall tales" at home; he told them to his friends at school, and he told them in Italy, and in every tale Ernest stood so tall that nobody could miss him.

Ernest was lucky. At Fossalta he had been a real hero, and newspapers had told the real story of how he had acted "beyond the call of duty!" Ernest came home feeling a lot less like a trick rabbit than ever before, but it did him no good; even his wounds did not help Grace Hall see Ernest as a man. The feeling of terror, that he was nothing and could be made to disappear, stayed with him.

Doing something hard, like writing very well, or catching a trout when the trout weren't biting, made the feeling go away. Sitting around only made him feel worse. Doing anything at all felt better than doing nothing, as if in action Ernest could prove he was still there.

The terror came and went for the rest of his life. There were years when Ernest wrote well and years when he fished when he wasn't writing, years when he was strong and happy. Then later, at the end, there were years when he couldn't keep the terror away.

What was true and what was not true? The same question always came up. It made Ernest want to find something he could trust, something that never pretended to be anything other than what it was. Ernest turned to himself. He decided he could really know what he felt, not what anyone else said he should feel, only what he felt. Ernest decided to trust his own eyes and ears. On this decision Ernest built his life.

Ernest was a private man. He never named the day on which he decided to be himself. Maybe he never made a decision at all, maybe it just grew until Ernest found he was too old to play make-believe. Ernest escaped into reality, but it wasn't enough. He had to spend the rest of his life nailing the world down by writing about it, as if only by writing about it could he be sure it was there.

Paris was very different from Oak Park in January 1922 when Ernest and Hadley moved into an apartment in an old building on the rue du Cardinal Lemoine. Two thousand years before Oak Park became a town, Roman soldiers marched along the road which later became the street on which Ernest and Hadley lived.

In Paris there were many men who had been mutilated in the war, men whose faces were ruined. In Paris young men walked along the river and hugged and kissed their girls. In Paris everybody thought water was for fish to swim in, and they all drank wine. In Paris beautiful paintings hung in great palaces. In Paris a man could see a hundred bookstores in an hour. In Paris if a girl sang in the streets people stopped to listen, and threw money at her feet. In Paris everybody wanted to eat good food every day.

On some streets there were whores, and there were nightclubs where only women danced with women, and there were other nightclubs just for men, and in many small hotels two people could rent a room for an hour if they wanted to. A man could pay to see a live sex show or go to see a marble statue by Michelangelo. A woman could buy a dress for a thousand dollars or a rag to cover her back from the secondhand clothes man.

Paris was a big city with a great cathedral, wide boulevards, and crowded cafés. There were many theaters and beautiful houses and many great men and women from all over the world.

Ernest liked Paris. He liked the local dance hall where people danced and got drunk; it smelled and it was noisy, but the people who went there liked it. Every morning when he got up, Ernest liked the feeling that he could do whatever he wanted to do with his day. He boxed with his friends and sometimes, even though he was bigger and stronger and a better boxer than they were, he punched too hard and hurt them, and sometimes he was gentle. He went to the racetrack and bet on the horses and to the six-day bicycle races and bet on the riders. He drank at the Ritz Bar and in the cafés, and he went to see his friends and drank with them. He enjoyed himself. He made friends with jockeys and waiters, writers, anybody he met, anybody he liked.

The only people he didn't like were the ones who talked too much about themselves, who thought art was wonderful and said so all the time. They made Ernest mad. To Ernest, their talk only served to cover up the fact that they did nothing.

Ernest worked. He used his freedom; he didn't waste any of it; he used it to enjoy himself, but above all he used it to test himself, to see if he could write the way he wanted to.

Ernest knew the short words and the long ones; he tried different sentences with different words, and he tried different paragraphs with different sentences. He put words together and pulled sentences apart. He put paragraphs together and pulled stories apart. He listened to what he wrote, and then he wrote it again. He changed a long sentence into three short ones. He put five short sentences into a long one, and listened. He always listened.

Ernest worked alone, sometimes in his room, sometimes in a café. If anyone interrupted him he hated it. He found it painful to be interrupted when he was writing; it felt as if he had been caught when he was defenseless. Ernest used himself when he wrote. He pushed everything out of his way in the search for his feelings. If he could turn what he found into words, then his stories might do what he wanted them to; they might make the man who read them see what he had seen.

If Ernest had allowed Oak Park to choose he

would have become a doctor, a lawyer, a minister, or a respected member of the business community, and if he had insisted on becoming a writer he would at least have written by the rules and there would have been no fight; everything would have gone the way it was supposed to. But Ernest didn't want things that way, even if it meant he would have to fight. It didn't matter if his way was harder, as long as he chose the way. If he was free to put words and sentences together the way he wanted to, in a way which meant that other men might feel as he felt, then he had a chance to be the man he wanted to be. Just as with any fight which a man chooses himself, the harder it became the more Ernest tried to win. As long as he fought he had a chance and there was no fear that he would feel like nothing.

Ernest went to the museum in the Luxembourg Gardens; it was only a five-minute walk from the rue du Cardinal Lemoine; he looked at the paintings by Monet and by Cézanne. He said they taught him more about how to write than most writers had. Over and over he went to see how Monet had done it, how he had painted so as to make Ernest see water lilies floating on a pond, see clouds in the sky above the pond, even see frogs which Monet had not painted. And Ernest tried to learn from Cézanne; how he made the heat rise from a mountain, how he made the skin of an apple look cool. Paint wasn't real, but then words weren't either. The problem was how to use them so they seemed real.

Every time he began a sentence Ernest found he could write it in hundreds of ways, or not write it at all. Which was the best way, the one way to make somebody believe what the sentence said? The questions were, "What do I want to say?" and, "Why say it?" and, "Now that I am going to say it, is it better not to?" and, "How much more should I say?" There was no end to the questions and Ernest tried to answer all of them. And there was no end to the difficulty.

Ernest said writing was a serious job. He liked to laugh and kid around and enjoy himself, but writing was "deadly serious." Ernest called himself crazy names when he drank and sang in the local dance hall; he liked the noise and the fun and the people liked him. But when he wrote, he had to be alone. He compared writing to the slow, measured construction of a building. Ernest was not looking for a quick victory. He was willing for the world to take a hundred years to decide whether or not he wrote well. Ernest worked on his sen-

tences; he put himself into his words; he committed himself to what they said, and he hoped his best was good enough to live.

Words ran through Ernest's life; he knew their power; he was used to hearing men twist words in order to twist other men, bending words so they could bend others to their will. Ernest knew the minister who stood in his pulpit becoming more and more inflamed by the sound of his own voice, his words growing more eloquent as he fired the zeal of his congregation, until the congregation became so convinced that his words were the true words of God that they began to spread his words throughout the world, in the hope of making others believe as they believed.

And Ernest knew that "sin" was a word that hurt and that "weak" explained why he sinned and that "strength" was what he needed to fight sin, and he also knew that to "obey" the word of God, always the word, was the only "right" way. Ernest was afraid of words.

But when his father taught him the names of the birds: "golden-winged warbler," "indigo bunting," "meadowlark," and the names of the fish: "spotted bass," "yellow perch," "rainbow trout," Ernest loved these words. He loved them as much as he hated his mother's words: "noble purpose," "higher development," "day of opportunity."

Often words were used in ways which Ernest found immoral. Powerful men spoke of peace when they made war; they spoke of sacrifice, never their own, and they tried to get more power for themselves, even if others had to die so they could get it.

Men abused the best words; they said "love" and felt hate; kind words hid cruel acts. And so many good words had been misused to the point of seeming false that Ernest came to hate not virtue itself but the man who repeated the word "virtue" too often.

It was all done with words. Words were used to do almost anything, to persuade, to deceive, to seduce. And Ernest didn't like it at all. He did not like an empty promise, a word twisted out of its real shape. When Ernest wrote he made no promises. He tried to sharpen his words until they could cut through anything, and then he tried to use them to write the truth.

Ernest made his own rules. First, he refused to do to others what he did not want them to do to him. Ernest was not going to imitate Oak Park; he would never push other people around with words. He would respect their feelings.

If the law of silence could exist, Ernest decided it could also be broken, but it must not be broken with twisted words and dreams. Ernest saw the real world; he needed to find a way to share it, using only words and the truth, and never using either as a weapon. Ernest was not a cold man who looked at the world as a thing separate from him; he was tied to everything he saw by his feelings. He decided to use his feelings about the world as the link between himself and other people; through his stories he was going to share the world with them. To do this Ernest had to touch their feelings. It was easy to know how he was not going to do this, he only had to think about the lies he hated.

A liar obeyed no rules; he blew up his words, shouted them, shoved them, turned them around, as long as his words ended by making somebody believe they were true. Once that happened, once a man had been convinced, he could be made to do anything. Ernest knew that words could be used as strings to play with a man; he knew a man could be turned upside down with words, if there were no rules. Without rules, words only had to seem true. If lies did need to be hammered in, and Ernest was certain they did, then the truth had to be left alone.

Not only did the truth have to be free but the words in which the truth appeared also had to be free. Above all, the writer needed to be free from the desire to make everybody believe his way. Ernest hoped his words would lead others to see what he had seen, but he was not going to attempt to convince them of it; they would have to do that on their own.

It was as if Ernest decided to offer half the apple he had been eating to a friend, in the hope that his friend would taste what Ernest had tasted. But there were rules to follow with a friend, and if he said, "No, thank you," you didn't ram the apple down his throat. Ernest felt the same about words.

When he wrote about the ammunition factory which exploded near Milan a few days after he arrived in Italy in 1918, Ernest did not say that the bodies of the men and women which were blown up were anything other than bodies which were scattered by a sudden and violent explosion. Ernest did not try to be convincing. He avoided saying that what he saw was "horrible"; he refused to say it was "sickening." Instead, he looked for what it was about the scattered bodies which had made him sick, and this he put into plain words so that we too could see. "Fragments of the bodies," Ernest wrote, were "found a considerable distance away in the fields, they being carried farther by their own weight."

Ernest allows us to feel as we choose about the explosion.

Life in Paris was not all words. Whether he went to Constantinople, to New York, Madrid, Toronto, or Venice, Ernest came back to Paris. For years Paris was his city, and forever Paris was a city he loved.

He enjoyed the oysters with cold white wine, and the bookstalls along the river, and the fish which were caught in the river and were very good if they were fried. He enjoyed sitting in the sun reading, eating sausages and drinking red wine, and watching the fish being caught; watching the long, wide, black barges moving slowly on their way upstream and quickly downstream, the barge captain's wife hanging up her laundry, her dog running up and down barking. He enjoyed the geraniums which the woman had neatly planted by the wheel house in the stern where her husband stood at the wheel. A hundred barges went by on a busy afternoon.

Ernest liked the beer and the good potato salad with olive oil and pepper which he ate with the beer. And he liked cold salmon from the Loire River served with a green sauce. He liked the smell every time he walked into a bakery and he liked the hard sound the gravel made as he walked through the Luxembourg Gardens on his way to see the mountains and the apples painted by Cézanne, and he liked to hear the music the accordion made late at night in the local dance hall.

If it was cold, Ernest liked an Eau de Vie de Poire, which smelled like a bushel of pears and made him feel warm because it was a strong, clear alcohol with a pure, sharp, pear taste.

In 1922 everything tasted good in Paris: the rose-red radishes, the Camembert, the flower market, the two-room apartment with no bathroom; making love right after lunch, going to the zoo, talking with new friends about new books.

Ernest and Hadley went to Switzerland. They loved the snow; Ernest wished his old friends from Michigan could come to ski with him. He went bobsledding and found out he could get killed on a bobsled, and he heard about an avalanche which buried a man and his wife.

In the spring the chestnut trees in Paris were full of tall flowers; a tree had either white or pink blossoms, and on one street all the blossoms were the same color because that was the way the trees had been planted.

In Paris, for the first time, Ernest and his work and his life were one. Afterward he always tried to keep it that way. Ernest spent no empty hours; he missed nothing. He observed the details of his life and he used them every day; if Ernest had not written he might have felt as if he were nothing.

He saw and he wrote about an accident at the racetrack; he saw and he wrote about a gigolo who killed himself late at night; and about a whore with one leg and the priest who wanted her; he saw a riot and he wrote about one man who was proud and afraid at the same time.

Ernest remembered being a boy in Michigan and he often wrote about that, and about how much he loved to fish. He remembered how his mother had bullied his father, and how she lay in the dark so she would see nothing she didn't want to see, how she blamed everything on his father, how he preferred to be in the woods with his father away from his mother even though he knew his mother had asked to see him, how he had wished his father would stand up to his mother, but how his father never did. And he remembered how his mother had bullied him when he came back from the war, even though he came back wounded and with medals, how much she had wished he would become a "credit to his community," and how much he had wanted to write instead. And Ernest wrote about his father being bullied, and about himself, how he was bullied into lying when he didn't want to lie. Ernest said he was hurt, not so much because it hurt him to be bullied, but because it hurt more to see that his father was a coward.

Ernest made friends with reporters in Paris, and he went to Anglo-American Press Club meetings, and he horsed around with his friends. Together they made a lot of noise and laughed a lot, and drank whiskey, told each other lies and talked about boxers and jockeys. Ernest became a friend of Sylvia Beach who ran a bookstore. Sylvia loaned him books and Ernest bought books from her and they were friends forever. Ernest listened to what Gertrude Stein told him about writing; what she said made sense to him. She thought he wrote well, but that he could write better, much better.

Soon after he arrived in Paris, Ernest again began to write articles for the *Toronto Star;* he would have preferred to work on his own stories,

but he and Hadley needed the money to add to her small income. Ernest wrote about anything that interested him, from commercial tuna fishing on the Atlantic coast of Spain, to the election of a pope. The managing editor of the paper liked the way Ernest wrote; he printed almost every article which Ernest sent him, and he asked Ernest to cover news stories which interested the *Star*. First, he sent Ernest to an International Conference in Genoa where Ernest saw "statesmen" from thirty-four countries. The "statesmen" did not impress Ernest with their statesmen-like qualities; instead they struck him as frauds who only knew how to seek their own profit through deception. Ernest avoided them as much as he could and went to see the slums of Genoa to see what it was like to be in misery, rather than listen to the "statesmen" tell him what they wanted him to believe.

In June 1922 Ernest took Hadley to Italy to show her where he had been during the war. From the hospital in Milan where he had known Agnes they went to Schio, and from Schio to Fossalta, but Fossalta was no longer destroyed; it was rebuilt and ugly. Nowhere did Ernest find anything to show Hadley; the trenches and the shell holes had all disappeared. Even the spot where he'd been hit was hard to find. The war was dead.

Summer in Paris, more articles for the *Star*, dancing in the streets at night to celebrate the 14th of July, fireworks at night, accordions and bagpipes playing all night, Ernest dressed like a French fisherman, dancing and drinking lots of wine, and in August he and Hadley went off to Germany to fish for trout in the Black Forest with friends from the States, and in the fall a telegram came from the *Star* asking Ernest to go to the Near East to report on the war between Turkey and Greece. Hadley didn't want Ernest to go. On the 25th of September, Ernest left on the Orient Express, and on the 29th he arrived in Constantinople.

This war was different from the first war Ernest had seen; in this war, the soldiers spoke Turkish and Greek; in the first they had spoken Italian, French, German and English. In the first war, the soldiers had been Catholic and Protestant; in this war they were Moslem and Orthodox. But the rats and the dead, and the mud and the pain were the same.

Ernest caught malaria; his fever went way up; he sweated heavily and he shook with chills. From Turkey he went to Greece where he watched the refugees from the war moving slowly in the rain; mile after mile of tired people, tired, cold, and afraid of dying. In October, Ernest told the readers of the *Star* that he had seen a woman giving birth in the rain while her daughter watched and cried, and later Ernest wrote about ''women with dead babies'' who would not ''give up their dead babies.'' There was ''nothing you could do,'' you just ''had to take them away finally.'' When Ernest came back to Paris from the war his head was covered with lice.

Ernest hoped to see his first book, a few short stories and a few poems. He wrote Agnes to tell her he was married, living in Paris, and that, soon, he expected to be a published author. He continued to complain bitterly about writers who didn't write; ''scum'' Ernest called them, as if the fact that they posed as something they were not could threaten him, as if in their deception Ernest found a never-forgotten pain.

Again Ernest left Paris for another International Conference, this time in Lausanne, in Switzerland. The ''statesmen'' spoke for peace, for peace was what they preferred this time; while at other times they preferred war. Ernest worked steadily sending cabled news reports back across the Atlantic.

As soon as the conference was over, Hadley joined Ernest and they went off to ski. They had a good time together; they drank brandy in the evening sitting by a big fire after spending the day racing down the snow in the cold. Ernest often went bobsledding; he liked the speed and the feeling of the wind cutting into him. One afternoon Ernest watched as a steady rain began to loosen the deep snow. He knew how dangerous this was; in a few hours he saw avalanche after avalanche crash into the valley. In the local newspaper the next day Ernest read about the people who died.

In Switzerland, Hadley told Ernest she was pregnant. They took a train south, celebrated in Milan, and traveled on to the shores of the Mediterranean where they stayed in Rapallo at the Hotel Splendide. The service was excellent, the gardens filled with flowers, and the sea was a bright blue. Ernest wanted to write but he found he couldn't, and this made him miserable, but his first year in Europe, his first free year, had been happy. If he felt like watching barges on the Seine he watched; if he felt like betting on the third horse in the fifth race at Auteuil he bet; if he wanted to be alone and write in a café he went to a café and he wrote, and if he was thirsty he ordered a drink.

During the year, Ernest saw the misery of another war, and he saw misery in the slums of Genoa while the statesmen were busy making speeches about a better world. Ernest watched these old men at their long green tables talking for days and weeks, and then he heard them go home and announce with pride how much good they had done. The old men reminded Ernest of the young men who sat forever at marble café tables and talked about what wonderful artists they were. It didn't matter if they were old or young; if they told lies, Ernest had contempt for them.

A lot of people liked Ernest, and some didn't. Many talked about how kind and generous he was, how friendly he could be; they said he was really charming. And others said he was mean and often suspicious, as if he had been cheated and was afraid of being cheated again.

From the warm flower gardens of Rapallo, Ernest and Hadley went north to Cortina d'Ampezzo where it was cold. Ernest was happier in Cortina because he wrote better. He worked hard trying to make his words fit into sentences, trying to make his sentences fit into paragraphs, trying to make what he felt work inside somebody else. He cut out the useless words, hoping that the words he left on the paper were the right ones.

In the spring the snow melted in the mountains, and Ernest put away his skis and took out his fishing rods. He went on writing as the weather grew warmer.

In the spring of 1923 Ernest went to a bullfight in Madrid. He thought the bullfight was like a war; when a soldier was killed he didn't stand up to take a bow when the war was over, and if a matador was killed he never stood up to bow either. Ernest liked a thing boiled down to what it really was; he liked to feel that it never tried to be something it was not. Death in a bullfight was death; nothing in a bullfight was anything other than itself. A wound was a wound; if it became infected and the infection was not stopped, the infection spread and the wounded man died, and before he died the pain from his wound was often so bad that the doctor had to give the man morphine.

Ernest saw how blue the entrails of a horse look when they are spilled, and he saw how dark the bull's blood was when it first rose out of the wound made by the picador, and how bright it became in the sun when it ran down the bull's shoulder. Ernest saw fear control the men, and in turn he watched the men try to control their fear, but no matter how hard a man tried, if he could not do it he could not fake it; his actions made it impossible for him to deceive the crowd. When a man chose the place to stand, and stood there, his legs still, and, holding the red cloth out in his left hand, brought the bull slowly past, keeping his legs still when the bull's left horn moved near them, then the crowd knew the man was in control of his fear. But if the man suddenly snapped his legs away from the horn, they knew his fear controlled him.

Six times in two hours the bull came into the ring; six times a man stood with the bull and, knowing the bull was trying to kill him, the man tried to control the bull's attack, tried to shape this attack into a series of repeated charges each of which clearly showed that the man could order the bull into the exact rhythm he chose, and not the one the bull chose. The ideal rhythm existed, but no one ever found it; the man's fear did not allow him to come near it.

Every man in the arena was afraid; Ernest knew that and the crowd knew it. Every soldier was afraid, but there wasn't always a war to go to. For the price of a ticket Ernest found he could study how a man acted when he was afraid.

Ernest always studied what interested him. He studied how to tie a trout fly, and how to cast it the right way to the right spot in the stream, because he wanted to catch fish. He studied the behavior of birds, their flight paths, their feeding habits, and how to handle his gun, because he wanted to shoot birds. Ernest studied men because he wanted to write. It was easy to watch a man drinking at a bar, sitting in his office, walking down the street, making a speech or kissing a girl; watching a man do a lot of things was easy; if you looked and listened you could learn a lot about him and still not know how he would act in front of a firing squad. Ernest wanted to see what a man would do if he was about to lose his life. Ernest said every true story ends in death, and so if he was going to write stories he had to know how a man acted in front of death.

A man couldn't hide in the bullring; whatever he did was true. If he was a cheat, and could only pretend to be brave, his cheating was there to be seen; there was no chance that it could be mistaken for anything else. A coward in the bullring was a coward; a liar was a liar, and neither coward

nor liar nor hero ever spoke a word; they were known only by their actions. A man with dignity moved with dignity; an awkward man moved awkwardly. A short heavy man was just that, and a tall skinny man with the legs of a heron looked only like himself.

From the first trumpet call to the death of the last bull, a man was exposed in the arèna. Once he committed himself, a man could not turn back; he could leave the bullring if he was carried wounded into the infirmary, or if, having refused to face the bull, he was arrested by the police and taken to jail. Ernest went from bullfight to bullfight. For two hours in the late afternoon he found life concentrated in a drama he had never expected to see. The commitment which a man made when he entered the arena moved Ernest in the same way as the men at Fossalta had moved him.

No one in the arena could deceive with words; the arena was not a café where a man could pose as anything; it was not an International Conference where statesmen pretended to feel what they never felt, and it certainly was not Oak Park. The bullring was different; no man was safe in the arena, safe behind a mask of words put up to keep himself from being seen.

Ernest believed a man had to hold on to his life, at least he had to try to. It didn't matter if he died, if he had tried to last as long as he could, but in trying to last a man couldn't do it any way he chose; he had to try hard, to do what he set out to do, to be a soldier and not run away even if his fear made him sick, to be a matador even if the bull made his throat so dry he couldn't swallow, to be a poet even if he was scared because he had no idea what words to write, to be a mother even if her child was a monster, to be whatever. As long as a man never gave up being something Ernest was for him. But if a man put on an act, Ernest turned against him for making himself seem to be something he was not.

Ernest liked men who never gave up, and he wrote about them. When he was a young man he wrote about his friend Maera; Maera the matador who didn't stop because of the pain, who got angry at his own pain because it wouldn't let him do what he wanted to do. And twenty-five years later, Ernest wrote about an old man who went far out to sea, an old man who did what he wasn't supposed to be able to do, who held on even when his pain was too great, even when his fish was too big.

Ernest had stuck to his way when he broke from

Oak Park; the safe way would have been to grow into a pillar of the community and live the way a pillar does. The safe way would have been to write according to the old rules instead of making up sentences using his own rules; it would have meant writing about things which were safe and not about what he felt.

Ernest committed himself to his way. No one pushed him into it; no one said "Write!" No one said "Break the rules. Make up your own rules!" And certainly, nobody ever said "Go as far as you want and see what happens!" but Ernest tried to.

Ernest liked the idea that the crowd came to a bullfight to be moved; he liked the Spanish phrase *dar emoción,* to give emotion, and he liked the fact that in his performance the matador tried to give the crowd emotion. The crowd not only wanted to be given, but it was also ready to give. Whichever way the bullfight crowd was moved, it never hid its feelings. From the moment the matador appeared before the people he was exposed to their love and their hate. If they were moved by the precise and beautiful rhythm which the matador created, they punctuated his work with a cry. Each time the matador moved, they gave him their cry, and each time their cry grew louder until the matador, the bull, and the crowd were all acting together.

But if the matador slipped into shameless behavior; if he repeatedly allowed his fear to dominate him; then the crowd turned on him in disgust. They hated to see his cowardice, for if he was a coward what right did the man have to pretend to be a matador; what right did he have to cheat them of the price they paid for their tickets, a price they paid in order to see a man rise above his fear? With each act of deceit the crowd's anger grew until it filled the arena and the streets beyond.

If the matador changed, the crowd changed; if cowardice turned into courage the arena was again filled with a cry. No one pretended to feel one way if he felt another; the crowd was honest in both its cry and its hate. Nothing was farther removed from the quiet afternoons in Oak Park than the hours Ernest spent at the bullfights, between 5:00 and 7:00, in the spring and the summer of 1923.

In the summer Ernest went to Pamplona for the first time, to the *feria* of San Fermín which began every year on the seventh day of the seventh month. In the Basque country, in the southern foothills of the Pyrenees, Ernest saw a bullfight every afternoon for a week; he saw the bulls run through the streets of the city at six o'clock every morning, and he saw the entire city explode: in fireworks, in dancing, in crowds, in wine, in merry-go-rounds and ferris wheels, in tests of bravery and strength, in parades, and in contests between one brass band and another. Ernest stayed up all night, and fell asleep for an hour on a bench at first dawn, before getting up to drink wine for breakfast. He danced in the streets. He ran into the arena with the bulls. He joined a procession and wandered with giant kings and queens through the crowded city; and he watched their huge-headed royal courtiers scare the children of Pamplona by banging them on the head with inflated pigs' bladders. The children loved the great moving statues even if they were afraid. Ernest remembered everything about the *feria* of San Fermín; he went back to it, again and again, for the rest of his life.

Ernest made friends in Pamplona; he met the matadors; he ate with them; he ate lots of lamb; he went to the garlic market near the amusement park; he watched the gypsies sell their horses in the shade of the grove of trees beneath the high walls of the city, and he saw the Holy Virgin being carried through the streets and he went into the cathedral and saw the people praying to God, and every afternoon Ernest went to the bullfight.

When the *feria* was over, Ernest and Hadley went back to Paris. The music from the dance hall on the rue du Cardinal Lemoine felt tame after the music in the bullring; the streets of the Latin Quarter felt empty after the streets of Pamplona. Nothing was ever the same after Ernest went to Spain; he loved Spain and her people forever and he knew Spain from Málaga to Bilbao, from Valencia to Vigo.

Ernest worried; he didn't have enough time to write; too many everyday things kept interrupting; Hadley didn't feel well and Ernest had to take care of her; and plans had to be made to go to Canada where she was going to have her baby.

Ernest wanted to see his first book. More than anything else he wanted to hold his book in his hands and know that others could read what he had written. He wrote about a love affair which began in Milan and ended when a letter came saying it was all over; he wrote about a young man lying wounded at Fossalta; about a matador who was hated by the crowd, about another matador who was a drunk; he wrote about a horse which had been gored, about a hanging in Chicago, and two murders in Kansas City, and he wrote about a boy whose father was a jockey in Paris, and about how the jockey was killed when his horse didn't clear a jump in a steeplechase race at Auteuil, and about making love on a boat dock at the edge of a lake in Michigan, and how the girl cried.

Ten days before he went to Canada, Ernest held the sheets of his first book, *Three Stories and Ten Poems.* It felt thin, but it was his; a book by Ernest Hemingway. Then Ernest said good-bye to everybody, and everybody said, "Hurry back to Paris," and on the 15th of August Ernest and Hadley sailed.

In Toronto, Ernest started to work for the *Star* as a regular reporter, but the new editor did not like Ernest, and Ernest did not like him. Even though he traveled on assignment in Canada and the United States, and even though it was near, Ernest did not go to Oak Park. Ed Hemingway had to mail the wedding presents which had been left behind in Oak Park to Toronto.

Ernest and Hadley started to live in their new apartment, but there was no dance hall downstairs, no Cézanne paintings five minutes away, no river where Ernest could sit and read and watch the barges go by. The new building in which Ernest lived was called Cedarvale Mansions; the rue du Cardinal Lemoine felt far away.

One night in October, while Ernest was on his way from New York to Toronto, Hadley gave birth to a son, John Hadley Nicanor Hemingway; Nicanor celebrated Ernest's memory of the great matador, Nicanor Villalta, whom he had met in Pamplona in July.

His friends in Paris sent Ernest copies of his first book. He kept them very carefully and he looked at them often. Ernest wrote to his friends saying that he couldn't stand Cedarvale Mansions any longer; he had to come home to Paris, he said. Soon it was decided; Ernest, Hadley and the baby would sail back in a few months.

At Christmas copies of Ernest's second book, *in our time,* arrived from Paris. Only 170 copies of it had been printed, but it was a book, a book of his, and Ernest put *in our time* on the shelf next to *Three Stories and Ten Poems.* People said they were good books; they said the author was "deadly serious about his writing," that he wanted his work to be perfect and that he would do anything to make it perfect.

At the end of the year Ernest made one quick trip to Oak Park. He went alone. As soon as he returned to Toronto, Ernest began to leave; he handed in his resignation to the *Star,* packed, went to a farewell party, and took the train to New York to catch the boat on the 19th of January.

In Paris, Ernest and Hadley needed a larger apartment. They moved to the rue Notre Dame des Champs, a name Ernest liked very much; their new apartment was near their friends, near Gertrude Stein and Ezra Pound, near the Luxembourg Gardens, near a good café, and only a fifteen-minute walk from the river. By March, Ernest was happily settled, and he stopped worrying. He had only been away a few months, but during those months he had become an author and a father. Ernest read the first reviews of his work. They were good. He wrote and published short stories in small magazines, and he was told by other writers that he would soon be famous. Ernest was a disciplined writer, a disciplined man; he wrote early in the morning when it was quiet; he wrote slowly, going over his words again and again, going over his feelings and his memory, trying to get down on paper exactly what he remembered. He tried a new idea, to leave out part of a story, hoping that if he wrote well enough his reader would imagine what he had left out. Ernest said what he felt about people he disliked in a bitter way, as if his reason for disliking them gave him a license to hunt them down on paper. Ernest hurt people, but it never seemed to bother him for he thought he had the right to say whatever he chose.

In the summer Ernest went back to Spain, back to the bullfights, to Nicanor Villalta, Maera, Gitanillo de Triana. He couldn't wait to go back to Pamplona; he wanted to see everything again. And Pamplona was great. At six o'clock in the morning, after the bulls had run through the streets from the corral at the edge of the city to the corral behind the bullring, Ernest and a thousand other young men played at being matadors in the arena when a young bull with padded horns was let loose. The animal ran among the young men throwing them in every direction, and the audience laughed, but the young men were serious.

When the *feria* was over, Ernest went fishing near Pamplona in the Irati River. It was like Michigan, only it was in Spain. The forests were large, the streams were filled with trout, and there was nobody around. After the crowds and cries of Pamplona it felt good to be in the mountains. Ernest loved the Irati. He was happy there in July 1924, as happy as he would ever be. Ernest fished near a waterfall; the beech trees and the pines moved slowly in the summer wind; his son was in Paris with his nurse; in a few days Ernest would see him, and he would feel how strong he was. The two books he had written were on a shelf in their apartment on the rue Notre Dame des Champs; the reviews had been good, and there were many more stories Ernest wanted to tell.

In the high mountains to the north the snow was melting; the water in the river was as cold as ice and the bottles of white wine which lay in the river were just as cold. The wine tasted good with the trout. As he lay back against the trunk of a fallen tree Ernest listened to the waterfall and the leaves; he loved Hadley; she was a generous woman, and she loved him. He thought of the *feria* he had just been to, and all the *ferias* he would go to next year, and the year after, and the books he would write about the people and the places he was going to see. In a week Ernest was going to be twenty-five years old.

Ernest spoke as an author. He said himself what others had been saying, that he was a "deadly serious" writer; he insisted that he must see and he insisted that he must fight to say what he had seen. He spoke of his eyes as if they were holy.

Ernest wanted to be a great writer. He wanted to raise up the true things he had seen until, with his imagination, he was able to make them truer than they had ever been. When the short, careful scenes of bullfighting which Ernest had drawn in his second book were compared to the bullfight etchings of Goya, Ernest was moved because he thought Goya was a great artist.

Ernest's feelings came out in his stories. He loved anybody who never gave up, anybody who went on, even if by going on it meant he would be killed. Ernest felt that in the end everybody gets hit, but just because a man knew he was going to lose was no reason to quit; with luck he could fight and last for a while. A man like Maera only became angry at his pain when he was hurt. Until he fell, Maera stood as straight as he could.

Ernest showed how much he hated the "god-damn phonys" who never fought, and he showed his disgust for those who were too afraid to fight, who only made gestures to keep from being hurt again.

Ernest's feelings for the man who fought were as strong as his feelings against the man who didn't, as if he were torn between what he hoped to be and what he refused to be.

At times Ernest was willing to say what he felt and explain what he hoped to do in his writing, but just as often he was completely unwilling to talk about anything except baseball and boxing.

Just before Christmas Ernest wanted to get away from the rain in Paris. He and Hadley and their baby went to a village in Austria, to a small family pension, where they all spent the winter in the sun and snow for only a few dollars a week. Every day Ernest was on his skis; he loved the powder snow, the high rock peaks, the glaciers, the chamois, and all the food served in the pension; he ate venison in wine, thick gravy on his potatoes, rich puddings, and he drank a dozen different kinds of beer. During the day Ernest was out in the sun, and at night he played poker and drank *eau-de-vie* made from cherries. He grew a beard.

By mail Ernest kept in touch with publishers in New York. In February 1925 the first offer came from an American publisher who wanted to publish *In Our Time,* not the original, thin volume, *in our time,* but a new and larger book, whose title was now to be written in capital letters. It was to be a book of brief and precise scenes, and many short stories. The publisher was afraid of two stories, because Ernest had written about sex as if it was real, not as if it was something to be hidden; one story was dirty and would have to be changed; the other was so clear about the fact that a man and a woman made love that it simply could not be published. Ernest was not surprised; he had always known people like this, and he was finding out they didn't all live in Oak Park.

Back in Paris, another letter came, this time from a magazine editor who said that a story which Ernest had submitted to him was a great story, really a great story, but that it was "too strong" for his readers. If "too strong" meant the story of a man who was down, who tried to fight his way up, who was willing to risk his life to get up, and who, on his way, was wounded and failed, then the editor was certainly right. Ernest hated the letter; he hated anyone who pretended that people don't get hurt.

Ernest signed a contract for *In Our Time,* and he also wrote warning the editor-in-chief not to change a word in his stories. *In Our Time* gave Ernest a good feeling. He was sure that anybody could enjoy his stories; they weren't written for the doctors of philosophy, but he thought the doctors would like them; they were written for anyone who wanted to see the world the way it was. Ernest hoped that would include a lot of people.

In the spring of 1925 a friend invited Ernest and Hadley over for a drink. One of the girls who had been invited was Pauline Pfeiffer, an American from Arkansas, a young woman with a lot of money who worked in Paris on *Vogue* magazine. Pauline didn't like Ernest, but it wasn't long before people thought that Pauline wanted Ernest to notice her.

That same spring a letter came from an editor in New York, Maxwell Perkins. He had written Ernest because an author of his, Scott Fitzgerald, had told him that Ernest Hemingway was one day going to be a great writer. Ernest answered, saying he would be glad to offer a book to Charles Scribner, the publisher where Perkins worked, but that for the moment he had nothing to send, having just signed a contract with another publisher. Ernest added that he might write a book about bullfighting one day, a big book. In May, Ernest met Scott Fitzgerald in a bar. The two writers drank champagne together; they took a trip together; they met each others' wives, and Ernest liked Scott's novel, *The Great Gatsby.*

In June, Ernest began a novel about a young man in the First World War who was wounded at Fossalta and then fell in love with a nurse in Milan. After a few pages he stopped.

In July it was time to go to Pamplona; the *feria* always began on July 7th, just two weeks before his birthday; Ernest liked that. Before the bullfights began, Ernest wanted to fish the Irati River; he thought of the year before when he'd first seen the river; he thought of how the fishing and the bulls so close together had made something perfect. But the Irati had been ruined; it was filled with the junk of a logging company; the forest was being cut down, the fish killed off. And Pamplona wasn't what it had been the past two years either. Ernest's friends brought their love affairs from the Latin Quarter to the *feria,* and this didn't help Ernest enjoy himself; the quarrels which the lovers brought with them kept intruding on the *feria,* but this did not stop Ernest from using them in the first novel he wrote.

In Madrid, within a few days of leaving Pamplona, Ernest started to write another novel. This time he did not stop. It was based on the people he had just left and on the events he had just seen. Only a few weeks before he began to write about

him, Ernest had met a young matador named Cayetano Ordóñez in Pamplona. Ernest thought Cayetano was the best he had ever seen and he introduced him to his friends and to Hadley. Something in Cayetano, something in what happened between Cayetano and Ernest's friends, and something in Ernest himself suddenly came together in a way which moved Ernest to write as he had never written before.

Ernest wrote in Madrid and he saw Cayetano in the Madrid bullring. Cayetano went to Valencia; Ernest followed. Ernest wrote in Valencia and he saw Cayetano perform again. The fireworks in Valencia were the greatest Ernest had ever seen; they shook the city, and they lit up the city. Ernest liked the explosions of sound and color, and he stayed up late every night to see them, but he started to write again early every morning.

Ernest had his birthday. He went on writing. The *feria* in Valencia ended at the end of the month. Ernest went back to Madrid. He wrote there. He and Hadley went north to San Sebastian and he continued to write, and on into France to Hendaye and he wrote in Hendaye, and when Hadley went back to Paris to get their apartment ready, Ernest stayed on alone in Hendaye and wrote. Then Ernest went back to Paris to write, and he wrote throughout August and into September, until on the 21st of September he wrote "The End" on the last page of his first novel. Ernest felt empty.

He worried about the title. He'd been calling his novel, *Fiesta,* but Ernest didn't like that anymore, and from a list of titles he finally chose *The Sun Also Rises.* Ernest had found his title in the Bible, in the words of a preacher who said that even though all the generations of men are born and then die, the earth goes on and "The sun also rises." The preacher's idea fit into what Ernest had seen. He knew that each generation must die, and that the earth was in no way changed by its death. He had seen the dawn come up in Michigan ever since he was a boy; he had seen the dawn in Italy during the war, and he had seen the dead. Ernest liked the dawn more than any other time of day.

There was still work to be done on the novel—cutting, changing, adding, making it clearer—but the work, the first work, was done and Ernest felt he had done it well. He felt like celebrating. He borrowed too much money, and he spent too much money to buy a painting to give Hadley for her birthday. The painting made Ernest happy; it was by Joan Miró; it was of a Spanish farm; it was big and it made Ernest think he was in Spain when he looked at it.

In Our Time was published in New York. Ernest was the only one who thought people would buy his book. Some critics began to say that Ernest wrote in a way no one else had ever written, that he was taking English apart and putting it back together in a new way. Some liked it and some didn't. Some thought his stories were "strong," "true," "hard," and some thought they weren't stories at all. Some said his way of writing was his own, and a few said he copied others. Ernest hated to be compared to anyone; he always fought to be himself, not just in his life but in his stories

Ernest wrote a quick, short satire to strike at the idea that he imitated other writers. His friends told him not to; Hadley said "No," but Ernest did it. He felt he had to defend himself against an unfair attack. The satire was vicious, but Ernest felt it served his purpose; it let everybody know they couldn't say anything they wanted to about him and get away with it.

From Oak Park, Ernest heard that his writing was "brutal," that it should be more "joyful," that it should "raise up" its readers, not lower them into "vulgarity." Grace Hall was disgusted. She felt Ernest had ignored the "spiritual heights"; that he had chosen the gutter over "the whole world full of beauty."

It hurt when Ernest learned his father was so shocked at his son's harsh words that he felt he had to return Ernest's books to the publisher because he could not have them in the house. Ernest had broken the rules, writing as he did, and neither Grace Hall nor Ed Hemingway forgave him. They had no choice; the make-believe world which they knew did not accept the painful stories which Ernest wrote. Grace Hall refused to see the "ugly" at any time; Ed Hemingway said it was all right to speak of syphilis in the doctor's office, but not in the living room.

Just as Ernest's Italian friends—VIVA ER-NESTO VIVA!—had violated Oak Park when they gave their big parties, so Ernest violated Oak Park when he wrote about what was, and not what ought to be. He stuck to what he knew to be true above all dreams and he was not forgiven for this. Even if people were in pain, even if they did what they should not do, it was better never to say so. If a handsome young man chose to mutilate

his genitals because of his twisted sense of religious purity it should be kept a secret; but Ernest chose to write about it.

At the end of 1925 Ernest, Hadley, and their son were back in Austria. The mountains were dangerous; an avalanche had killed nine; skiing was forbidden. Pauline Pfeiffer had become a good friend of Hadley's. She had made a point of this ever since she began to hope that Ernest would pay attention to her, and she had also become a friend of Ernest's. Now Pauline was in love with Ernest and now she went to Austria to spend Christmas with her friends the Hemingways. It was pleasant for Ernest to have two young women love him at the same time; at first it was fun, then difficult, but in the end it was painful.

Early in 1926 Ernest had to go to New York to straighten out his publishers; he had two books to place, his novel and his satire, and there were problems to be settled. Hadley decided to stay in the mountains with her son while Ernest was away, but Pauline followed Ernest to Paris, urging him to let her sail to New York with him. By now she wanted Ernest whether he was Hadley's husband or not, and Ernest had begun to want both Hadley and Pauline.

Ernest sailed alone knowing he was in trouble, but not having any idea what to do about it. In New York he changed publishers. He chose Scribners on Fifth Avenue to publish both new books and for the rest of his life Scribners was Ernest's American publisher. Maxwell Perkins, Ernest's new editor, became a good friend, one of the few men whose advice Ernest asked for and listened to.

A few weeks in New York were enough. In Oak Park Ernest's parents wondered if he would come home, but he did not; he went back to Paris and to the trouble he had left there. Pauline was waiting. Instead of going to Hadley in Austria, Ernest stayed in Paris with Pauline. Even though she was a Catholic, Pauline Pfeiffer had decided to marry a man she hoped would soon be divorced.

Ernest was happy and miserable. He couldn't choose and he didn't want to have to choose. When he went to Austria he felt so badly he wanted to die. He sat down to edit his novel, but he thought of new novels, and new short stories. Ernest was confused and didn't know what to do. He wondered about dying, about jumping off a ship to disappear under the waves, and he wondered about being wiped out by an avalanche, but nothing he wondered about did any good.

Going back to Paris didn't help either. One day Hadley said she knew, and Ernest became angry and blamed her for his trouble. If he had said "No" to Pauline and stuck to his word Ernest could have broken away. But he didn't say "No" and he didn't say "Yes" and things fell apart.

Ernest went to Spain alone and felt sorry for himself. In Madrid he wrote and went to the first bullfights of the season, but he couldn't stay still; he went back to France to see Hadley, to see Scott Fitzgerald and show him his new novel, to worry, to wonder what to do, to feel badly because he was doing something he felt he should not do, and to try to write. Ernest stayed with Fitzgerald and a dozen friends on the French Riviera, and then he moved to a hotel with Hadley and Pauline. They swam together; they ate together; they went out together, the three of them, and then the three of them went to Pamplona.

Pauline was set. She felt she was going to get what she wanted, and she was right. In August, Ernest and Hadley separated; Ernest went to live in a friend's apartment in the south of Paris, and Hadley went to live in a hotel; their apartment on the rue Notre Dame des Champs was empty.

Ernest often blamed Pauline for taking him away from Hadley, felt sorry that he had been taken away, spoke as if Pauline had made him do something against his wishes. Ernest always spoke of Hadley with love. Months later he said he still might go back to her; he wanted to. It wasn't easy; Ernest was in pain and he didn't like it.

From New York came the news that pain was not what editors wanted, the pain which comes from knowing that nothing is the way we want it to be, and knowing that many of the things which happen every day are terrible. "Too terrible" was exactly what the editor said about the story Ernest sent him, "too terrible" for the readers of the magazine to see in print that the world was not as beautiful as they hoped. Anything "too terrible" could not be published; the pain would be too great.

Some news was good. Max Perkins thought *The Sun Also Rises* was like life itself. Reading it, he said, felt as if he were seeing what Ernest had seen. This was good news; this was what Ernest wanted. He had spent too many years living with people who said "too terrible" every day and he was sick of it.

Ernest was torn. Work was going well, but life was not. His stories were translated into French and German; more and more people read his work; for the first time he was published in England; book sales in the United States grew month by month and at the same time the price he could ask for a new story rose. Not only were most reviews good, but what meant much more to Ernest than any review was the fact that people enjoyed reading what he wrote; his words, which he had so carefully chosen to tell others how he felt, were being read. It made Ernest feel as he never had before, as if he might never again feel like nothing.

Ernest was becoming famous, but he was sad. He said that the people in his novel were people who hurt themselves, who hurt others, and who didn't know how to stop hurting. This was the way he thought about himself and Hadley and Pauline. Ernest hurt as much in his life as the characters he had written about hurt in theirs. He said he was unhappy. He had no idea what to do. He cried and he prayed. Ernest tried to cover up his pain by being rude, by pretending to be beyond pain, by saying he'd beat up any guy he didn't like.

Pauline was in Arkansas with her family. When she told her mother she was going to marry a man who was married, her mother worried a lot about the woman the man was married to. Pauline's mother thought the other woman might suffer.

In Paris, Ernest thought about Hadley and he didn't like it; he knew he was wrong and he felt he had no right to be wrong. Ernest became bitter and he struck out with his fists and with the meanest words he could find.

More pain came from Oak Park. Grace Hall wrote to say that her life was a "heaven on earth" because it was dedicated to beauty. She could not understand why Ernest had written "one of the filthiest books." She wondered why her son no longer loved virtue, why he cared only for sin. She spoke of her prayers in which she hoped Ernest would discover good and shun evil. Grace Hall urged Ernest to devote his life, as she had always devoted hers, to making the world a happy place. She urged him to stop drinking liquor, to rise up, to call upon God in his hour of need, and she urged him to stop writing filth. Grace Hall urged all this, as she had ever since Ernest was born.

In January 1927 Ernest and Hadley were divorced. Ernest felt badly. He took a trip by car to

Italy with friends. Ernest was certain he had done something bad by breaking away from a good and loving woman. His guilt seemed to come from long ago, and when it struck, Ernest could only cry and pray.

In May, Ernest married Pauline. They went south to the Mediterranean; Ernest fished and wrote. In July, Ernest and Pauline went to Pamplona. A week later Ernest was twenty-eight years old, and a few days later he went back to Valencia to see the fireworks fill the sky every night, to see more bullfights, to hear the firecrackers explode at noon, to hear the best brass bands in Spain.

Ernest's life had changed; he had a new wife and the memory of having done something which hurt. Pauline had money, so much money that Ernest didn't have to stay in cheap hotels, didn't have to save, didn't need to write for newspapers in order to pay the rent. He was free in a way he had never been free; he could do what he wanted and not have to think about how much it cost.

From the time he first left Oak Park in 1917 until he married Pauline in 1927, Ernest had to fight; he had to break out of the world of make-believe; he had to feel death at Fossalta and feel the pain of his wounds; he had to live as he wanted and not as others chose, and he had to write as no one else had ever written. It had been hard. Ernest would have found it much easier to follow the way open to him, but he wanted his life, and he took it.

Max Perkins published a fourth book by Ernest, a new book of short stories, and immediately it sold well. It seemed that Ernest could do no wrong when he wrote; everyone enjoyed his stories, except those who found them to be "dirty" and about "vulgar" people.

Ernest read what people said about him, all of it, the articles in the press, the letters sent to him, and he became angry every time he was told to "clean up" his "dirty" world. To Ernest this meant he was supposed to lie. But there were many who said he wrote with a knife, cutting the pain from our lives so as to show it to us so we might know better what to do with it. They agreed with Ernest that silence was a lie and they said he wrote the truth.

Ernest cared too much about what people said; he acted as if he didn't, but he did care; he knew it was dangerous, that it could make him change the way he wrote and he didn't want this to happen.

Ernest wanted to write using his own words, put together his way. He lived to do this.

The year 1928 was important in Ernest's life. It began in Paris, when a large, glass skylight crashed on his head. He had pulled the chain which operated the broken skylight instead of the chain which operated the toilet he had just finished using. He was badly cut. Ernest was sewed up and had a new scar, none of which mattered at all except that the skylight proved that Ernest was a famous man.

International news services in Paris picked up the story of the author and the skylight and broadcast it around the world. Anxious cables crossed the Atlantic from the family; anxious editors who got in the act sent more cables; newspapers in Europe and America ran the story. An accident was turned into an event. Ernest was famous; he had become Ernest Hemingway.

For the rest of his life the press used Ernest. He became what they wanted him to be. Whatever he did or said, and whatever happened to him, was so blown up that it became impossible to see Ernest. He was treated not as a man who walks as other men, who hurts as much, who does as much wrong and wishes he didn't, but as a legend.

Ernest was restless in the spring; he wanted to go somewhere he had never been. He loved Paris; he still went down to the river to eat sausages and watch the barges go by, but he wanted to move and in April he and Pauline sailed to Havana and on to Key West, Florida.

Ernest explored the sea, the mangrove islands, the beaches, the local bars, and all the people he met in the bars. Ernest saw fish and birds he'd never seen; he felt the thick tropical heat for the first time, and the heavy rains which came and went quickly. He loved what he found, and he made the sea and the villages and cities along the edge of the sea his home. Ernest went to Africa, to China, and Peru; he always went back to Paris; he always went back to Spain, but the sea near Florida, near Cuba, would be his forever and his favorite part of the sea was the Gulf Stream. He called it his "great, deep blue river."

Soon after he reached Florida, Ernest learned by accident that his parents were also in Florida. Ernest saw them and his father made him sad. Ed Hemingway was gray and thin; he seemed ill at ease in clothes which had become too big for him. He was anxious about money and anxious about himself. Grace Hall looked fine and announced that she had never been healthier.

Ernest became a father for the second time in June; he and Pauline called their son Patrick. In July, Ernest missed the *feria* in Pamplona for the first time since 1923. All summer he was homesick for Spain and in the fall he was homesick for Paris.

Then in October, Ernest went to Oak Park; he hadn't been there for years. His father looked worse than he had in Florida, worse than Ernest remembered ever having seen him.

Grace Hall was well. She showed Ernest her beautiful new paintings with pride. "All's right with the world," Grace Hall said in the article written about her in the local Oak Park newspaper. "All's right with the world" was what Grace Hall had answered when the reporter who was interviewing her about her new paintings asked her what she thought about artists who were less optimistic about life than she was. Grace Hall, it was reported, always laughed at the dark side of life, only painted beauty and said that she was a happy woman.

Ernest returned to Florida, but three weeks later, in November, Ernest suddenly came back to Oak Park. Ed Hemingway was dead. He had shot himself in the head with his revolver. Grace Hall had heard the shot.

Ed Hemingway had worked very hard all his life. He was an excellent doctor, a generous man, a man who loved wild places and wild animals. He was a good cook who made wonderful pickles and loved to give them away; he always tried to be kind, but he was forced by his strict sense of right and wrong to be too hard on everyone. He always thought of others, but as a father he tried to help too much, and he hurt his children sometimes.

Ed Hemingway told no one why he killed himself; there was no one reason. Illness, money, anger, sadness, arguments, fear, the end of hope—all added up to a feeling of defeat, a defeat he could not forget.

It hurt to think that his father had been in pain, but Ernest remembered the days when they went fishing together, when they walked through the woods and his father talked about the animals and the plants and the lakes and streams, and how he had quickly learned everything he'd heard his father say and had never forgotten it. Ed Hemingway gave Ernest what he loved most and Ernest kept it.

The Gulf Stream and the Michigan woods were different; in the Gulf Stream a fish often weighed hundreds of pounds, a thousand or more at times.

In Michigan, a man could eat three or four trout for his supper, but the feeling in the woods and on the sea was the same, the feeling of being far away and of not knowing what was ahead. It was a feeling Ernest shared with his father. Ernest was sorry he could never take his father fishing with him on the "great, deep blue river," but most of all Ernest was sorry his father had never stood up to his mother.

After the funeral Ernest went back to Florida. Writing and fishing became his way of life, a way he stuck to. He wrote in the morning; he fished in the afternoon; he liked it that way; he liked the early-morning cool air. He awoke, to remember, to think, and to write, often in the same room where he'd slept. He liked to write, even though it was the hardest thing in the world to do well; it made him feel alive. To put himself into every word was the way Ernest liked to start the day, but he didn't want to be alone all day. After five or six hours, maybe seven, he was too tired, so by lunch, or by eleven if he'd started early, or by two if he'd started late, he'd stop.

Having spent himself and his morning working alone, Ernest wanted to move around in the afternoon, to go fishing and then go to the bars, to talk, to make friends, to find out as much as he could about everybody, and to find out correctly. Ernest wanted to hear what was being said; Key West was a good place for that because everybody went around saying what was on his mind.

Ernest liked the bars. Everybody was hot; everybody sweated, and everybody wanted a drink. The people in Key West liked Ernest, liked to drink and talk with him. He listened when they told him what they did and how they felt; lots of people were poor, and they told about how hard it was to live, how they could get killed at sea, how they had to fight to get along, and how even when they fought they didn't get anywhere. There weren't many phonys and all around there was the sea.

Key West was a small, scattered village on a narrow piece of land; when there was a storm, waves came onto the flat land. From the boat dock Ernest could leave Key West, leave his work behind, his wife, his friends, leave everything and everybody. At sea he could look as far as the horizon; at sea he could make his own world, choose who went with him, drink what he wanted, eat and sleep any time, read, fish, talk, watch the waves, or look at the clouds.

Ernest liked to stop at a beach that had no

name and swim alone and watch the brown pelicans. They flew slowly in a straight line, then suddenly, their wings folded back, from high up they dove straight into the water, disappeared in a white splash, and came up with a fish. And high against the blue, Ernest watched the black frigate birds gliding in long, slow curves.

Ernest began to study the fish in the Gulf Stream; he studied carefully, just as he had in Michigan when he was a boy, until he knew under which rock and near which reeds he would find trout, just as he studied death during the war in Italy, and his friends who hurt themselves in Paris and Pamplona. Very little, if anything, escaped him.

The Gulf Stream curves up and across the Atlantic Ocean. Near Florida and Cuba it is often a mile deep and up to eighty miles wide, and of all the fish in the Stream, the one Ernest studied the most was the marlin, and of all the fish—the wahoo, the tuna, the dolphin, the bonito, the grouper, the mako, the kingfish, the tarpon, the sailfish—the one he liked to catch most was the marlin.

His taste in fish was the same as his taste in men; he liked fish that fought if they had to, smart strong fish. The marlin was a fish, but it made Ernest think of a great bird, and a great horse; the marlin spread its pectoral fins like wings and seemed to fly, and the marlin was as strong and as nervous as a stallion; it moved beautifully and its colors were dark and alive.

To love a marlin was one thing, to catch one another. A man had to be in shape; he had to be strong, and as smart as the fish, and he had to be fair to catch the marlin honestly. Ernest loved to do something difficult and do it well; it was one of the things he loved most, and catching fish in the Gulf Stream according to the rules and with success demanded the kind of attention and total effort which he was ready to give when he decided to win.

Ernest did nothing halfway; if he was going to catch marlin he was going to do it as well as it had ever been done, or better. Writing was serious, so was fishing. To write well Ernest paid attention; he looked at words, studied them, found out what they did, how they changed, which were the good ones and the bad ones, then he worked hard putting together everything he had learned, and if he was lucky he wrote well. Fishing for marlin was the same; first Ernest listened to others, those who knew how to fish. He remembered what they said,

then he went to find out for himself, checking to see if they were right. He did this because he knew there were no quick answers; as a matter of fact, he went on checking as long as he fished, or wrote, or did anything, because he knew he could never know all the answers, and often what he had thought was a right answer turned out to be wrong, even if he had worked hard to find it.

It is impossible to study an animal that can't be seen, an animal that is born, and grows, and changes its sex in the ocean. Ernest found out there were nothing but questions about marlin, and that all the answers were only guesses. Strangest of all was the fact that it was difficult to know what kind of marlin it was even after the fish was in the boat. The different marlin had different names: striped, silvery, blue, black, white, but the names only described what the marlin looked like. The name didn't explain if these were different fish or if they were all the same fish at different ages. And it was difficult to decide on the sex of the fish because one fish might be a male one year and a female the next.

And there were questions to be answered about what the marlin ate, at what time of day, at what depth, and whether or not the marlin preferred to eat a fish which skipped quickly on the surface, or moved slowly a few feet below the surface. And questions about what direction marlin took in the morning, in the evening, in the summer, in the winter. Did marlin travel straight or in circles? At what depth did they travel and did they swim with or against a current, or did they do both? Does the wind affect a marlin's behavior? If the sun is out do they do one thing, and another if the sun is covered with clouds? And there were endless questions about which rods, which reels, which hooks were the best and finally, what was the best way to catch the marlin once he was hooked? Ernest wanted to know it all.

Ernest liked the feeling of being connected to a marlin. To stand or sit in a boat holding the rod which held the marlin, to feel the sudden great rush when the fish was hooked, to hold this power, to control this power with his hands, his shoulders, his back, his legs; this was a feeling which gave Ernest pleasure.

If a marlin was played for a long time before being brought in, sharks often attacked it. Ernest hated this. It hurt to think of the sharks destroying his marlin; it was as if the sharks were taking something precious away from him; almost as if they were attacking him. To protect his fish from the sharks, Ernest brought in his marlin faster than anyone else. He put all his strength into the fight, and he was strong. He never rested. If he rested, Ernest said, it meant the marlin could rest also and regain his strength. Ernest didn't play the marlin on the hook as if it were a trout; he fought it as if it were a wild horse. In thirty minutes Ernest caught a marlin. The marlin Ernest brought in were not mangled by sharks.

Coming home late in the afternoon when the sun was going down, Ernest looked at his marlin, part fish, part bird, part horse, and as he drank his beer he'd think of how many times the marlin had leaped out of the sea, and he'd think about it over and over again.

Ernest knew it hadn't been a fair fight; he said so. He knew it could not be fair unless the fisherman was hooked in the mouth also but, as he said, that would eliminate all fishermen.

Ernest fished in the Gulf Stream from 1928 to 1960.

When Ernest finished his second novel, he invited Max Perkins to come down from New York; at dawn every day he took his editor out fishing, and brought him back to shore in the evening. Ernest liked to share what he liked and Max Perkins, who rarely ever left his editor's desk, had the best time of his life. He also liked the new novel; he thought *A Farewell to Arms* was excellent; he predicted success, and he said he hoped to go fishing again with the author. When Max Perkins went back to New York he was very red from the sun.

A Farewell to Arms was written ten years after Ernest lived the story he wrote. In 1918 he went to war; in 1928 he wrote about war, about the pain, the love, the wounds, the battles, the retreats, the tears, the terrible waste, the explosions, and the dead.

Going fishing with Max every day, all day, was Ernest's way of celebrating the end of his novel. It was impossible for him to know whether what he had written was good or bad; he was still too close to his own feelings about the story to be able to decide. He turned to his friends who were writers, and asked them what they thought. He waited while they read, eagerly hoping to hear they liked his book; it felt as if he was being judged, and he was as impatient as any man waiting for the jury to bring their decision into court. The friends liked *A*

Farewell to Arms; they said they were moved; they said it was true, and Ernest was happy.

War was one of the most important things to Ernest, and he said what he felt about it in his book, about what war did to people, and what people did to make war. Ernest said that war meant everlasting pain, and that make·believe could never make such pain go away. If nobody felt safe when they read his stories it was because the world is not a safe place; if people felt afraid it was because there was good reason to be. In the spring of 1929 Ernest took his family back to Paris.

In Key West he'd been homesick for Paris; now in Paris he was homesick for Key West. It wasn't that he was not glad to be where he was; it was just that there were different things he liked and it was impossible to put them all together. If fireworks in Valencia could have been combined with bullfights in Pamplona, with the Gulf Stream and Paris and Michigan added, then Ernest would have been as happy as any man could be.

Ernest thought for a long time, and very carefully, before he decided exactly what he wanted to say, exactly what feeling he wanted to give, and in his mind there were not two different ways of saying one thing; there was only one. Though he knew he could be wrong Ernest felt he had chosen the right way. Therefore, when the magazine editors to whom Max Perkins showed Ernest's stories tried to change Ernest's words, he became angry. The editor in whose magazine *A Farewell to Arms* was to be serialized wanted to change Ernest's novel. Ernest refused. Reluctantly, and only because he was forced to, Ernest gave in on one point; he allowed dashes to be used instead of the "dirty" words he had written, but he defended his "dirty" words by saying that they were true.

By summer Ernest finished editing his novel. He traveled south from Paris as eagerly as if he hadn't been to Spain in many years. Having been away for one year felt like a long time to him. He missed the dry hot weather, so dry that in the summer a man's lips cracked and bled; he missed the trumpets which announced the bullfights late in the afternoon; he missed the thick grilled shrimps which were harvested from the sea, cooked, and eaten in less than an hour; he missed being with people whom he trusted more than any others; he missed the fireworks which filled the sky, and the barrels of wine, and the roast lamb, and the garlic, and the religious processions, and the gypsy horse markets. Ernest wanted to see the walls of Avila which seemed to grow out of the earth, and he wanted to look up at the high aqueduct which had stood gracefully for two thousand years in Segovia. And he wanted to walk through the cool pine forests in the mountains near Madrid, and go to Ronda where bullfighting had begun, near the southern coast and from which Africa could be seen on a clear day. And Ernest wanted to hear Spanish spoken everywhere he went.

Ernest adopted people he admired, from whom he could learn. They were people who were very much themselves, who acted as only they saw fit. Ernest met an American bullfighter, Sidney Franklin, and adopted him. He traveled with Sidney from one bullfight to another, and became his friend. For an American to be a bullfighter was strange, to be a good one, and Franklin was good, was unheard of. By adopting somebody Ernest added to himself, as if by doing this he could know the other person better and write about him more truthfully.

In the fall in Paris, which was the time when Ernest liked to be in Paris more than any other place, when the rust-brown chestnut leaves covered the boulevards, good news came from New York. *A Farewell to Arms* was a great success.

Ernest was as gentle and as kind as possible; all was right with the world. He didn't threaten to punch anybody; he took his friends to lunch and showed them his book, and had a good time. Before he was thirty Ernest was a famous author.

Ernest never put down a word he didn't believe in. He may have seen a thing as he wanted it to be, and not as it really was, but he tried to see it right. He never chose to be false to earn a dollar, nor to please someone. His one rule was to be true to himself and he kept to it. Because he worked this way he felt hurt when he was attacked and when he was hurt Ernest reacted brutally. For those who thought he was "filthy" Ernest had nothing but contempt and he threatened them with his anger. Ernest said their accusations were false.

But there was a kind of filth which was real; this was the easy talk, exaggerated and repeated with no regard for anything but the pleasure of the speaker and the person listening. Somebody said to somebody, that they had heard that the author, the famous and handsome young author of *The Sun Also Rises* and *A Farewell to Arms,* that they had heard he beat up his wife, that he was a pervert, and that his wife was too. And others said

they knew that Ernest had knocked out this man and that man and still another man. And there were those who knew that Ernest had not knocked these men out but had instead been knocked out by them. To some Ernest was a brute; to others he was a coward. These were the lies that amused; the cheap and stupid gossip was the real lie, not the pain which Ernest wrote about, which was ignored by those who refused to see it.

Ernest tried to protect himself from others; he didn't want to be invaded. He wanted to be private and didn't want anyone searching for his motives and his problems. He warned people off by seeming to be tougher than he was. On and off over the years Ernest boxed with his friends in Paris. He didn't always box according to the strict rules he believed in. He knew he should, but he didn't. He knew tricks which were unfair; still he used them, giving the excuse that he had to learn them when he was young, when his life had been rough. He knew his life had not been hard, in the sense that he had never been poor, never been locked in by dirty city streets, never fought his way out of a tight spot in an alley, but he did feel that he had been hurt; he did feel that he had been cornered, and that he had had to fight his way out, but he didn't want to talk about it.

His life had felt rough to Ernest but he was afraid no one would agree with him. To say he had lived in a big, new house on a beautiful street with a mother who sang beautifully and a father who was a fine doctor would not exactly sound very painful; no one would believe in his pain if he didn't make things sound much worse than they had been. And so Ernest invented a more obvious pain than the one he felt inside and, claiming to have been hurt in ways which could be easily believed, he said his childhood had been tough.

Being made to feel that his tears and his anger meant nothing, and that he could only do wrong, had left Ernest feeling raw, as if he were exposed to all the pain in the world. But it was dangerous to admit this; if he did, anybody could take advantage of him and hurt him over and over again; however, if he acted tough they might be more careful and he would not get hurt.

Ernest liked to be with people; he had many good friends everywhere. He only needed to warn when someone moved in too close. No one was allowed to discover how easy it was to hurt him. Ernest did not like to feel this way; it made him anxious to act tough, and this only made him act tougher. But he refused to be seen as a tender man, so sensitive that he felt not just his own pain but every man's.

Ernest acted as if he had no right to his tears and he buried them in his books. But Ernest was a tough man. If tough means uncomplaining; if it means not taking the easy way out; if it means being willing to do something that is difficult or dangerous for a long time, then Ernest certainly was tough.

In 1930 Ernest was thirty-one years old. His life was half over. He went on living as he had, writing about what he knew well, loving to fish more than anything else except writing, hating what he thought were lies.

Ernest fished in the Gulf Stream. Once, cut off from the world by a storm, he was isolated on a tropical island like a pirate. Ernest was as happy as he could be. He was always happier far away from cities, far from where rules are made and enforced.

When he was young Ernest ran off to the prairie, and went camping in the woods; now he sailed the Gulf Stream and made plans to go hunting in Africa. But he did not go to Africa, not yet; instead, he went hunting out West and, though for many years he drove back and forth across the United States from Florida to Wyoming, Ernest never turned in the direction of Oak Park.

In Wyoming, Ernest found bears and elk, in mountains and valleys that were more beautiful than any he had ever seen; and in the streams which ran through the valleys Ernest found trout. After sweating in the thick wet air of the tropics for months, Ernest loved the cold nights and dry days in the north. He went off on long pack trips; for weeks at a time he rode; he hunted and he fished, and joked around and ate, and drank with other men who also loved being far away. They lived around a campfire far from any road, and Ernest was as happy as when he had felt like a pirate in the Gulf Stream.

Ernest grew a beard at sea and grew a beard in the mountains; he ate marlin steaks and he ate bear steaks. He studied the stars in Key West and in Wyoming, and he compared them and learned the differences between the southern and the northern sky. When he went away there was time to enjoy the world, the sunrise, the clouds, the sunset, the rain, the wind, and the friends he had chosen. There was nobody to tell him what to do on a pack trip, nobody to make him feel he was wrong.

Year after year Ernest moved back and forth between the sea and the mountains with such regularity and such pleasure that he seemed to be spending his life just as he chose. Ernest wanted to live this way, not according to a thousand rules. He was a lucky man; Ernest found what he loved and he found the time to love it. He enjoyed feeling a boat move under his feet, a horse move between his legs and he was caught up in the hope of seeing a marlin or an elk.

At sea Ernest wanted to test himself against the power of the great fish—part bird, part horse—to see the fish jump from beneath the waves, so high that its blue body stood out against the storm clouds. Riding through the forest day after day, Ernest focused on finding a bull elk, and what would happen when he did. In which direction would the wind be blowing? How near could he approach? Should he approach on foot or on horse? Would the elk run or hide if he was scared? At what distance could he be certain of killing the elk with one shot? Ernest was obsessed with trying to find out who would win and how he would win.

When he was hunting, Ernest had no time to think about himself; he concentrated on his immediate needs. He thought about choosing the best campsite, finding a good supply of water, about the availability of dry wood; he thought about the weather and what to do if it rained hard and there was a flash flood, or what to do if the forest was dry and lightning struck. His concentration made Ernest feel alive. He kept track of every hour he spent in every forest and valley, and he used all he knew whenever he had the chance; it gave Ernest a sense of his own power and a sense of belonging in the world. Ernest liked to feel powerful but he enjoyed even more the feeling that he belonged; it made the world seem like a good place.

As he discovered when he was a boy, there are no lies in the forest. Ernest liked being free from lies; it made him feel safe.

If every year Ernest spent months fishing and hunting, he also spent months writing. Just as the two sides of a coin face in opposite directions, Ernest lived his life in two different ways. He was either under the sky enjoying the whole world around him, forgetting the things he didn't want to think about, hoping to catch the biggest fish of his life, running to get a shot at an antelope before the antelope reached the safety of the trees, drinking anything he wanted to drink, pumping bullets into a shark to keep it from attacking the marlin a friend had hooked . . . or Ernest was alone in a room writing.

Ernest used his life when he wrote; he used everything he ever did and everything that ever happened to him. He set no limits on what he wrote; his job was to draw a true picture. The one thing Ernest would not do was turn something into something it was not.

Ernest did not think of the truth as a noble goal toward which he was marching; he liked neither noble goals nor the noble words which accompanied them. Ernest was a dedicated man but the last thing he would ever have done was say so; he believed in doing the right thing. He knew how empty words can be, how quickly they can deceive. Ernest never said "the truth will make you free," but he spent his life writing as if he believed it.

Some men displayed their pain; Ernest kept his in, using it only when he wrote. Pain was one of his important tools, but Ernest did not debase it by drawing attention to himself. Ernest drew a sharp line between his life and his work; he wanted his stories to be seen but he wanted to be left alone; only his writing mattered; only his ability to turn himself into a story was important. It was as if Ernest had said, "Don't look at me. Look at my words."

Ernest is in his stories, all of him; nothing is missing. But Ernest hid behind his stories; he never wrote that he hated Grace Hall. He did not point and say, "This is my mother. She always complained and thought she was better than everybody and wanted her own way and did anything to get it." Ernest never wrote that Grace Hall was a bully and a fake; he never said it in one story, but he said it in many. It was not his way to write, "I hate you. You loved yourself. You didn't love me. You hurt me." Ernest did not choose to be the author of a book about the author, in which the author reveals himself. Instead he wrote many stories.

Ernest wanted to write, not about his pain and not about his fear, but about pain and fear. He could have written psychological essays, but the essay was not his way, any more than the autobiography was.

To do what he wanted, Ernest had to discover what made him feel the way he did. First he had to find all the pieces which, when they were put together, made him feel bad, or happy, or sad. He trained himself to feel the world, to see and hear and taste and smell it, until he knew the world. He became as sensitive as he did to every shadow and whisper, because he had to. No act of will can make a man know the world as Ernest did; only a man who has to know in order to survive can do this. Ernest needed to bear witness to the real world. Acting as if he were being hunted with deadly lies, Ernest armed himself with the proof that the lies were lies. Then he wrote down the proof that others might defend themselves.

Whether they were the lies of a mother who pretends to love her son, or the lies of a politician who convinces the youth of his nation that duty calls them to battle, in order to gain more power for himself, Ernest gave evidence against them. But he did not come out and say, "I accuse!" Instead, he wrote a story in which lies are told, in which "dear" becomes a weapon in the mouth of the wife who only seems to be a loving wife.

Ernest never preached. He never said, "This is a sin!" He had heard too many sermons in which too many things were called sins not to be disgusted by them. Ernest never told anyone what to think nor how to feel. He left a man free to decide for himself. If he told his story well, Ernest thought it must be clear that instead of "dear" the loving wife was saying "damn."

Ernest did not single out lies because they were sins, but because they hurt people. The soldier whose body was torn apart to satisfy the politician suffered from the lies he was told; the husband who gave in to his wife who said "dear" suffered from her lies. It was their pain which made Ernest care and it was in pain that he felt close to them.

Ernest said that all stories end in death, if correctly told, and so no matter how hard we fight to live we end up defeated. But we are here and we must go on. Ernest took sides with those who hurt; in his stories he joins every man who tries hard, so hard that it almost kills him, but who keeps on until in the end he dies. Death never let a man down; it was real and always waiting. Ernest studied death everywhere.

At thirty-one Ernest wrote *Death in the Afternoon*. He hoped to give a feeling of what a bullfight was by putting together a countless number of the pieces he had gathered in the bullring ever since he first went to Spain in 1923. Over the years he had found each piece by making himself know the bullfight world, a world as strange to a man from Oak Park as any that can be imagined, a world of horses being disemboweled, of blaring trumpets, of crowds that shriek their hate and their love, a world of gold and red, and of death every afternoon.

If the new book was about death and the agony which comes before death, it was also a celebration of all that Ernest loved in Spain. These were the two sides of Ernest, the one side which had to see death and the other side which enjoyed life for all it was worth. The two sides fought. Ernest never denied either; with one eye on the grave he kept the other fixed on the next day's fishing trip.

From his own childhood Ernest knew pain, and from the explosion at Fossalta, and from the accidents which struck him; an arm broken in a car crash was broken so terribly that for months Ernest was in constant agony in a hospital. But though he knew pain, looked at it, and wrote about it, Ernest was not blinded by it; he saw pain as one part of the world which also gave him the women he loved, his friends, all the onion sandwiches he could eat, and the ocean and the sun.

Ernest went to Spain to finish *Death in the Afternoon*. He was never far from death; either he gave it with a gun or a fishing rod, or he went to see death in a bullring. The sight of death, however, was never as bad as feeling down. When all sense of power went out of him, Ernest felt like nothing; his words failed to say what he wanted them to, and he felt he would stay down forever. But Ernest always came back. He came back up to feeling that the world was his.

It was impossible for him to escape the idea that he didn't matter, and that what he did was wrong. Because he felt this way Ernest learned how to stand it, and it never got too bad for too long. It was just like any other fight; Ernest had to know how to last until he came out on top.

Ernest spent most of 1933 on top of the world even though the year began badly. Hollywood made a movie of *A Farewell to Arms* and changed the end from what Ernest had written. In anger he called the movie a "monstrosity." Monsters violate what we are used to seeing, and the Hollywood ending to his novel violated the truth; the lie was up there on the screen for everyone to see. Ernest believed there are no happy endings; it was sickening to see the tears and the despair he had written about turned into a row of smiles. It reminded Ernest of the way Oak Park turned the real world into a pretty dream.

In the spring Ernest went to sea; for two months he caught a marlin every day in the Gulf Stream.

Then he went to Spain to hunt wild boar and watch the bullfights in August. In the fall he went to France to hunt deer and shoot pheasants, and in November Ernest sailed from Marseille to Africa. The safari he had planned for so long was real at last.

To Ernest the Gulf Stream was ten thousand Michigan lakes rolled into one great current; East Africa was ten thousand Michigan woods and fields, greater and more wonderful, far more wonderful than Ernest had dreamed. Life moved like a strong river across the high plain; great herds grazed with the rains and the sun, drinking, giving birth, dying, and returning to the earth; the cats ate the sick, the old, and the young who were unprotected. The giraffes moved high above the herds and the cats, and above them flew the birds. Along the edge of the plain the elephants moved slowly in and out of the forest.

Ernest felt as if he had burst into a new world; the animals were new, kudu and eland, rhino and waterbuck; the people and their languages were new, the Kikuyu, the Kamba and the Masai; even some of the stars at night were new.

With Ernest on safari there was a white hunter, Philip Percival, Pauline, a friend, and the Africans who worked for Percival. They lived on the plains or in the forest with the animals, apart from the world of villages and cities.

Percival was a gentleman; Ernest liked him, and Percival discovered quickly that Ernest wanted to learn everything about the animals and the people who came to hunt them, and the land and the people who lived on it. Ernest listened to Percival; he made no notes but he paid careful attention and he remembered. Later, when he came back from Africa, Ernest turned all he had seen and heard in Africa into stories. While he was hunting he didn't write.

For two and a half months Ernest lived on safari. In the midst of his happiness Ernest felt the dark side; he watched black flies cluster and eat their way across a lion's wound; he saw how the flies made the lion suffer; it seemed as if there was always something to make suffering worse. Ernest became sick, and no matter how hard he fought to be well, his sickness forced him to fly out in a rescue plane from the safari camp he loved to a hospital in Nairobi.

And on safari Ernest suffered because he had to win. He could not spend weeks hoping to shoot an antelope, track it, bring it down with one shot in the shoulder, and enjoy it if another man shot a bigger and a better antelope. Ernest's antelope had to be the best; his novel had to be the best. Life was a fight; Ernest never made a secret of it. He said he was glad to put his stories up against the stories any other man had written, but not against Tolstoi and Dostoievsky. Most of the time Ernest felt he would win; some fights might end in a draw, but in the ring against the Russians he was sure to lose and so, he said, he preferred not to fight them. Ernest wanted to enjoy without fighting; he knew it would be better if he could. Having to win spoiled things; it ate away in places it shouldn't.

But there was a wonderful side to the safari, free from illness, and flies, and the need to win, filled with the sun rising over the far edge of the great plain, filled with a great mountain, filled with every living animal a man could want to see. His first safari was not yet over when Ernest started to plan the next. As soon as he stopped hunting, Ernest went to fish in the Indian Ocean and while he was fishing he dreamed of the day he would return, and fish all the way from the Mediterranean down the Red Sea and into the Indian Ocean. Ernest was not to be stopped; he went on and on as far and as long as he could.

From Africa, Ernest went to Paris and in Paris he read that a man had taken the trouble to write that Ernest was dumb, that he was an unfeeling and unthinking brute. Out in Wyoming, the cowboys who went hunting bear with Ernest, and the fishermen in Florida who went after marlin with him, and the Kikuyu tribesmen in Africa who helped Ernest track lion, all enjoyed being with Ernest and he enjoyed them.

Ernest didn't like people who appoint themselves to criticize others; they reminded him all too much of Oak Park. Ernest also felt that too many men are willing to earn money by picking at other men, and then complaining about the pickings. Ernest felt it was not useful and it certainly was unpleasant. They were a breed Ernest could do without and he made it very clear, which only annoyed the breed more. It was their pretension which angered Ernest, the pretension which allowed them to think they had the right to tell others how to live and write, when they had not distinguished themselves either in the field of living or writing.

Ernest didn't stay long in Paris; he moved on to New York. Across the East River in Brooklyn he did something he had wanted to do for a long

time; he ordered a fishing boat built to his exact specifications.

Ernest christened her *Pilar,* after the patron saint of Zaragoza. He sailed on her year after year with his wives, his sons, and his friends. He lived on *Pilar* at anchor in tropical bays where no one could find him; he steered her through storms when he was afraid he and *Pilar* might both go down. Ernest took care of *Pilar* when a hurricane threatened her, tying her up, watching over her during the night until all danger was past. He repaired her and he painted her and he was happy fishing from her deck.

Back in Key West, Ernest began to turn his life in Africa into his next book; he aimed at being more truthful than ever before. He wrote, and he waited for *Pilar* to be delivered, and he planned where to go with her when she arrived. Ernest felt good; he wrote about all the things he loved to see and do and he named the many places he loved, but he left out Oak Park, as if he loved every place he had ever gone, but not the place he came from.

At thirty-five Ernest was proud of not being "a god-damn phony"; proud of enjoying his life so much that most of the time he looked forward to the dawn of the next day as the best part of the day. And he was famous, and as he became more famous more people told more stories about him and, whether or not they were true, with each new story his fame grew. Some despised him for being a phony himself; others felt he was the best they had ever known. From these stories, and from the hate and the love which people felt for him, the legend of Ernest Hemingway grew. The legend made him a giant, and Ernest got lost. It was also said that he came to believe in the legend himself, that he acted like a living giant; if he did, it was only his answer to those who saw him as one.

Ernest went on wanting to write better than he had ever written and fish better than he had ever fished. Ernest didn't think he had won just because he was famous. He sailed to the island of Bimini in *Pilar.* He issued a challenge to anyone who wanted to box and he tried to bring tuna and marlin into his boat faster than anyone had ever done it. He boasted of catching a fish of almost a thousand pounds in half an hour. Speed was important; it kept the sharks away from the fish he had hooked. Ernest had to be strong to box all comers and strong to bring in big fish in record time. He was proud of his strength and of his victories; he liked to tell about them and, as all victories do, they grew when they were told.

When he finished his book about Africa, Ernest was optimistic. He was sure he had done what he had set out to do, put his reader into the shoes he had worn on safari. Just as he had issued a challenge in Bimini to anyone who wanted to step into the ring with him, now he issued a challenge with his new book. He felt ready to defend his title. He dared people to say his book wasn't the best, and just as they did when he published *Death in the Afternoon,* many took up the challenge and said *Green Hills of Africa* was the worst. They took the opportunity to attack Ernest, striking at the man through his work, showing how much they disapproved of his going to bullfights, sneering at his safari, saying that his fishing was foolish. Maybe they were jealous or maybe his pride made them mad; whatever the reason, they hit Ernest and not what he wrote.

Ernest thought this was unjust; he thought they had no right to find fault with his political opinions, when he had none beyond thinking that all politicians were frauds. When he said this, fault was found with Ernest's lack of opinion; he was declared undedicated to his fellow man. Ernest refused to allow himself to be used by any men who were only out to benefit themselves. To take sides politically, as a writer, was to be castrated; it meant submitting to the will of another and to Ernest this spelled death. He not only had a right to his thoughts and feelings, but he had an obligation to keep them free; he would put them at the service of the world as he saw it, not as some politician said it was. Ernest believed that the truth about how one man felt about another man, the truth about how one man acted toward another, was far more important than the "truth" as told by a politician in a speech.

One morning Ernest rushed to a Government work camp after a hurricane had struck Florida. He saw more dead that day, he said, than at any other time since the war. Ernest was angry; he took the side of the victims, accusing the politicians of ignoring their camp, of not rescuing the men in time to save them from the hurricane. He had taken far better care of *Pilar* than the Government had of its men, he said.

Ernest studied the dead. He described how bloated and black they became in death. He collected pictures of them and he kept the pictures. The truth was simple; men in power did not care

for men who had no power. Ernest knew this and it was up to him to say so. It was his job. It was not his job to join the powerful.

Ernest was true to himself, to the one rule he obeyed above all others which demanded that he write about the world as he saw it. Ever since the night he was hit at Fossalta, Ernest had spoken against war, and against those who make war; not the soldiers who fight and die, but those who lie to them.

In 1936 a civil war broke out in Spain, and the insane lies which always accompany war immediately filled newspapers and radios around the world. Each side claimed to be good; each side proved the other side was evil, and both were certain that God would give them victory, and that justice would triumph. In the meantime, men were mutilated and the list of the dead grew each day. Ernest was certain that the war in Spain would soon lead to another and a larger war, a war that would fill the world with mountains of dead.

When a man nears forty he starts to repeat himself, doing what he knows best, making the same mistakes he has made before; rarely doing anything unexpected. In Key West, Ernest got ready to go hunting in Wyoming; at the same time he also wanted to go fishing in Bimini; he kept planning another safari in Africa, and he worried about dying. It would be a terrible thing when the day came for him to shoot himself, he said, but he reassured himself that he loved life. He began to write a novel set in Key West.

Ernest felt he should go to Spain, because he loved Spain and because he wanted to see the war, but his job was to finish his book first.

At the end of 1936 in a bar in Key West, Ernest met Martha Gellhorn, a young blond woman who was a writer. Ernest liked Martha, and he immediately began to be as charming as he could when he was with her. Martha met Pauline, just as Pauline met Hadley, but Pauline was suspicious from the beginning, whereas Hadley had suspected nothing for a long time.

The next year Ernest decided to go to Spain. He would go, he said, as an "antiwar correspondent." He would try to warn the United States of the danger ahead, hoping, he added, to help his country stay out of the next World War.

New York, Paris, Barcelona, Alicante, Valencia, Madrid. As soon as he reached Madrid, Ernest drove to the front; he had never watched anything from a distance, and he didn't plan to change his habits just because he could be killed. He wanted to see entire battles and he wanted to talk to the men who fought them. And again, Ernest wanted to know how he felt when his own life was in danger.

But Ernest didn't have to go to the front to find out; death was all around him in Madrid. The hotel where he lived was hit by exploding shells; people were killed in the streets every hour; bullets and shrapnel were more common in the city than in some sectors of the front.

Ernest studied what interested him. He examined battle plans; discussed strategy with commanding officers; spent hours talking military tactics, and everywhere he went Ernest impressed the professional soldiers with his knowledge of the science of war. Ernest had to know how something was done, whether it was catching a trout in a Michigan stream or capturing a city in Spain. How something was done was real. Only if he knew how did Ernest feel he could write the truth.

Ernest was cheerful. He was learning and he felt that this would make him write better than ever before. To be with men who were fighting to survive gave Ernest the feeling that he was with his own kind. Ernest insisted on living, even though he was constantly threatened by death, and he enjoyed being with others who insisted on doing the same. Going to war was like joining a club where all the members played the same game. The daily victory over death made Ernest feel more alive, as if he had the power to win over and over again.

Ernest made new friends with generals and lieutenants and privates, with Spaniards, Russians, and Americans, with doctors, tank drivers, waiters, and chauffeurs; anyone he met might become his friend. Often Ernest drove northwest out of Madrid to the Guadarrama Mountains. He saw the troops fight in the pine forest; he saw the enemy planes; listened to the guerilla fighters and wondered when victory would come, and if it would come.

Martha Gellhorn came to Madrid as a war correspondent. She lived in the same hotel as Ernest, and they went to the front together. Pauline was in Key West with her two sons.

The war was a political war; it was not a war fought to conquer an enemy land. Spain was her own enemy; she stole from herself; killed herself; Spaniard raped Spaniard. Ernest saw this and he took sides with the people. He helped to make a film which would be used to raise money to buy ambulances. Just as in World War I, Ernest wanted to help the wounded.

Suddenly in the spring Ernest left. Paris, New York, Key West. At home, Ernest settled down to edit his novel. And then he did something very unusual; he gave a speech in New York in a theater to a meeting of writers. Ernest was met with an ovation. He told the crowd that he had one goal and that he thought it should be every writer's goal: to "write truly" and "in such a way that it becomes part of the experience of the person who reads it."

Ernest had built his life on this; he had, however, never before stood up in public and said it. He went on believing it until he died. Whenever he wrote, Ernest tried to make a new piece of the universe, so new and so true that whoever read his words would feel forever that he had lived what Ernest had written.

Because he refused to join one side, Ernest did not act politically. He leaned toward the Republicans in the Spanish Civil War, against the Fascists, but that was because he believed in freedom, not because he believed in one political party over another. He saw good and evil on both sides because he saw through the lies which both sides told.

For once Ernest set out to work for a cause. He went to the White House to show the movie he had helped to make in Spain, hoping to urge President Roosevelt to side with the Republicans, and he went to Hollywood hoping to raise money for ambulances. Then Ernest went back to Key West, but not for long. After a few weeks' fishing he went straight back to war. From the fall of 1937 until early 1938 Ernest stayed in Spain; many times he was almost killed.

Ernest's new novel was published in the States. The usual happened. The novel immediately sold very well, but the fight was on. Some critics attacked; some liked the novel. It seemed to Ernest that it was a lot easier to complain than it was to write; it didn't seem fair, but the most unfair was when the complaints were about him, and not what he wrote. Ernest should have been used to this by the time he was thirty-eight, but he wasn't. He never learned to ignore the people who found fault with him. Ernest called them murderers instead of dismissing them as fools.

Ernest and Martha spent Christmas together in Barcelona while Pauline waited for her husband in

Paris. She still hoped to save her marriage. When Ernest came to Paris he fought with Pauline because of Martha. From Paris, Ernest went back to New York and south again to Key West. It seemed as if he couldn't stop moving.

Just as he had felt remorse when he left Hadley, Ernest was unhappy because he was leaving Pauline. He became more suspicious of others when he felt badly. He put more and more people into the class of the critics who were "out to get him." And as if he felt he was committing a sin, and would be caught and hurt for it, Ernest grew more wary. His only escape was to sail into the Gulf Stream on *Pilar*. Catching marlin brought relief, but after the fish were caught Ernest had to sail back to shore. He could not sail away forever on his boat, but he could return to war and try to forget.

Within three months of leaving Spain, Ernest was back. Just as he had to fish and had to hunt, Ernest had to go to war. He felt strangely better near the bombs and the exploding artillery shells.

In his hotel room in Madrid, Ernest wrote stories for magazines in which he tried to make the readers feel what it was like to be at war. With words he tried to turn one lost man standing by one bridge into all lost men. In his stories Ernest wrote what he knew about feeling hurt. He felt better when he wrote, as if he were able to get rid of his pain by putting it into words; it was a way of trying to feel less helpless; and when he wrote about men who were brave and strong it was a way of helping himself feel braver and stronger.

When he was not writing, when he was at war, Ernest was the first to help the wounded. Ernest was not just a man of words; when there was danger he acted; he kneeled down at the side of men who had fallen; he cleaned the blood from their faces, put on their bandages, tried to make them comfortable, and if they were dying he gently spoke the last words which they heard. The "critic" who said Ernest was a brutal man, who complained that his values were not high enough, never lay in the mud with a leg blown off with Ernest at his side.

Ernest left Spain, left the war, and went home to Key West. Wherever he went he made it clear that he hated the Fascists, hated the war, that he cared for freedom and the people, and that he didn't care for politicians anywhere.

That summer Ernest decided to start a new book of short stories in which he wanted to write what he had learned in Spain. The new book would be so great that with this one blow Ernest felt he would knock out all the critics at once; never again would they be able to attack.

From Florida, Ernest went out to Wyoming, but he couldn't stay away from Spain, and after a few weeks he sailed from New York on his way back to the war. Over and over again Ernest was almost killed. When the war was almost over Ernest left for the last time, to go home.

In March 1939 in Havana, Ernest sat down to write a novel set in the Guadarrama Mountains near Madrid, a novel about the men and the women who fought in the Spanish Civil War. Ernest worked steadily for a year and a half; he worked harder at the job of writing this book than he ever had in his life.

On his fortieth birthday, Ernest was more excited about his life than ever before. Every day began with his book, and the book went well. All morning Ernest lived with his feelings and his words and in the afternoon he sailed in the Gulf Stream on *Pilar*. He wrote and he fished; half work and half play made Ernest a happy man. Nothing in the world interested him except his book. After six months Ernest switched from writing and fishing to writing and hunting, from the Gulf Stream to the Rockies.

Ernest was in Wyoming when the next World War began in the fall of 1939. He was not tempted to go back to war; he was too busy writing about it. The new war did not surprise Ernest; it was just an extension of the one in Spain.

Ernest went west to Idaho; from the first day he saw the village of Ketchum, Ernest liked the place and the people. He quickly made new friends and one day when they were talking about their mothers and fathers Ernest said that Grace Hall was a bitch. His friends objected; they thought his language was too rude to use about his mother, but Ernest reassured them that he would not have said Grace Hall was a bitch if she had not really been a bitch, and if he had not really hated her.

Just before Christmas, Ernest returned to Havana. He and Martha had been living together for many months, even though he was still married to Pauline. Divorce had been discussed. Finca Vigía, Lookout Farm, was the name of the large house and property fifteen miles outside Havana where Ernest went to live early in 1940. Ernest liked the

143

name of his new house; he thought it suited him.

Whether he was in Idaho, or in his new house in Cuba, or whether the world was at war, or the sun moved on its appointed course across the sky, really didn't matter at all to Ernest; he was writing a story and that was all he cared about. Every day he counted the words he wrote; he counted them very carefully and he told his friends how many there were: 385, 404, 462, 551, 388, 817, 275, 654. Ernest felt drugged by his words; he could not escape them. Ernest was held by his story. He had to write it. Ernest said this was a disease, and if it was, so were fishing and hunting and going to war, because they also held him.

The title which Ernest gave to his novel showed how he felt, not just about men at war but about all men. The Bible had always been one of his favorite places to look for titles; he had found *The Sun Also Rises* there, but this time neither the Bible nor Shakespeare were of any help.

Ernest read an English poet who said that every time one man died, no matter who, and no matter where, he felt that man's death because he was "involved in Mankinde." There was never any point in asking "for whom the bell tolls" because it always "tolls for thee." This was exactly the feeling Ernest wanted to give and he immediately called his novel *For Whom the Bell Tolls,* a title to be expected from a man ready to kneel at the side of another man who was hurt.

A letter came from Grace Hall. She almost never wrote because for many years Ernest had made it clear that he did not want to hear from her. Grace Hall wrote to say that someone had told her that Ernest was writing a novel; she hoped, Grace Hall said, that for once in his life Ernest would write "something constructive." She, who never knelt beside anyone, but who so often spoke in praise of helping others, was worried about discovering filth in her son's latest book.

The words which Ernest gave to the hero of his novel were the same words he used in his life; the hero was sad because his mother was a tyrant, sadder still because his father was too weak to fight back. The hero's father killed himself with a pistol; the hero never forgave his mother, nor did Ernest ever forgive Grace Hall.

Ernest was a rich man at forty; he could write anywhere in the world; he could choose to live in New Zealand or Sweden, in Rio or Peking, but he chose to buy a house near Havana and live in it for twenty years. Havana is only a mile from the Gulf Stream and Ernest's house was near the harbor where *Pilar* lay at anchor. Escape was easy, not just escape, but the pleasure of fighting the marlin, the underwater horse with wings.

In 1940 Havana was a place where Ernest could shoot live pigeons at a private club down the road from his house; where Ernest could legally raise fighting cocks and bet on them; where he could meet and talk with his favorite whore at his favorite bar. Havana was a place to which people came to see live sex shows for a price, where anybody could get a drink of whatever he wanted at any time, where all kinds of dope were sold. There were factories in Havana where they made rum and there were gambling casinos. As long as a man had money, in Havana he could have all the fun he wanted.

And Havana was a beautiful city. The hotels and beach clubs were large and comfortable, the avenues were wide, the streets were lined with trees, the markets filled with the colors of every tropical fruit. And there were restaurants where you could eat good French food, good Spanish, Chinese or Indian food, and you could eat all the fresh fish you wanted, including marlin steaks. And there were places in Havana where you could hear an opera, see a play, a movie, bet on a jai alai game, watch a dog run and bet on the dog, or a horse and bet on the horse.

At the entrance to the harbor a great castle was built to protect the galleons which held the gold and silver the Spanish conquerors stole from the Indian empires in Mexico and Peru. The galleons waited in Havana before sailing to deliver the wealth of the New World to the King of Spain.

In Havana in 1940 you could dress up like a millionaire or you could walk around in old shorts; there were no rules and nobody bothered you. Havana was as wide open as Oak Park was closed.

By the fall Ernest had finished writing; he was busy working with his editor. Ernest made some minor changes, but he would not change what he had written about death, not one word, no matter what anybody said. If what he had written was terrifying, so much the better; that was the way the world was, and he would not pretend it was any other way. Ernest did not agree that because something was painful it was in bad taste; only a lie was in bad taste in his opinion; and to lie about death would be the worst lie.

Ernest dedicated his book to Martha, and by the end of the year Martha became his wife;

Ernest said he preferred living with her legally.

Within one year *For Whom the Bell Tolls* sold more than a half million copies; a writer whose dream was to be read, Ernest saw his dream come true. Within that year Ernest read that his book was "great," "beautiful," and "true," and he also read that he was "rude," "vain," and "arrogant."

He reacted with pleasure and anger. Ernest was angry to read that many people felt he was wrong not to have taken a firm political position. Those on the right were angry that he had rejected them; those on the left were even angrier that he had not sided with the left. Neither right nor left respected the side Ernest took, which was not political. Both right and left were only interested in themselves, not in the men who died at the front.

Ernest went to China to another war; he and Martha went together as war correspondents. He did the same thing with the war in China as he had in Spain; he studied it. He went everywhere, by river boat, by cart, by plane and by pony, and he never avoided the front line.

Ernest watched eighty thousand men building an airfield with their hands; afterward he said that he felt as if he had seen the pyramids of Egypt being built. The eighty thousand men in China sang as they worked. Ernest felt they wanted to win; he felt close to them and he did not forget them.

While Ernest was at war he was denied a literary prize by the President of Columbia University in New York because the President did not wish his great university to be linked with trash. The principal of Oak Park High who looked for dirty meanings in the jokes which students published in the school newspaper would have applauded the university president who refused to give Ernest what many felt he deserved.

Ernest came home. Instead of traveling between Key West and Wyoming, Ernest now began to travel between Havana and Idaho. He did this for the rest of his life. Taylor Williams was a guide in Ketchum. He became a friend of Ernest's, a good friend, the kind Ernest liked best; a man who was honest, who said what he liked and disliked, who never faked anything, who knew what he was doing and did it well; a man who was aware that life was often both complicated and painful, but who did not sit around and worry about it. Taylor liked Ernest; he was a hard man to please, but he was always glad to be with Ernest, and, Taylor said, Ernest was a man to be with when things were difficult. It wasn't, Taylor added, just that Ernest liked it when things were hard; Ernest was a better man, Taylor said, when things were hard. Taylor believed that the more Ernest was asked to give the more he gave.

In December 1941 the United States was attacked by Japan. Even though he hated war, once his country was at war Ernest felt they should fight to win. Ernest decided to fight in a very strange way. He convinced the staff at the United States Embassy in Havana that he could help to win if he was officially helped to do two things. First, Ernest was to be allowed to create a private intelligence agency; his friends would act as secret agents, and he as chief agent would bring the intelligence in to the Embassy. Secondly, Ernest was to be supplied with the weapons necessary to transform *Pilar* from a fishing boat into a submarine chaser. Ernest felt that his great knowledge of the sea would permit him to find enemy submarines when they surfaced. Once found, *Pilar* would approach slowly, disguised as a fishing boat, and then suddenly, at the last moment, Ernest and his crew would man their hidden machine guns and mow down the German sailors while, at the same time, throwing grenades down the open submarine tower.

Ernest's power of persuasion was such that the United States Ambassador agreed to all that Ernest asked. Ernest gathered his friends: jai alai players, priests, waiters, fishermen, farmers, rich men, poor men, anyone Ernest felt he could trust, and the intelligence agency went to work. They worked together and they drank together, and now and then Ernest secretly reported to his superiors.

Pilar was filled with explosives; she set out to sea and the chase was on. Never did Ernest doubt that he would succeed. Through the summer, fall and winter of 1942 and all through 1943, Ernest looked for submarines. He often heard German U-boat captains talking on the radio, but only once did he see a submarine far away, and it quickly disappeared.

When Ernest was not at sea, all the pals who served as crew on *Pilar,* and all the secret agents, and all the other old friends, and the new friends met for drinks and meals at the Finca. Ernest was rich and friendly and everyone knew he liked to have a good time. It was a three-ring circus and Ernest enjoyed it. He stopped writing completely and there were no fixed hours to eat or sleep. Champagne, absinthe, red wine, white wine, rum, vodka, brandy, gin, beer, scotch, bourbon.

French, English, Spanish, Basque, American. Noon or midnight, the front gate to Ernest's property was never closed.

Martha didn't like it and Ernest didn't like her criticism. Martha said Ernest didn't make any sense; he was too blown up with his own self-importance, she said. He hated it when Martha went away and did what she wanted, and he hated it when she came back and told him that he only cared about himself. Ernest made it clear that he refused to be told what to do by his wife, but, in turn, he expected her to do exactly as she was told by him. Above all he wanted to be certain that he could not be hurt by her, and he felt that if he had the final word he would be safe.

To be safe was important to Ernest. When he felt threatened, a black rage overcame him, a rage which he let loose in any direction. It seemed to Ernest that he was being ignored if anyone defied him, and he could not stand being ignored; it made him feel as if he were nothing at all. The smaller he felt the more Ernest needed to explode.

As he grew more and more anxious, Ernest needed to be reassured that he indeed was not nothing, that he was a writer, a fisherman, a hunter, a boxer, a man! The easy and quick way to make him feel better was to say, "Yes." When he felt badly Ernest started down; the worse he felt the worse he acted.

Fighting with Martha made Ernest drink more, which made Martha angrier. There was no way out. The more he drank the more Martha felt like leaving; and the more Ernest felt as if he was being abandoned, just when he needed Martha most, the more he became enraged. Ernest had no intention of ever being bullied like his father; having seen his father act like a coward was enough; he was never going to let this happen to him. Ernest wanted to be free to come and go, to give orders and have them followed, to know he was not going to be hurt by a woman. Once was enough.

For two and a half years Ernest did not write; during this time his last book sold a million copies, but not writing depressed Ernest and often made him mean. He wanted to write but he didn't; he wanted to see the war in Europe but he didn't go. He liked his pigeon-shooting club; he liked the Gulf Stream; he liked the double frozen daiquiris at his favorite bar. He liked his friends, his house and his dozen servants, his private pool, his big comfortable car, the good food at home and the jai alai games in town.

Martha came and went as she pleased; she traveled as a war correspondent, and she urged Ernest to do the same. She thought that the life Ernest led in Havana, playing at war, not writing a word and drinking too much, was bad for him. But Ernest would not move. Then, just before it was too late to see the big show in Europe, Ernest left Havana and went to New York a few weeks before D-Day. From May 1944 until January 1945, Ernest lived it up as he never had before.

In New York he enjoyed his usual five-pound can of caviar with friends. At the last minute one Sunday, Ernest remembered to send a Mother's Day telegram to his "old bitch," and a few days later, he flew to London.

Ernest's ancestors were English but he had never been to England. He stayed at one of the best hotels in London, and within a day of his arrival his room was a circus filled with old and new friends. Ernest's life moved more and more quickly. He met a young, blond American foreign correspondent at lunch; her name was Mary Welsh. Ernest liked her and he began his courtship immediately. He went to a party and after the party he hit his head badly in an automobile crash. He went to the hospital and worried about his accident because he was afraid it would keep him from going to France on D-Day. He had terrible headaches even when he left the hospital.

On the night of June 5th, Ernest sailed to Normandy with the greatest fleet ever assembled, and at dawn he saw the greatest invasion. He went with the troops to the edge of the beach but he was not allowed to land, and had to return to London. When he heard that Martha had landed on D-Day, Ernest was angry; he did not like being defeated by anyone, and especially not by his wife. In London, Ernest was happy to see Mary Welsh. He found her charming and he was in turn charming himself. Ernest saved his anger for Martha who, he felt, was continuing to be cruel to him, and in turn he was rude to her.

Ernest wanted to go bombing with the Royal Air Force; he wanted to see how they did it and know how he would feel on a bombing mission. He had never gone bombing and he was excited by the idea. When he was actually over the target Ernest's only disappointment came from the fact that dropping the bombs took no more than a few seconds and he didn't have enough time to study what was done and how it was done. He asked for a repeat run over the target area in order to see better, but was refused by the pilot who did not want to be hit by the German antiaircraft guns; other planes ahead of them had already been hit and crashed. Ernest was full of questions about everything; he wanted to know as much as the bomber pilots who had been bombing for years.

After his bombing trip Ernest wanted to go up in a fighter plane. He did, on a night reconnaissance flight, and he urged the pilot to chase the German rockets which flashed across the Channel on their way to London, and he urged the pilot to shoot down the rockets so he could see it done. Ernest took no notes on what happened; he trusted his memory. The pilot remembered that Ernest was excited and happy to be in the middle of the action, as if he'd been sixteen years old. Back on the ground, Ernest did not stop talking about courage and the need for it, and how it was found and lost.

From the war in the air Ernest went to the war on land, in Normandy. From an armored division he went to an infantry division, and from a division he went to a regiment, the 22nd Regiment. The commanding officer was Colonel Lanham; Ernest stayed for ten days and they became friends. From the time Ernest had left Havana in May, till he began crossing France in July, he had moved quickly; now he began to go even faster.

He captured a Mercedes Benz and a motorcycle from the enemy; he traveled with the troops; he armed himself; he moved ahead of the troops; he was pinned down by enemy fire; he escaped; he studied the movement of the armies with the generals; he walked the streets of the villages with the infantry squads.

People wanted to talk to Ernest about books, but he only wanted to hear about war. Wherever he went, Ernest took along his private supply of hand grenades and submachine guns. As a little boy Ernest had liked weapons ever since the day he'd threatened to shoot his mother for calling him her "dolly." In Normandy, Ernest had more weapons of his own than ever before. Weapons gave Ernest a feeling of having the power he wanted. He said he liked to fight even though he knew he should not like it, and he said that he fought against being killed, that it made him feel as if he had more of a chance to win if he had the power to kill.

Between Normandy and Paris, in July and August, Ernest helped his side win the war. No one asked him to, but he decided to be a scout for the army. Even though he was supposed to be writing magazine articles, Ernest did not write; instead he moved ahead, and tried to find the Germans and warn his friends where the enemy was so the enemy could be destroyed. It was as if Ernest were the link between his side and the enemy.

Being a scout on a motorcycle was not very different from being a scout with pen and paper. When he wrote Ernest insisted it was his job to give the truth to his readers. Knowing what lay ahead was all-important. If a man knew what life was going to be like, he was a lot better off than if he didn't. It was because he believed this that Ernest wrote. He had seen; he had been hurt; he knew how he had been hurt, and he knew that if he had known before how it would happen, if only there had been someone to warn him of what was coming, then maybe he would not have been hurt so badly. Ernest didn't think he was better or different from anybody else, nor did he feel he was the only one who knew what life was like; he just wanted to say what he had found, in the hope of making it easier for others. He wanted to give them an advantage he had never had.

Near Paris, Ernest organized French guerilla fighters into a band of intelligence scouts. He acted as their chief and as a scout himself, and he communicated the information they gathered to the U.S. Army officers in charge of the battle. Ernest was brave; he took no stupid chances with his life, but he risked it to find out where the Germans were.

Ernest was there on the day Paris was liberated from the Germans. He cried like everybody else; he was happy, very happy, like everybody else, but he found that Paris was dangerous because there were still a few Germans and French traitors who wanted to fight and their guns killed a lot of people. On the 25th of August, 1944, the city which more people love than any other city had a party. Ernest was a guest at the party but he also acted as a host.

He crossed the Seine, drove through the Bois de Boulogne near the racetrack where he'd gone to bet on the horses with Hadley twenty years before, up Avenue Foch, around the Arc, down the Champs Elysées, across the Place de la Concorde, stopped his jeep in front of the Ritz, and walked into the hotel.

Ernest said he liberated the Ritz. He felt at home there. He settled into a room, and gave a party and the party went on in his room and in the bar downstairs all day and all night. Everybody drank everything there was to drink and it was free; everybody hugged and kissed and smiled inside the Ritz and all over Paris, everybody except those who died in the streets that day. Ernest stayed at the Ritz while the fighting troops moved around the city on their way to Germany. Ernest entertained all the time; his room at the Ritz was like a royal court; some of his guests found their host to be polite; others said he was rude and went away. Ernest was never alone. Old friends came to stay at the Ritz and soon Mary Welsh arrived from London and she too stayed there. Ernest was immediately glad to see Mary; he said he'd missed her every day. The Ritz was like Ernest's private champagne club. Ernest felt free to tell club members that, in his mind, his mother was a prize-winning, all-time, famous bitch. Even at the Ritz in Paris, in September 1944, Ernest did not forgive Grace Hall.

Ernest liked the champagne and the Ritz, but he had to go. He couldn't stay too long where everybody was having a good time; he had to go where men were fighting and dying. He drove away in his jeep in the direction of the front to find his friend Colonel Lanham and the 22nd Infantry Regiment.

During the rest of the year Ernest lived in the strangest way possible; he chose to travel back and forth between the greatest luxury and the greatest horror. Never before and never again did Ernest show as clearly how much he was a man of extremes; he began now to commute between life and death.

Ernest went from room 31 at the Ritz, 15 Place Vendôme, Paris, to a hole in a forest where no one lived but where many were dying. At the Ritz on the ground floor the concierge would do anything for Ernest; in the bar the best champagne was served and the driest martini was mixed; bright display cases of rare jewels and perfume lit up the long corridors; on the forest floor there were only leaves and dead men. At the Ritz there was a maid and a valet to care for Ernest in his room, and waiters to bring him what he wished when he asked for it; in the forest there were men who prayed they wouldn't die in pain.

Ernest was torn between the Ritz and the forest; he wanted to be with Mary and he wanted to be with his friends in battle. In Paris, Ernest felt he must go to Lanham and his men, as if they needed Ernest to be with them when they were in danger. When there was a lull in the battle and the dead were buried and the wounded were in hospitals, only then did Ernest leave and go back to the Ritz. But when the battle started up again, a

week or a month later, Ernest would once more go from room 31 to the forest. He said the forest in eastern France reminded him of Michigan where he had first gone hunting with his father.

Ernest reached Germany with Lanham. The regiment came up against the German Westwall and the fighting became harder and the list of the dead grew longer. Ernest did not stand back. The ground was filled with antipersonnel mines, which if stepped on would blow up a man's genitals; the air was filled with exploding metal and the screams of the wounded. The Westwall was broken and the regiment moved on into Germany.

Ernest remembered the morning when American artillery killed American soldiers by accident; he remembered the soldier who had been run over by so many trucks that he didn't look like a soldier, and the soldier who was killed by flames and the dog who was eating him.

Ernest said he knew he should not be so happy. He said the summer and the fall of 1944 were the happiest in his life. He spoke in extremes, just as he lived. At war, Ernest was never lonely; everything was very clear, very real, and being real it was easy to understand what was happening, and just as easy to know what to do. When the fight was on there was no time to feel the pain which came when Ernest didn't know what to do. It was easy to know who the enemy was in a fight. The enemy didn't pretend to love you; the enemy never lied; he wanted to get you, and if you wanted to live it was up to you to get him first.

Ernest knew that war was horrible, but he found that war was not complicated. In battle he knew who his friends were; he never had to suspect his friends at the front, but at a café or at home he could never be sure who was really on his side.

Ernest stayed in the snow and mud in the heaviest fighting at the front. Casualties grew into the thousands; the regiment suffered terribly and Ernest stayed. The regimental combat officers found Ernest to be a good friend; he was helpful in every way a man can be; he was always in a good mood, never seeming depressed. The men were moved by the fact that Ernest chose to be with them in the worst danger instead of in room 31 at the Ritz. At last, in December, the regiment was pulled out of the front line; the men who were alive were given a rest. That day Ernest was almost killed by a German bomber.

By now, Ernest was through with Martha and he was certain he wanted to marry Mary. When he saw Martha in Luxembourg he was purposely rude; when he saw Mary in Paris he courted her. Ernest decided he had seen enough war. He thought of going home to the Finca, to *Pilar* and the Gulf Stream, and he wanted Mary to come with him.

Suddenly just before Christmas, the Germans counterattacked. The entire allied line was in danger. Ernest, even though he was sick in bed at the Ritz, quickly decided he had to go to his regiment, and for the last time he drove to the front. He stayed with his friends; he saw the fight and the victory, and in January 1945 he drove back to Paris. Ernest never again went to war.

In February, when Lanham came to Paris on leave, Ernest was eager and ready to celebrate his friend's arrival at the Ritz. Ernest was happy to introduce his friend the Colonel to his friend Mary, and he was so happy when Lanham gave him a present of matched machine pistols, and so full of champagne, that he propped up a photograph of Mary's husband on top of the toilet and proceeded to use his new weapons to blast away at the photograph. The toilet bowl exploded; the pipes burst; there was a flood. Mary was so angry she said she never wanted to see Ernest again.

The Ritz hotel staff came running to see the disaster and Ernest explained to them, in French, that the disaster had been caused by his friend. The Colonel, Ernest said, had sat down to empty his bowels and an immensely powerful explosion had followed. Now it was time to fix things up, Ernest added.

In March, Ernest went home to Cuba. He had written almost nothing in four years, except a few dispatches. He said it was time to write again.

At home Ernest was depressed. Just because he had everything did not help Ernest get through a day and a night. The worst times were when there was nothing going on around him to draw his attention away from himself; then, Ernest would fall into blank despair. He didn't write and this made him feel more desperate and more useless; his job was, after all, to write and if he couldn't do it then he certainly didn't add up to much. His empty hours were filled with nothing at all.

Ernest couldn't stand being alone, waiting for Mary to come to him. Only when he was writing did Ernest enjoy being by himself, for then, alone with pencil and paper, he could find something to do with himself. During the war it had been easy not to write; there had been a lot to do, spies to catch, submarines to sink, rockets to shoot down, an invasion, landing craft, bombs, and a great city to liberate from the enemy. The enemy had always been there; if the enemy was not under the sea in his submarine, he was behind a row of trees in Normandy or in a cement blockhouse in the Westwall. The enemy made it easy to know where to look for danger, but after the war the enemy was gone, and Ernest was stuck with himself; he felt the danger in himself but he could do nothing about it.

He drank too much liquor; he had headaches; he spoke slowly and couldn't remember the words he wanted. He still suffered from the accident in London, from the severe concussion, which he had pretended was not severe so that he could sail with the invasion fleet on D-Day. Ernest was in bad shape, but he pulled himself up. He tried to stop drinking; he exercised a lot, ate less, fished, swam, lay in the sun, tried to sleep enough, and wrote a little as if he were learning to write all over again; the idea was to make himself fine before Mary arrived. He even tried to think good thoughts, but that was very difficult, he said.

Mary came to Cuba in May 1945, and the world was wonderful again. Mary loved the tropics, the sea, the marlin, all the cats at the Finca, *Pilar,* Havana, and she loved Ernest, and Ernest loved her very much.

When Mary went to Chicago, Ernest refused to go with her; he had no intention of being within ten minutes of Grace Hall. Ernest announced that his mother was filled with false purity, and false love. He preferred to enjoy life, he said, and to try to love his neighbor.

When Colonel Lanham and his wife came to visit Ernest and Mary at the Finca, Ernest showed his friend from the war all the fun he could: cockfights, jai-alai games, boxing bouts, pigeon shooting, marlin fishing. Ernest made a point of telling the Lanhams how he felt about his parents. He said his mother was a bitch; he said she had bullied his father to death, and, Ernest added, he still hated her and loved him. Mrs. Lanham did not like Ernest. She thought he hated all women, not just Grace Hall, that it was very hard for Ernest to love any woman, that he really only enjoyed being with men, as if he'd never forgotten how happy he'd been with his friends in the Michigan woods.

The Finca soon went back to being the same three-ring circus which Martha had hated: boxers, hotel owners, editors, ball players, movie stars, and anybody else Ernest could find, and anybody else who could get a free drink and a free meal at the great writer's house outside Havana.

Ernest was divorced from Martha, and Mary was divorced from the man who caused Ernest to destroy the toilet at the Ritz; and so, in May 1946, Ernest and Mary were married in Havana. Their wedding day ended in a fight.

Ernest was an extreme man, not just extreme in choosing to live in luxury one day and in mud the next, but in the way he felt and in the way he acted. He'd enjoy lunch with a truck driver and dinner with Marlene Dietrich, he'd eat a pound of caviar and drink Charles Heidsieck champagne, or he'd chew on an onion and wash it down with a beer; he'd love you like a father or tell you he should kill you. Ernest spoke of the finest or the worst, the bravest or the most cowardly. He seemed to be torn between taking over the world and giving in to it, between sitting on the throne, and putting his forehead on the ground in front of the throne.

When Ernest hoped, he felt that nothing could be more wonderful than to make a piece of the universe out of words, and think that this piece, which he had made, would never die. It made Ernest feel as if he might live forever and this was a wonderful feeling to have, but it was often followed by the feeling that he would die the next day. In the middle of life death was very close.

Ernest wanted to show Mary how beautiful Idaho was. In the middle of summer they set out together to cross the country by car. Ernest had taught Mary how to fish in Cuba; now he wanted to teach her how to hunt. The weather was lovely and they enjoyed the trip. Mary was pregnant. One morning Mary woke up in pain. She hurt so much that Ernest took her quickly to the local hospital where he found out that she was in immediate danger of dying from an abnormal pregnancy. When he felt there was no hope of saving Mary's life, the doctor urged Ernest to say good-bye to her. Ernest refused. He ordered the doctor and the nurses to give Mary transfusions of blood and plasma. Soon another doctor arrived who continued the treatment which Ernest had begun. At the end of the week Mary left the hospital and, with Ernest, continued her trip west to Idaho.

It was strange, Ernest thought, how fate could suddenly change, but sometimes, if he tried hard or was lucky, he could get out of the way in time to escape.

Mary loved Idaho as much as she loved Cuba. Ernest took her gambling; he took her to meet his friends; he took her up in the mountains, and as far as they looked they saw more mountains. One afternoon a woman, who had gone shooting with Ernest and his friends, almost killed Ernest by accident; she fired her shotgun so close to his head that she burned his hair.

Ernest and Mary traveled; they went back and forth between Havana and New York, and Paris and Italy. They drove through the Alps, skied, and stayed in happy splendor at the Gritti Palace in Venice. Wherever they went, they saw old friends and made new ones. Ernest's Italian publisher gave Ernest the best news he could hear; Ernest's books sold better than any others in Italy; everyone read Ernest's books, the professors, the rich, the young, the unknown, the soldiers, the housewives.

In 1948 Ernest went back to Fossalta to look for the exact place where he was wounded in 1918. The last time he had been to Fossalta was when he had brought Hadley to look for the same place.

Ernest wrote and he felt that his words meant nothing, and he went on writing until he felt his words were better than ever. He sold stories to the movies for a lot of money, fifty and seventy-five thousand dollars a story, and he grew richer and he worried a lot about paying his taxes.

Ernest lived very well. Wherever he went he ordered the best; it was never too good for him. If the bartender where Ernest was staying did not make a bloody mary the way Ernest liked, Ernest carefully taught him how, so that whenever Ernest walked in to the bar he was certain of being served his way. Wherever he went, Ernest stayed in the best room, sat at the best table, and everyone knew who he was and many said he was the best writer.

Ernest liked being a champion. He loved a champ himself: Babe Ruth, Shakespeare, Cézanne. Ernest often acted like a champ, big, strong, and commanding. When he felt well, Ernest felt as if the world was his, and he treated it as if it were there to please him. He traveled with a full bag of books so that he could enjoy reading what he wanted whenever he wanted. Ernest liked to order a good Burgundy with a goof beef stew before going to the races at Longchamp on a cold day in Paris. He liked to invite his friends for gin and campari before dinner in Cortina d'Ampezzo after spending the day skiing in the sun. He shot ducks at dawn from a blind in the

Venetian lagoon because he liked to shoot well, because he enjoyed the dawn and because the ducks tasted good. When he stayed at a friend's house near Venice, the friend took two of the paintings in his collection down from the wall and put them near Ernest's bed so Ernest could see the paintings better when he woke up; one was painted by Goya, the other by El Greco. The friend knew that Ernest liked both Goya and El Greco.

After dinner in Venice, after drinking a lot of white wine with the best grilled fish from the Adriatic, Ernest sang. He sang songs in Italian, in English, and in Spanish, and if he hit a sour note it didn't matter because he was having a good time. Some friends at dinner said they had heard that Ernest might win the Nobel Prize.

In the spring Ernest and Mary sailed from Europe on their way home to Havana. Ernest was unhappy; he said he was sad and that he knew what sadness was and that he felt the world was empty. He began to go back and forth between being rude and polite, except that he was more often rude; and back and forth between mean and kind, except that he was most often mean. He did exactly as he chose. He hurt Mary. He was bored. He invented stories about himself. And he showed the disgust he felt for anyone who did not please him, and he was angry not just when things went badly but also when they went well. Ernest slipped on *Pilar*'s deck one day. He hit his head badly and he lost a lot of blood. His headaches came back and Ernest felt worse.

A new book was published. Some said it proved Ernest was a champion. The greatest writer to have lived since Shakespeare, one man said; others said Ernest and his book were bad. Ernest paid attention to every word said about him, and swung between feeling wonderful and terrible. He pretended not to care, but that was because he pretended to be tough. It was dangerous to let anybody know that he depended on how they felt about him. If they found out, it could be the end. Ernest knew lions and wolves never attack the strongest animal in the herd.

Ernest abused people near him. He insulted Mary and he looked at his friends suspiciously as if they could easily turn into enemies. But Ernest could be soft; he could smile and mean it; he could fix you a drink and wait to see if you really enjoyed it; he could listen to you, and give you the feeling that what you said was more important that what he said. The trouble was that Ernest went from good to bad, and back to good again, in a way that made it hard to follow him.

When Ernest wrote he felt better than when he didn't. It was not just that he was doing his job and felt virtuous, but that he was using himself, his feelings and his thoughts, in a very real way. When Ernest wrote, he felt alive. When he used himself it proved he was there in the room doing what he said was the hardest thing to do in the world. No one could ignore him; no one could dismiss his feelings; no one could turn away from his tears, because they were in his words, written down, soon to be printed, soon to be read and maybe to be read forever. Ernest often said he felt empty after he'd been writing, as if he had taken something from inside himself, something he could touch, and put it into words.

Of the many painful things which Ernest saw, the most painful was to see his mother twist away from him as if he did not exist. Whenever he was not the boy Grace Hall dreamed of, Ernest felt the cold pain of not existing, and then, if he pleased her and fit into her dream of the good boy, he felt her love and his pain went away until it came back the next time she twisted.

Before he was nineteen, Ernest saw the men and women who had been shattered by the explosion in the suburbs in Milan, and he felt himself covered with his own blood and the blood of the wounded soldier he carried to safety on the night they were both hit at Fossalta, and he saw men spin on a bull's horn in the arenas of Spain, and he saw women who wouldn't give up their dead babies.

Wherever he went Ernest felt his own pain and saw the pain of others. He put it all into words, from the pain of the boy who grew up being forced to lie to his mother, from this little boy's pain to the pain of the old man who stood by a bridge lost in the middle of a war. Ernest felt better after he put his pain into words, as if he had gotten something out which was cutting into him, but the pain always came back. Ernest never got rid of his first pain.

Grace Hall Hemingway died in 1951. Ernest did not go to her funeral. He refused to go near his dead mother just as he refused to go near her when she was alive. On the day Grace Hall died, Ernest said he hated her; he said he did not think she had been happy during her life and that he hoped she had not died happily.

Ernest looked through the family album in which Grace Hall wrote, "Ernest Miller Hemingway came to town . . . and the Robins sang their sweetest song to welcome the little stranger to this beautiful world." He thought of the hate which tied him to his mother for as long as he could remember, and of the world which was not the way she said it was.

Grace Hall expected Ernest to be a coward like his father, demanded that her son bend to her as her husband had done. She never dreamed that Ernest would do anything but please her, love her, never dreamed that her son would oppose her will. Ernest was certain that Grace Hall had hated his "guts" as much as he hated hers. She had warned Ernest never, never to disobey her; if he did, she said, he would always be sorry. Ed Hemingway, Grace Hall said, had once had the nerve to disobey and she had made him pay for the rest of his life.

To live Ernest had to hate Grace Hall, even if by hating her it meant he could never be free of her. His hate cut two ways; it helped him to know who he was, but it was also painful.

Ernest acted as if it was dangerous for anybody to ask questions about him; he gave the feeling that he thought there was danger in his being found out, as if he had done something terrible and was certain he would be made to suffer terribly for it. Ernest fought the idea of anyone writing about him; he even said he'd hit the author. He did not want to be spied upon, he said, and he added that it made him sick to talk about himself. Ernest seemed more willing to face enemy guns than himself.

Grace Hall died. Pauline died. Charles Scribner, Ernest's publisher who was an old and a close and respected friend, died. And one day a kitchen maid at the Finca killed herself. But there was always *Pilar* and the Gulf Stream. Ernest loved the Gulf Stream; he swam in it, studied it, fished in it a thousand times, was afraid he might die in it, loved to be rocked to sleep by its waves, and loved to watch the wind blow across the Stream and see it change color.

Ernest surprised himself when he wrote *The Old Man and the Sea.* He wrote it quickly and easily in less than two months. For years Ernest had thought of the story of an old man who went far out to sea, and during the years, Ernest had turned the story around, added to it, forgotten it, and remembered it; and one day he sat down to write, and every day as he sat writing, all the work he had put into the story was there to help him. Never before and never again did he write as fast

and as well. Ernest was on top of the world and, while he was on top, a dream came true.

Life magazine decided to print *The Old Man and the Sea,* every word of it, in one issue. All at once Ernest was given 5,000,000 readers. Ernest thought it was the most wonderful present in the world, more wonderful than all the prizes put together. The book proved he was still the champion, alive and kicking. The critics said Ernest was better than ever, and they said it over and over again. Never before had Ernest written a story which moved so many people so deeply. He could not understand what he had done. He had gone beyond his dream; he had written the story of one man, one old fisherman, and the world was saying that he had written the story of everyman. Ernest had caught the biggest fish of his life and he was very happy.

It was the right time to become better in every way, Ernest decided. There were certainly many areas in which he could improve; never, never be rude, always think of others before thinking of himself, worry less, be more understanding, try to be as healthy as possible, cut way down on the liquor, swim extra laps every day in the pool. Mary was very happy. The grounds of the Finca were always filled with flowers; they seemed more beautiful when *The Old Man and the Sea* came out in *Life* magazine than they ever had. Ernest was as good as he could be.

The numbers came rolling in. *Life* sold 5,300,-000 copies. In the United States the book sold 3,000 copies a week. In England the book sold 2,000 copies a week. And it was being translated into many foreign languages. Letters came every day in the mail, from friends and strangers, from all over the world, and each wrote to say he loved the story Ernest had written.

Some people said Ernest had filled his book with symbols, but Ernest said, "No!" There were no symbols, he repeated; everything in his book was what it was; the old man was an old man; the sea was the sea; the boy was a boy; the fish was a fish; the sharks were sharks. He had written a true story, Ernest said, not a dream.

By the end of 1952 Hollywood was talking about the movie of *The Old Man and the Sea.* Ernest liked the idea but he had another idea he liked better. He was hoping to go back to Africa, and early in 1953 he decided he also wanted to go back to Spain.

Even though he was on top of the world, Ernest fell back into his fear of being found out and fought angrily with whoever wanted to write about him, denying anyone the right to dig into his private world, saying that it made him feel as if he were being pursued by secret police. To be discovered was a threat he could not face, a danger from which he had to run.

And then Ernest started to go back. He sailed to France on his way to Spain, back to Pamplona, back to the bulls, back to Madrid, to the paintings in the Prado, to the Guadarrama Mountains where the men and the women in *For Whom the Bell Tolls* fought and died, back to Valencia, to the greatest fireworks in the world, to dinner at the beach where the best paella is served as the yellow moon comes up out of the sea.

Ernest was happy to be in Spain. His birthday fell between the fixed dates of the *feria* in Pamplona and the *feria* in Valencia. Ernest was fifty-four years old. He felt young being in Pamplona, hearing the same tunes played on the same flutes, and the same rhythms on the same drums as he had thirty years before, when he saw his first bullfight. Ernest saw an old friend who lived in Pamplona. The friend was older, and so was Ernest, and they talked about the days when they were young before Ernest had written a book, before anyone had heard of Ernest Hemingway.

And in Pamplona in July 1953 Ernest made a new friend, Antonio Ordóñez. Antonio was the son of Cayetano Ordóñez, an old friend whom Ernest first met when he went to Pamplona with Hadley. Ernest had thought Cayetano was a good matador and he had put him in his first novel, but now Antonio appeared in the arena at five o'clock in the afternoon and Ernest thought Antonio was a better matador, much better than his father. Ernest thought of bringing *Death in the Afternoon* up to date; he wanted to tell how a bullfight had changed in twenty years.

In August, Ernest went back to Africa. He sailed from Marseille, as he had twenty years before, but he sailed with Mary, not Pauline; and just as he had twenty years before, Philip Percival served as Ernest's guide on safari. The safari was comfortable; there were many large tents, showers, hot water, sheets, good wine, good food served on good china, servants to do every chore, and trucks and jeeps.

They lived in the middle of a game park beside a water hole, and there were more animals than any man could hope for. Ernest was back in the Garden of Eden; one evening he counted more than fifty elephants moving slowly on their way to drink; at night he lay in his bed and listened to the lions; in the morning he went to hunt. Ernest was happy. The weather was beautiful and Percival was full of good stories.

September, October, November, December; for four months Ernest lived on safari; for four months he lived with the animals. Nothing had changed in twenty years; one thing was exactly as it had always been: Ernest envied anyone who shot a bigger animal than he did.

Early in January 1954 Ernest offered Mary a private trip by plane to the lakes of East Africa and the forest of Central Africa. Ernest had never before taken a trip like it, and he eagerly looked forward to the day they would fly away, just the two of them and their pilot.

Ernest spent hours looking at his maps of East Africa. His maps told him exactly where places were. He loved all maps because he loved knowing all things exactly; he loved all place names because they were exact. Some of the names were African: Serengeti, Ngorongoro, Kilimanjaro, Shangugu, Kivu, Rubirizi, Bubango, Bwizibwera; and some were English, named after explorers and kings and queens: Stanley, Speke, Murchison, Edward, Albert, George, Victoria.

Ernest and Mary took off of the 21st of January. They flew south. On his left Ernest saw Mt. Kilimanjaro, 19,340 feet high, covered with snow. Once he had used the mountain in a story. He had packed enough in that one short story, Ernest said, to write three novels. They flew west. Below on the Serengeti they saw the great herds grazing on the great plain. From the air Ernest tried to pick out the exact spots where they had camped. The air was clear and as far as he could see the world was full of sky and earth and moving animals. Ernest felt he could be very happy living forever in East Africa.

They flew over the greatest African lake, named after the queen who ruled over the greatest empire; Lake Victoria stretched far away under the small plane, like a great inland sea. Along the flat shore Ernest saw groups of islands, canoes, and villages. Ahead he saw the mountains of Central Africa rising high above the thick green forest. Elephant, buffalo, giraffe, antelope, hippo, flocks of flamingo, herds of zebra; valleys, mountains, lakes, craters, rivers, plains; it felt to Ernest as if all Africa was his. They flew north.

On the third day of their private plane trip they

crashed. Ernest sprained one shoulder; Mary was in shock; the pilot was all right; the plane was useless; no one knew where they were and elephants were eating the bushes near them.

They built a fire and spent the night on the rocky slope of a hill. The next day they had no idea how to escape, until they were lucky. At the bottom of the hill Ernest saw a boat coming down the river. There were elephants between them and the river and it took hours to reach the safety of the boat. They were rescued. The boat sailed down the river into Lake Albert and dropped them off at Butiaba in Uganda where Ernest found out he was dead. The world had been told that Ernest Hemingway had died in a plane crash.

Ernest and Mary stayed just long enough to drive to the small airport in Butiaba and take off in another plane, but as they took off the plane crashed and began to burn. Mary and the pilot quickly escaped from the flames, but Ernest was not lucky. He was stuck inside the burning airplane and he was hurt. Ernest was already being burned when he tried to force open a door, but the door would not open. He bent his back, lowered his head, and hit the door as hard as he could with the top of his head. The door opened and Ernest crashed out. He had saved his life but he was badly hurt.

That night they drove over dirt tracks to a small hotel. Ernest was in great pain. In the morning they drove on to Entebbe on the shores of Lake Victoria. Ernest felt terrible. He was losing blood from his head; he could barely stand up; he saw two of everything. He was deaf, and when the deafness went away it was not long before it came back again. He vomited. His back felt broken. His intestines, his kidneys, his liver, and his spleen were hurt. His right shoulder and arm and his left leg ached. His face, head and arms were burned; he had a concussion, and he was in danger of dying.

When the newspaper reporters asked him how he was, Ernest stood up very straight and said he was fine. He assured them he had never felt better.

At fifty-four in Entebbe, Ernest had no more intention of admitting publicly that he could be hurt than he had had in Oak Park at the age of four. He lied about how he felt and he pretended to be a lot tougher than he was. From Entebbe Ernest went to Nairobi where he continued to play the part of the man who crashes twice and comes out feeling great.

Ernest could move only with difficulty. He was in constant serious pain and still he deceived others. From Nairobi Ernest went to the coast where he went deep-sea fishing in the Indian Ocean. Ernest wanted to catch a bigger fish than he had ever caught, even though he was weaker than he had ever been. Nothing was going to stop Ernest, nothing at all, and certainly not his pain.

Ernest and Mary lived in a camp near the coast where their chartered fishing boat was anchored. One morning Ernest was in such pain that he was not able to force himself to go fishing. He decided to spend the day resting in camp, but there was a fire near the camp, and Ernest went to help put out the fire, only Ernest was unable to help; he was too weak, and he fell into the flames. He burned himself badly and was in far worse pain when he tried to go to sleep that night than when he had gotten up that morning. Soon Ernest sailed from Mombassa to Venice; his second African trip was over.

One thing was not over; Ernest had found a new pleasure in life, reading about his own death. It began in Entebbe the morning after the second crash when Ernest first learned how he had died. Reading about his death gave Ernest a new feeling. No matter how close he had been to death, and no matter how often he had imagined that he might soon die, Ernest had never really thought of himself as being dead. Death had always been something that was going to happen in the future; now, reading his obituaries, it was as if he was dead, as if it was all over.

In Nairobi, Ernest found more obituaries and every day new obituaries came by mail from all over the world. Ernest collected them all, read them all, and carefully put them away to read again. He enjoyed his obituaries, spent a lot of time reading them, early in the morning, at noon and again in the evening. Mary told him it was bad for him to read them so often, but he continued in secret, and showed them to his friends.

Ernest knew how very rare it was for a man to sit and drink gin while reading about his death. It was almost unheard of, except in his case. Ernest knew it was unnatural for him to read the words, ERNEST HEMINGWAY IS DEAD, but it gave him a sense of magic, as if he alone knew how to die and come back to life. He felt as if all the good-luck charms he had carried all his life had suddenly put their secret power together, just to give him the greatest power of all.

On the long boat trip to Venice, Ernest stayed in

his cabin. When he reached Venice, he smiled when his picture was taken, and then he went to bed at the Gritti Palace. His friends thought he looked terrible, but he pretended to be fine. Ernest went on reading his obituaries like reviews; it had become, he said, a vice.

Ernest rested in Venice and he grew a little stronger. But he could not stay still. In May he made the long, tiring trip from Venice to Madrid by car to see the first important bullfights of the season, and then he drove back to Italy, to Genoa, to catch a boat to Havana. Ernest moved quickly from place to place but he had no strength. He came home to the Finca with a scrapbook full of death notices and the idea that he had come back to life. He was fifty-five years old but to his friends Ernest looked seventy.

The Nobel Prize for Literature was won by Ernest Hemingway in the fall of 1954. Ernest very much disliked certain words which the Nobel Prize Committee used to describe his work. They said it was "brutal," because they were too brutish themselves to see that Ernest had written about brutality only because he was sensitive to the pain which brutal people inflict on others, because he wanted to warn against brutality, and because he thought it was far better to live with one's eyes open rather than closed. The Committee also said Ernest was "callous," because they thought he was unfeeling, when the truth was that they were so callous themselves that they were incapable of seeing his feelings.

Grace Hall would have applauded the Committee's adjectives, and so would Oak Park; together they might have added their own favorite word to describe Ernest's stories, "dirty." But the Swedish Committee did think Ernest deserved their prize, despite his being "brutal" and "callous," and Ernest accepted it, though at first he hesitated because of the words he disliked. But Ernest would not go to Sweden to accept the prize; he said he was not well enough to travel. If a bullfight had been given in Stockholm to celebrate the prize-giving, Ernest would have been in the front row.

In his acceptance speech, which Ernest wrote and sent to the Committee, he said that, "a writer is driven far out past where he can go, out to where no one can help him." It sounded as if Ernest was writing about the old man who had gone far out to sea, beyond sight of land, to catch the biggest marlin of his life only to see the sharks eat up his marlin.

Now that he came equipped with the world's most famous prize, Ernest was a certified success, a guaranteed star, and the world came to his door in person, by phone, by letter, and by telegram. What had once been a three-ring circus at the Finca now became a festival.

Ernest was still suffering a year after the two crashes, but people expected him to meet their every demand; after all, he was Ernest Hemingway, a great celebrity, and a celebrity belongs to the public. But Ernest had never wanted to belong to anyone but himself; he had always fought to be himself. Ernest found the demands intolerable and painful. The world wanted him but Ernest didn't want the world; he only wanted the parts he had carefully chosen: the Gulf Stream, Spain, Paris, the Ritz, Venice, Havana, Kilimanjaro, the woods, the mountains; and Ernest only wanted to be with the people he chose to love, not those who announced loudly that they loved him.

In spite of his pain the demands went on and on. Everyone felt he had the right to see Ernest Hemingway, to know him, to sit with him, listen to him, praise him, interview him, instruct him, take from him. At the end of 1955 Ernest went to bed. He stayed there for almost two months, until 1956. When he got up Ernest felt so badly he wondered if he should shoot himself. Instead he went to Peru to help film *The Old Man and the Sea*. His job was to catch big marlin, and hold them while they jumped, as the cameras rolled.

In September, Ernest sailed for France. He wanted to see his friend Antonio Ordóñez at the end of the bullfight season. He and Mary drove down from the Ritz, to Logroño in the north of Spain. It rained and the hotel and the food were both bad, but Ernest was happy to see Antonio, happy as always to be back in Spain. He felt a little better.

Ernest was a star not just in Havana, New York and Paris, but he was a star in Logroño. In the arena, he was hailed as if he were himself a famous matador. El Premio Nobel, as Ernest was called, was given the front page of the newspapers, asked everywhere for his autograph, and honored by the dedication of the death of one bull after another. Ernest stood quietly at attention when a death was dedicated to him.

From Logroño, Ernest went south. He lived in large comfortable rooms in an almost empty large hotel in the foothills of the Guadarrama Mountains. It was cold and damp in the fall, but there were bright days full of sun. Ernest lived quietly.

He saw old friends. He spoke gently. He went to lunch at his favorite restaurant in Madrid where he had eaten with Martha during the Civil War, and he spoke as a friend to the waiters. He went on a picnic in the mountains and ate onion sandwiches among the pine trees and looked at the valley and the bridge he had imagined in *For Whom the Bell Tolls*.

And Ernest dreamed of going back to Africa. He wanted Antonio Ordóñez to come with him when the bullfight season ended; together they would hunt lions on the Serengeti Plain. Ernest invited Antonio and he began to make careful plans for his third safari.

But Ernest's old friend, Dr. Madinaveitia, who was the gentlest man in the world, but a strong man, told Ernest that he had no business going to Africa. Ernest was wrong, the doctor said. Ernest said he would go anyway; he wasn't too weak; he wasn't afraid; he could do it; he had always done what he wanted, and he always would.

Ernest went to the last bullfight *feria* of the year in Zaragoza, the Feria del Pilar. He liked the name. It was thirty-three years since Ernest had first gone to a bullfight *feria* with a group of friends. When he first went he had raised hell; he'd stayed up for days; there had been no way of stopping him, nor had there been any reason to. In 1956 Ernest sat and rested. He went to bed not long after dinner and, though he was up early, he was quiet all morning. Only at the bullfight in the afternoon, when Antonio was in the ring, did Ernest seem to be strong. He stood straight. He was alert. He was pleased to watch his friend who he felt was a great artist and a brave man; together they would soon hunt lions on the Serengeti Plain.

But the African dream died. Ernest went back to the Ritz to bed, on a diet, and he was allowed no alcohol. Ernest hated the diet; he hated not drinking whatever he wanted to drink; he hated his body.

In Havana the world looked black. There was nowhere to escape. Ernest even hurt when he was out in the Gulf Stream. Ernest was down; each time it was getting harder for him to get up again. Months went by. Ernest tried; he tried as hard as he could. He rested. He was depressed, and he waited and he hated to wait.

Then Ernest began to write again, about his first days in Paris with Hadley, when they lived above the dance hall where the accordion was played every night, when Ernest discovered how much he loved to sit by the edge of the Seine eating sausages, reading, watching the fishermen, when he first really started to write stories and hoped they would be good, when he had been very happy. Ernest was turning back to the time when the world was all his. He began to feel better. He was coming up. He always had. Now Ernest was sure he would stay up for a long time.

Mary felt happier about Ernest than she had in years. Together they planned a trip by car across the United States back to Idaho. Ernest was the old Ernest again, interested in everything, caring about everything. There was no detail about the trip which he didn't carefully plan. He had his maps, his binoculars, his mileage chart, and he knew exactly what weather to expect and what the terrain would be like. But Ernest felt he was going to die soon.

Ernest surprised his friends in Idaho; he had not been in Ketchum for a few years and they remembered another man. Ernest not only looked old, he seemed to be different.

Ernest went right back to hunting. He hoped to shoot as well as he had before the crashes in Africa. By the end of the year, by 1959, Ernest was satisfied; he was as good a shot as he had been six years before, and he was, for a while, feeling well again. But there was a lot to worry about.

In Cuba there was a revolution. One group, which said they loved freedom and all men, was trying to defeat another group which was in power. The ones in power acted like tyrants; their secret police mutilated people, hung them, shot them, beat them to death with clubs, and said this was necessary to maintain order. Ernest knew about the horror, and he knew he could not stop it. He worried about his friends being tortured, and he worried about losing his Finca. For twenty years Ernest had lived in Cuba, and it felt to him as if he was now going to lose his friends, his house, his boat, and his favorite bar all at once.

Ernest hated to lose anything. He liked to keep things. As a boy in Oak Park he started to save anything that reminded him of something he had done. It helped to remind him of himself. When he came home from the war, Ernest brought the uniform he had worn at Fossalta with him. The scars on his legs were not enough; Ernest had to keep his uniform with the holes in it to prove he had been hit. Ernest had saved bits and pieces of his life wherever he had gone; a menu from Paris, a bullet from Spain, a tooth from Africa, a shell from the sea, every piece of paper he had ever written on, laundry lists, road maps, bullfight tickets, receipts, obituaries, old letters, and champagne corks, and animal heads. Ernest had thrown nothing away. The Finca was full of ten thousand things which reminded Ernest of his life. And now he felt he was going to lose it all.

More and more friends died. Ernest went to their funerals, but funerals bothered him. Ernest decided to buy a house in Ketchum; he wanted his own place. Ernest wanted to write but he did not. He loved Idaho but he could not stay there, and though he was tired he found no rest. From Ketchum, Ernest set out on the highways back to Florida, back to Havana. He stayed a few weeks at the Finca and took off again back to Spain, back to the bullring.

In the early summer of 1959 Ernest began to live at a speed he had never lived before. It was as if he felt he would fall down if he stayed still. As if his life depended on it, Ernest went to one bullfight after another.

Ernest had decided to write an article on bullfighting for *Life* magazine and he had also decided that Antonio Ordóñez needed his pal, Ernest, to be with him at all times. Antonio was competing with his brother-in-law, Luis Miguel Dominguín. Seeing lots of money in this competition, the bullring impresarios blew it way up in order to attract large crowds. Ernest acted as if the competition was the most dramatic event in the history of bullfighting. He wanted Antonio to be judged the finest matador alive, and perhaps the finest ever. Ernest was going to help Antonio all along the way. It was going to be tough but Ernest would be there, just as he had been there when Lanham's regiment hit the German Westwall.

From city to city the bullfights followed one another, month after month: Málaga, Valencia, Madrid, Bilbao, Barcelona, Sevilla, Zaragoza, Pamplona. The bullfight world was one of constant motion and Antonio Ordóñez stood at its center. The season started slowly, but it quickly picked up speed, and as Antonio began to move faster and faster so did Ernest. They traveled in separate cars, but the cars took the same roads. They drove all night. They slept in the morning, and again Antonio killed two bulls. If they spent more than one night in a city it meant the city was celebrating its festival and the hotels, and the streets, and the restaurants, and the bullring were crowded. Ernest lived in a crowd; he was a famous man and the crowd loved him.

Ernest traveled with old friends, and with new friends, and with hangers on, with people who wanted to be photographed with him, with people who made a profit from knowing him, and with people who loved him. At lunch there were twenty people at Ernest's table, and at dinner there were twenty. At every meal there were guests who tried to sit near the Nobel Prize winner and every meal went on for hours. Ernest was never alone, and he was never still.

He was rude and he paid no attention to Mary when she hurt herself. He acted as if he were fifteen one moment, and as if he were eighty the next. Ernest made no sense. He seemed happy but he was not; he seemed strong but he was weak; nothing was the way he wanted it to be, but he wanted it to look all right. Photographs in the papers showed Ernest standing next to Antonio. Articles spoke of the partnership the two great men had formed. Antonio and Ernest knew the partnership was a joke; only the readers thought it was real.

When Antonio was gored, Ernest stopped running from city to city. He stayed beside Antonio and cared for him, and when the wound healed Ernest took off again: hotels, cars, phone calls, people, tickets, beer, papier-mâché giants, wine, parades, interviews, fireworks, bars, cafés, meals grabbed in the middle of the night under the moon, new rooms, trumpets, six bulls dead every afternoon, hundreds of miles driven at high speed and more phone calls and more beer and more people and more bulls and many more miles.

In the middle of the summer Mary gave a large birthday party to celebrate Ernest's sixtieth birthday. Antonio's wife sat on Ernest's right at the party; it was her birthday also. The weather, the party, the house and the girls were all beautiful. Mary had worked very hard; the food was excellent; the flamenco dancing was entertaining; the private fireworks and the private shooting gallery were lovely and unusual.

Friends came from all over the world, from Venice and Havana and Washington and London, from New York and New Delhi and Pamplona and Paris and Madrid—friends from a lifetime. It was a wonderful party. Antonio liked the party. He had a good time.

157

Ernest seemed to enjoy himself. He said he did. He kept shifting as if he couldn't decide whether he was having a good time or whether he was afraid. He made sense, and he made no sense. He smiled and said thank you for his presents, and then he said nothing when a friend spoke to him. A gentle word made him angry. A hand on his shoulder made him turn away quickly. Ernest acted as if he suspected some of his friends. He was young and gay with the beautiful girls and they thought he was fun. He was vulgar when no one else was and he was nasty to a man who was kind to him.

The party went on all night; it didn't end until after the sun came up the next day. From the birthday party in the south Ernest and his crowd, and Antonio and his men, drove north and east to Valencia. Wherever he went, Ernest moved like a king surrounded by his court and, like a king, he expected his court to obey.

Every day was a matter of life or death to Ernest, not just the death of the bulls, but Antonio's possible death when he faced the bulls. It was like war; any day Ernest might lose his friend. Again Antonio was wounded and again Ernest took care of him, and again he went back to the bullring when Antonio returned.

By late summer Mary could no longer stand it. She had suffered for months and she wanted to go, but Ernest would not go. He had to study Antonio's bullfights, he said, because he was going to write about them. Ernest would do nothing to please anyone but himself and Antonio; he seemed blind to the world outside the bullring.

In the fall, when the competition between Antonio and Luis Miguel ended, Ernest went back to the Ritz. He felt sick and he was angry with Mary, very angry, because she said he was behaving badly. Even though the fall had always been his favorite time in Paris, Ernest did not enjoy Paris in the fall of 1959, nor did he ever again enjoy anything as long as he lived. Ernest tried to; he faked it, but it was never true, even if he said it was.

Away from Spain and away from the bullfights, Ernest retreated more and more quickly. With Antonio, Ernest had had a reason to go on; Antonio had needed him. Ernest had had to be with his friend, to help his friend, and be ready to care for him when he was wounded, but back at the Ritz, away from the constant motion, Ernest had nowhere to go. He felt like nothing. He looked more like a mask of himself than himself. Ernest was

down and he would never be able to get up again, but he would not admit it, and he was not yet ready to stop fighting. But he did stop looking at people; he looked past them at nothing and he was often very quiet. Ernest worried about everything, but most of all he worried about what was going to happen to him.

Once more Ernest went over the well-worn route: Paris to New York to Havana. Ernest had always loved a trip; even if it was a trip he had made a hundred times there was always something new to see, but now Ernest saw nothing.

Later in the year Antonio and his wife came to Cuba. Ernest hoped to show Antonio the United States, between Florida and Idaho. He wanted Antonio to see what he had seen and enjoyed so often; but just as the dream that he and Antonio would hunt lions on the Serengeti Plain had died, the dream of hunting together in Idaho died. No sooner did Antonio arrive in Ketchum with Ernest than Antonio decided to go.

Ernest was hurt. His hope was gone and he had nothing to do. It was winter. He and Mary lived in their new house with the big rooms and the big windows. A month before Christmas, Mary fell on the hard frozen ground, smashed her left elbow and went to the hospital. She was in terrible pain and even after a long operation, the doctors were worried about her arm. Ernest was forced to help Mary; he was forced to do things for himself in his house and he didn't like it at all. He complained that he had become a maid and that, as a maid, he had no time to write.

But when Ernest tried to write his long-overdue article on bullfighting for *Life* magazine, he made a mess of it. *Life* had specifically asked him to write 10,000 words, not the 120,000 words he wrote. Ernest was a professional; he knew better than to do this, but he could not help himself; he had lost control.

At the end of 1959 Ernest wrote in Ketchum. He wrote in January 1960, when he insisted on going back to Cuba, and he wrote in February, in March, in April, and in May at the Finca. Ernest could not stop; the words came, more and more words about more and more bullfights, and still Ernest kept writing, as if the more words he put down on paper, the more he stood a chance of saving himself, as if the words to which he had always turned for help might in the end come to rescue him.

And during these months Ernest was afraid he was going blind. He believed that a rare disease was attacking him, and that he would soon lose his eyesight. And he felt that he was becoming confused and was losing his mind and he wrote words which made no sense as if to prove it.

A police patrol came to the Finca hoping to find a secret supply of weapons. They beat Ernest's dog to death. Ernest could do nothing about the police; he could do nothing about anything anymore.

But Ernest could worry. He worried all the time, not just about losing his eyes and his mind, and losing his dog, but he worried about his money which was safe in the bank; he worried about government agents who had no reason to arrest him; and he worried about Antonio who was a good friend.

Suddenly Ernest decided he must go to Spain. He must go back to death every afternoon. Antonio needed him. Ernest felt he had to go. On his way he went to see an eye specialist in New York and he found out that he had no rare disease. Ernest had only imagined that he was going blind.

Ernest spent his last birthday quietly in New York, no party, no friends from all over the world, no reason even to pretend that he was having a good time. Ernest was sixty-one years old and lost. Before he went back to Spain for the last time, Ernest began to be afraid that he was losing his memory. He had nothing more to lose on July 21st, 1960, except his life.

Even though his bullfight article was more than ten times too long, and even though it was finished, Ernest felt he must do more work on it, gather more information, talk to more people. He held on to his words as if they were his life.

Mary would not go back to Spain; she had suffered too much the year before. Ernest went quietly, alone. He flew directly to Madrid hoping that being near Antonio might help. His hope quickly died; each day was more painful for Ernest than the day before, each night longer than the night before.

Ernest behaved as if he suspected that his friends were plotting to kill him. He was sure that people were keeping secrets from him. Ernest was afraid of people, but he couldn't be alone. One hour he struck out in anger; he was loud and terrible; the next hour he sat alone and frightened. Ernest thought he was going to break. He gradually crawled away inside himself; sometimes he said nothing and did nothing for a long time.

Then Ernest would remember that he had always come back, always gotten up, never stayed

down, and he would feel sure that he could do it again; he would write again; he would fish and eat and love and shoot and drink again, and he would live a long time.

Antonio was wounded. The bullfight season was ending and Ernest was sick of everything; he said he was even sick of the bulls. Ernest felt certain about only one thing; everybody was against him. The critics were the ones who had always ganged up on him, but now it was the world. Wherever he looked Ernest saw danger. He went to bed in Madrid and stayed there.

Ernest crossed the Atlantic. He flew straight to New York and with Mary, took the train to Idaho.

The truth meant nothing to Ernest anymore. He only believed in his own bad dreams, and they were as bad as they could be. Ernest made them up with only one purpose, to hurt himself, by dreaming up stories in which people punished him: an airline was certain not to allow Ernest on their plane because his luggage weighed too much; Antonio was never going to speak to him again because Ernest had made mistakes in his bullfight article; a department store would refuse to let Ernest in their front door because his bill was unpaid; his lawyer, his wife, his friends were all going to leave him.

Wherever he turned Ernest expected a door to be slammed in his face because he had done something wrong, had broken a rule or made an error. One way or another Ernest had been bad. And it made no difference to Ernest if it was proven to him that he had done nothing wrong. Even if the airline begged Ernest to get on their plane with a ton of luggage; even if Antonio came to see Ernest in his bed and assured him he had made no mistakes, even if the department store insisted that Ernest had paid his bill, Ernest stuck to his idea that he was wrong.

On the telephone Ernest was suspicious. He was afraid to mention names because the police might overhear and catch him if they found out what he had done. The Internal Revenue Service was after him for tax errors; the Immigration Department wanted him for having illegally brought an alien into the country; the local sheriff was going to arrest him for having brushed a car's fender; the F.B.I. was looking for him because they thought he was guilty of taking a woman across state lines for immoral purposes. When he did not accuse himself of a specific crime, Ernest fell back on the idea that he must be guilty of something and that somebody out there must be coming to get him for it.

Ernest was not guilty. He had committed no crime. The only crime had been committed a long time ago in Oak Park against Ernest.

Ernest Miller Hemingway, who had come "to town wrapped in a light blue comforter" on July 21st, 1899, was taught that he must never, never be bad. Grace Hall was pleased that her son had learned his lesson so well before his fourth birthday. She took the trouble to express her pleasure in the words she wrote in the family scrapbook which she kept so carefully. "He gives himself a whipping with a stick when he has done wrong so Mama does not have to punish." It was not only Grace Hall who taught Ernest to be afraid of sin; her father, Ernest Hall, the man after whom she named her son, spoke out against sin every morning at the prayer meeting in the house where Ernest lived. Grandfather Ernest Hall taught Ernest how a man felt if he dared to sin. A sinner would "quiver in pain, in humiliation and in shame." And when he spoke of God, Grandfather Hall added, "We may turn from His fury and flee but there is no escape!"

Ernest never escaped. No matter where he went, Paris or Pamplona, Serengeti Plain or Gulf Stream, sin went with him. Sin was planted in Ernest for too long and by too many people to hope that he might ever escape. On Sunday, in church, Ernest had learned that "Sin is lethal!" On weekdays, at home and at school, he had been reminded that sin kills.

In Oak Park, life was a constant battle against sin; everyone looked for it; everyone was afraid of it; sin was the enemy! There was only one way to fight the enemy and that was to obey every rule, and there were a thousand rules in Oak Park, and God the Father was there to see that rules were obeyed, and Ed Hemingway was there to show Ernest the prison walls which held men who disobeyed. If he was obedient a boy could save his life and stay out of prison.

Sin scared the hell out of Ernest. At night he prayed that he had been a good boy during the day. The trouble was, a boy could never be sure if he had been good; he might have done something bad and not known it was bad. It was so hard to obey every rule, so hard to please his mother, his father, his teachers, his minister, his God; so hard that sometimes it wasn't worth trying, and a boy felt like giving up. But giving up was dangerous! If a boy was disobedient anything might happen; it was better not to think about it.

Ernest never gave up. He decided to fight Oak Park. He fought with every word he wrote. Oak Park closed its eyes; Ernest opened his. Oak Park demanded obedience; Ernest made his own rules. Oak Park said, "Flesh is evil." Ernest said, "Enjoy." Oak Park made believe the world was the way Oak Park wished it to be; Ernest said make-believe was a lie. But Ernest found it painful to fight Oak Park; it was like fighting against himself; Oak Park existed not only in Illinois but also in Ernest.

He hated being turned against himself; the fight made him angry and his anger was painful. Oak Park made Ernest feel as if he was dying and Ernest wanted to live forever. There was no way to win. Either Ernest stopped the fight because it hurt too much to go on, but if he stopped he lost, or he went on fighting and went on hurting.

It was a fight between those who always pretended to be right and Ernest who felt they were wrong. When he wrote about the women who would not give up their dead babies, Ernest was calling Oak Park a liar. He put his hatred of liars into his words; he used his words to hit them, to expose them, to warn of the pain which liars give, the slow pain of deception which lasts forever.

Ernest was made to think he was bad; this was the lie; this was the crime. The hot metal which struck him at Fossalta tore into his body, but the feeling that he was bad, which struck Ernest every day in Oak Park, tore into his mind. The wounds made by the metal healed, but the wound made by the feeling stayed open. When Ernest was first branded with sin he was hurt, but those who did the branding never heard his cry and Ernest was left with the cry stuck in his throat.

Ernest had quickly learned how dangerous it was to displease Grace Hall, and how it was even more dangerous to hate her; if he dared show his hatred, she made certain he knew how terrible this was, and this made him hate more. Ernest began to lie and say he loved when he did not, and he began to hate himself for lying. As one painful link was added to another, and as his pain grew, Ernest discovered that the world was not a perfect place full of love and lilies, but was instead a world which hurt him, and which then pretended his pain did not exist.

Ernest was lucky; he escaped. He discovered

the woods and the prairie, and found out that lies and pain weren't the only things. He loved the dawn and the colors of a trout and he loved snow and the sound it made when he stepped on it. And Ernest felt the love which his father felt for the things he loved, and he loved being far away with his father. They walked together through tall grass, and together they felt the water tug at their ankles when they stood fishing together in a stream. With his father, Ernest learned to help anyone who was hurt, and with his father he learned the truth. Ernest loved his father and his father loved him.

And so Ernest learned to live with hate and love, and he learned to keep an eye out for liars, and for people who told the truth. Ernest tried to be happy, and he often was, but he suffered from having been made his own enemy and from having been deceived when he knew nothing and was too weak to fight back. Until he learned to fight and use every word and sentence and story to make the world visible, Ernest felt lost and alone. When he learned to write he felt stronger, as if writing the truth gave him a chance of winning. Ernest spent his days looking at the world, and writing about it, and Ernest's days were full, as full of the world as he could make them. And during the day Ernest felt as if he was winning.

At night in his bad dreams, or if he was too tired to fight, or if he was quiet for too long, Ernest felt that the wound which never closed was still open and he would turn against himself. But Ernest was strong; if he went down, Ernest had always had the strength to get himself up. If he stayed down an hour, a day, a week, or even a month, he always came back to fight, as strong as before, and write again; Ernest always did, until he went down for the last time and the bad dreams took over his days and his nights.

Ernest had always believed in what he saw. Now, in the last year of his life, he only believed in what he did not see. He lived inside his dreams; the world around him was gone and Ernest never saw it again. Ernest went all the way back to the day when he first whipped himself, and every hour was filled with the pain of the wound which had never closed, and out of that wound poured the sins which filled his bad dreams, the deadly sins which had scared Ernest and had made him pray so hard to be good.

Ernest was tired. His shoulders were low; his cheeks had sunk; he didn't want to stand up straight. It was difficult for him to speak, and his

friends wanted to cry when they saw him. Ernest felt nothing but pain.

Ernest spent Christmas and New Year's Day 1961 in a famous hospital. The doctors tried to help him with kindness and with machines, but no machine ever helped a man with bad dreams. After each electric shock, Ernest looked forward to the next electric shock with terror. Ernest came home to Ketchum from the hospital late in January. The doctors said he was better, but Ernest came home with his dreams.

Ernest wanted to kill himself, but he was not allowed neither at home before he went to the hospital, nor in the hospital, nor when he came home. A few times he was stopped at the last moment.

Through the wide windows behind the couch, in the big living room of Ernest's house in Ketchum, the Rocky Mountains stretch far away into the north. Ernest sat with his back to the window. He sat still, almost as if he weren't there.

"I can't. I can't. I can't," he said.

Ernest was crying.

"I can't. I can't," he cried.

Ernest couldn't write.

"I can't."

He could not put his words together; he could not make them do what he wanted them to do, not anymore. To write well had always been the hardest thing to do, and the best of all the things Ernest had ever done. If he could have closed his damned wound and killed his bad dreams, Ernest could have gotten up and written another story and fought again. But he could not do it. Even though he tried, Ernest could not put his words into the shape of one sentence and take that sentence and put it in a paragraph.

Ernest wanted to forget that he couldn't write, but he could not even do that. He wanted to die, to stop remembering all the things he'd never do again: never make another friend, never hear an accordion in a Paris dance hall, never see a marlin jump out of the sea, never make a new piece of the universe out of words.

In April, Ernest tried to kill himself again. He was sent back to the same hospital, the same machine, and the same terror. Ernest lived in the hospital through May and most of June. Mary stayed in Ketchum without hope. She did everything she could do, but there was nothing to be done.

On the 26th of June the doctors allowed Ernest to go home a second time. Ernest had told them he wanted to get back to work and they had believed him. He had heard, he said, that all his books were selling well and this made him very happy. On the way to Idaho, Ernest worried that the police were going to catch him.

Ernest and Mary got back on the last day of June. In three weeks Ernest was going to be sixty-two years old, and in one week, on the 7th of July, the *feria* was going to begin in Pamplona. Early in the morning the bulls would run through the streets; everybody would dance to the pipes and the drums, and drink a lot of red wine, and go to the bullfight in the afternoon, and the next day they would do the same thing, and every other day until the *feria* ended. And ten days later the *feria* would begin in Valencia; the sky would fill with fireworks at night, and in the day the city would be filled with flowers.

The day after he came home, Ernest went out to see his friends. He had dinner in a restaurant, went to bed early, and on Sunday morning the 2nd of July, Ernest killed himself with a shotgun.

Below the house in which Ernest died a river runs from the high mountains to the desert in the south; the river runs quickly, jumping over rocks, swirling around dead trees, never stopping. Along the river tall, thin trees draw water up through their roots, and in the valley the grass is green. Deer come down to drink, and trout move steadily against the stream and then suddenly turn and swim to a quiet spot.

The river opens wide below the house into a deep pool; no rocks break the surface of the pool, and the cold water seems still, but the current is dangerous; it can pull a man down from the edge of the river and break him on the rocks below.

three
Oak Park to Ketchum

Oak Park Avenue
Oak Park, Illinois
1900

Ernest's grandfathe
Ernest Ha
and his mothe
Grace Hall Hemingwa
190

Ernest's father,
Dr. Clarence Edmonds
Hemingway

Ernest and his mother
October 1903

Ernest
Michigan
1901

The Hemingway living room.
Photographs of Ernest and hi
sister Marcelline are on the
wall.
600 North Kenilworth Avenu
Oak Park

Marcelline, Sunny, Dr. and
Mrs. Hemingway, Ursula, and
Ernest (from left to right)
Oak Park
1906

Grace Hall (fourth from left)
Ernest (second from right)
Michigan
1916

Ernest
Lake Walloon, Michigan

Ernest (right)
Upper Peninsula,
Michigan
1917

lock of geese
rom Ernest Hemingway's
rivate collection of
hotographs.

Michigan
1917

Oak Park High School
Class of 1917

World War I
From Ernest Hemingway's large
private collection of war
photographs.

Agnes von Kurowsky
(Catherine Barkley in
A Farewell to Arms)

Milan, Italy
September 1918

American Red Cross
ambulance convoy

Agnes (on Ernest's right)
Racetrack
Milan
October 1918

Ernest and his father
Oak Park
Spring 1919

Ernest and
his sister Marcelline
Oak Park
Summer 1919

Lake Walloon, Michigan
Summer 1920

Oak Park
1920

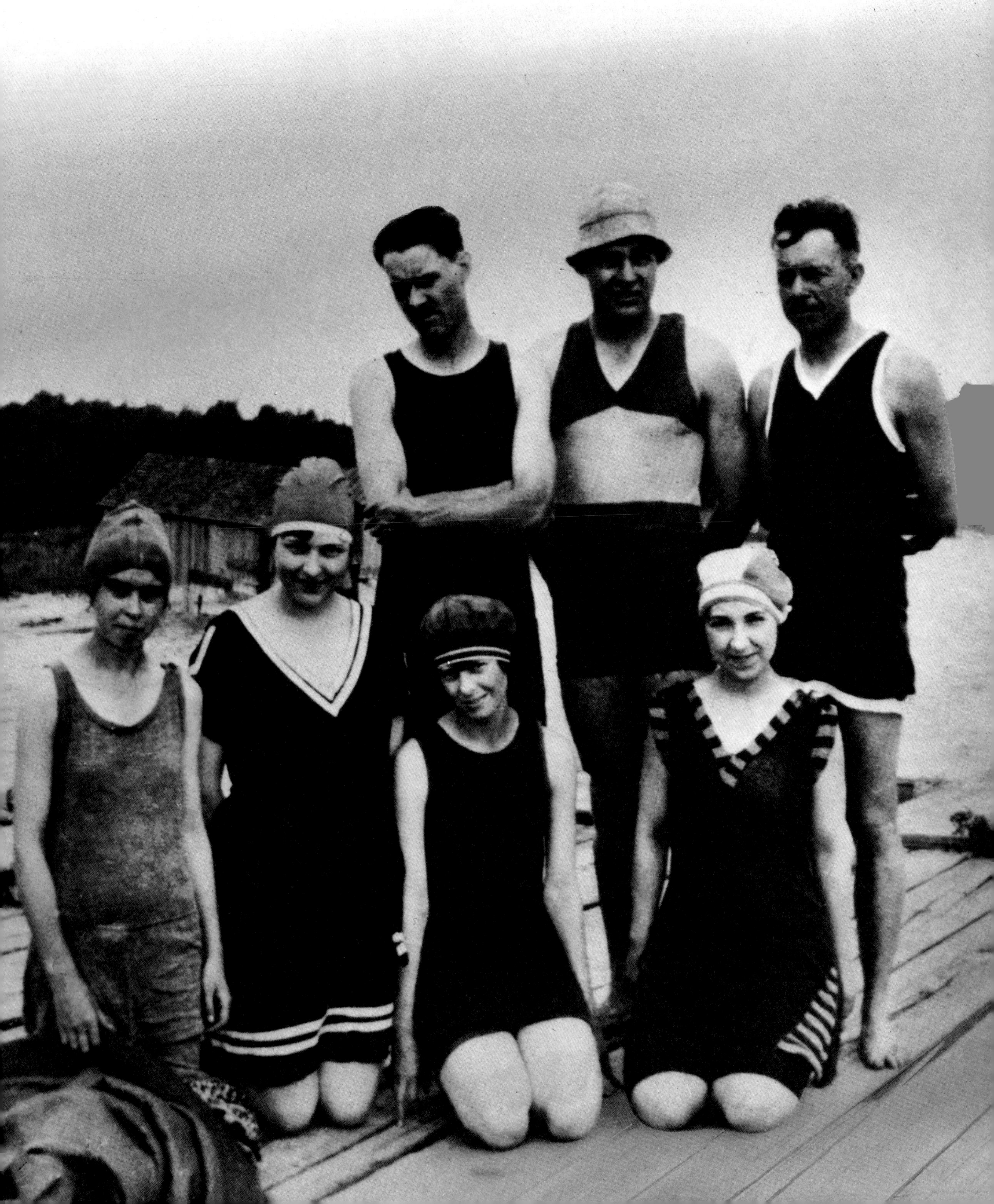

Ernest Hemingway and
Hadley Richardson
Oak Park
1921

The groom and friends
Horton Bay, Michigan
September 3, 1921

Paris

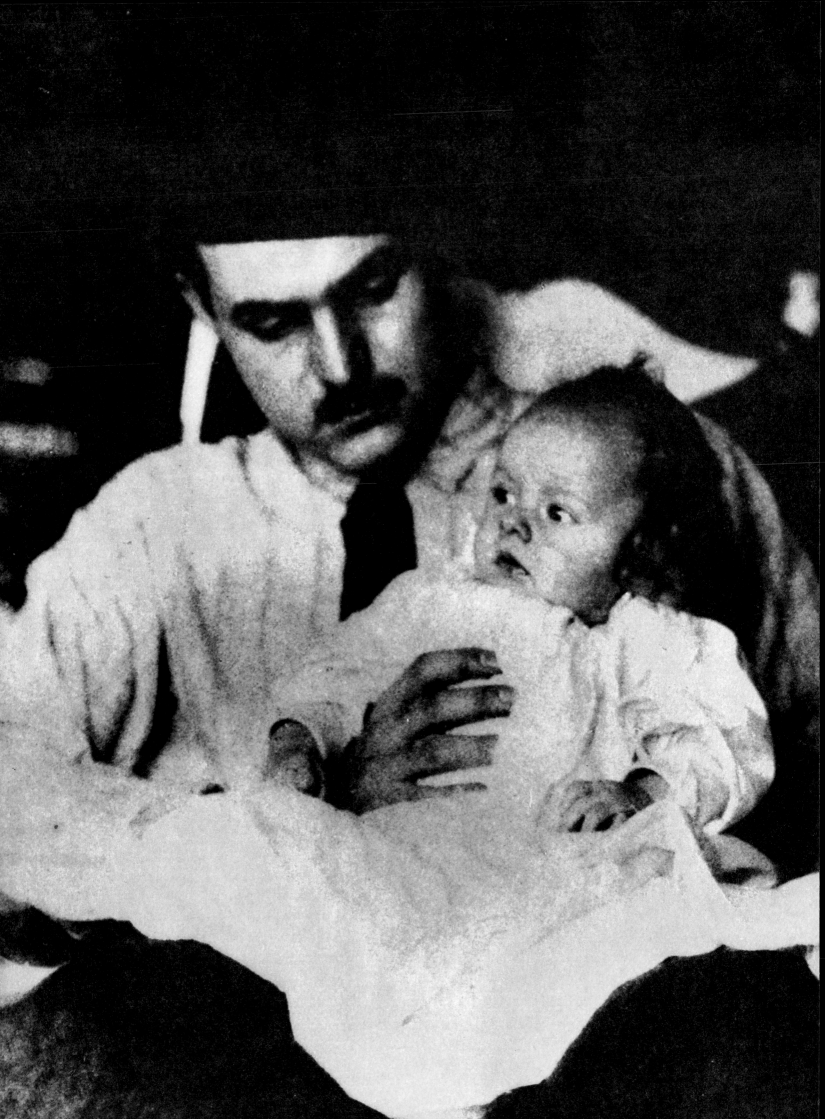

Ernest, Lady Duff Twysden
(Brett Ashley in *The Sun Also
Rises*), Hadley
Festival of San Fermín
Pamplona, Spain
July 1925

nest and his son John
ris
bruary 1924

Festival of San Fermín
Pamplona

Hadley
Hemingway (left) and
Pauline Pfeiffer
Schruns, Austria
January 1926

Ernest, Hadley, and John
Schruns, Austria
1926

Ernest and
Pauline Hemingway
San Sebastián, Spain
July 1927

Ernest and Pauline
at a bullfight.
La Coruña, Spain
1927

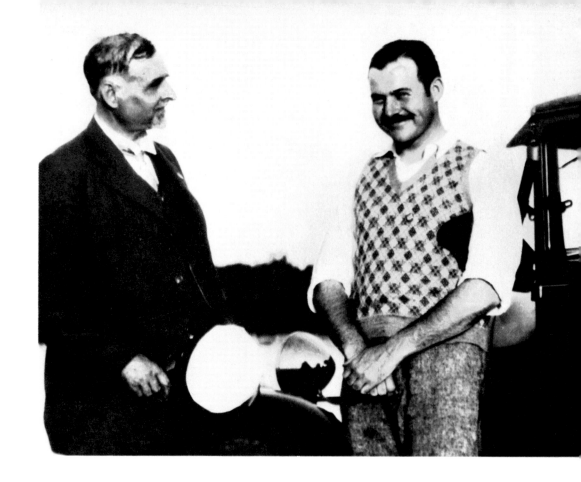

Sylvia Beach's bookstore,
Shakespeare and Company,
12, rue de L'Odéon.
Ernest is next to his
friend Sylvia.
Hemingway, Joyce, Fitzgerald,
Stein, Pound, Dos Passos, and Eliot
often stopped by.
Paris
March 1928

Ernest and his father

Ernest and Pauline
Key West, Florida
April 1928

Ernest on his way to East Africa
with Pauline, saying good-bye
to his son John at the
Gare de Lyon.
Paris
November 1933

Kenya
February 1934

Spanish Civil War
Guadalajara
April 1937

Gene Tunney, Bernard Gimbel,
Ernest, Jack Dempsey (left to right)
New York City
May 1937

Ernest, sailing to Europe on his
way back to the Spanish Civil War
is interviewed on the *Champlain.*
The press wants to know why Ernest
slapped Max Eastman in Maxwell
Perkins' office at Scribner's
a few days before. Ernest is
holding his book, *Death in the
Afternoon,* with which he says he
slapped him.
New York City
August 14, 1937

From Ernest's collection of photographs of war dead.

Ernest at the front near Madrid.
Spanish Civil War
1938

Ernest,
Martha, and Chinese
army officers
Chungking, China
April 1941

Ernest and his third wife,
Martha Gellhorn, on their
way to China.
On board the
S.S. *Matsonia*.
Hawaii
February 1941

Martha, Ernest, and (left to right)
his sons, Gregory, John, Patrick
Sun Valley, Idaho
September 1941

Ernest studying the invasion
with a naval officer off the
southern coast of England.
D-Day
June 6, 1944

Ernest and Colonel
Lanham at the front.
Germany
September 1944

Ernest with GIs
on their way
to France.
June 1944

Ernest and his fourth wife,
Mary Welsh, at his house,
Finca Vigía, near Havana.
Each is holding a *cesta* used
to play jai alai.
Cuba, 1946

Ernest and Mary entertaining
at the Finca.
Cuba, 1946

Lunch with a farmer
and his family.

Idaho
1947

Gary Cooper, Ernest, and
Tillie Arnold
Sun Valley Lodge
Idaho
January 1948

Ernest and Marlene Diet
New York (
November 1

Ernest and Mary
Cortina d'Ampezzo
Italy
1950

Ernest and Adriana
ancich (Renata in
*cross the River and into
e Trees*)
ritti Hotel
enice, Italy
)50

Ernest at the *apartado*, the
sorting of the bulls, at noon
Valencia, Spain
July 27, 1953

Ernest, Mary, and Juanito
Quintana (Montoya in *The Sun
Also Rises*) at a bullfight.
Valencia
July 29, 1953

Ernest and Mary at the last
bullfight of the *feria*, just
before leaving Spain on
their way to Africa.
Valencia
July 31, 1953

Antonio Ordóñez
(Pedro Romero
in *The Sun Also Rises* is
his father)
Valencia
July 1953

Philip Percival and Ernes
Salengai River camp
Kenya
August 1953

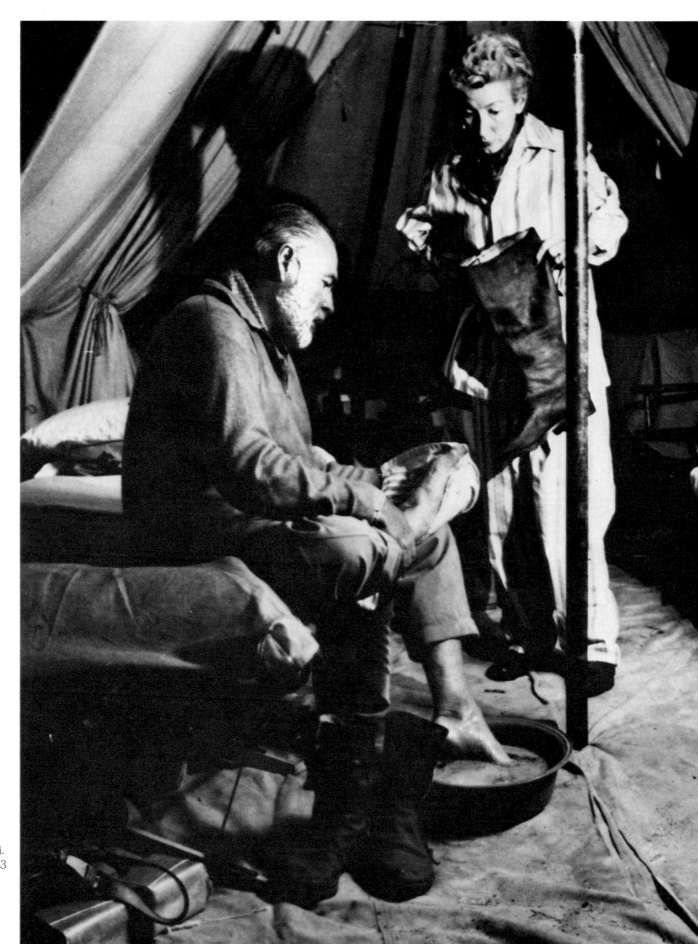

Ernest and Mary on safari.
September 1953

On safari
October 1953

nest, hunting scout,
d Masai herdsmen
enya
ptember 1953

Studying the track of a lion.
November 1953

Kimana camp
Kenya
January 1954

Ernest at the helm of his
boat, the *Pilar*.
Gulf Stream

"The Farm" by Joan Miró and a kudu head, on the wall.

Finca Vigía

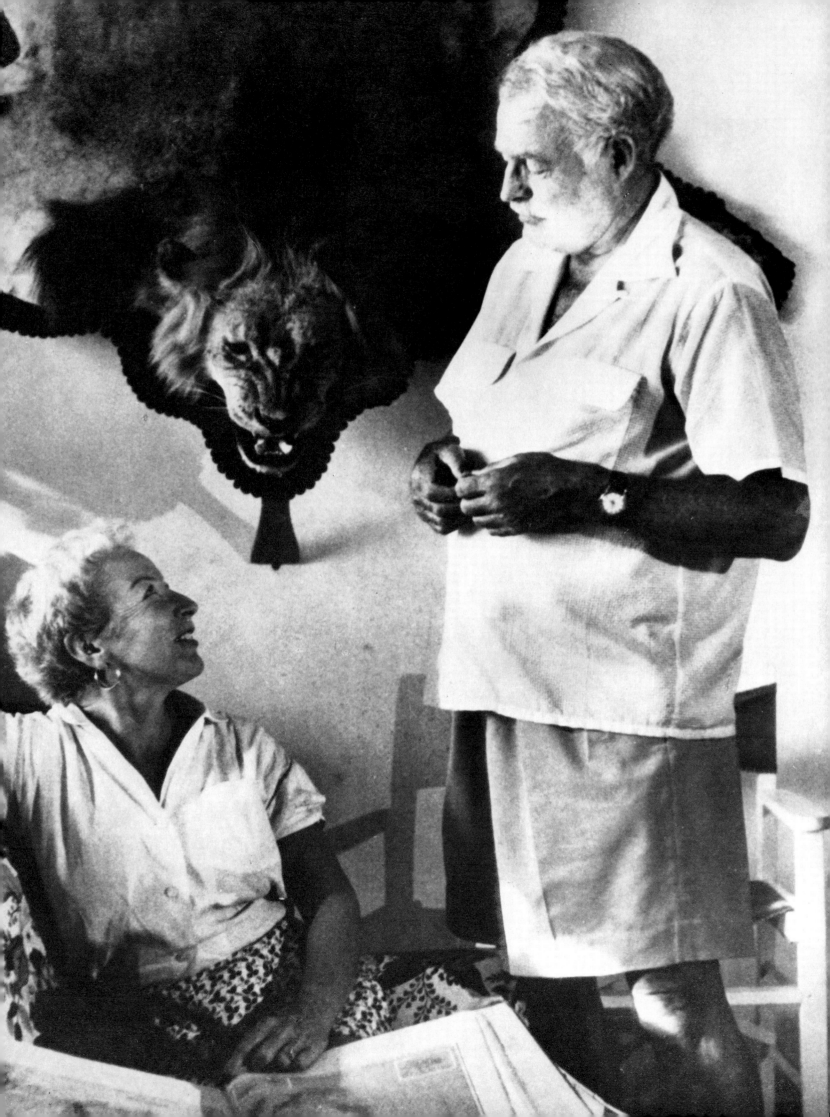

Ernest said he spoke
"elephant language" to his
friend in the circus.
Havana

Finca Vigía

On *Pilar*
Gulf Stream

Ernest helping to pull in a
fishing net at Cojimar, the
fishing village near Finca
Vigía.
1955

Ernest and Fidel Castro
Havana

One of the marlin that Ernest
caught while helping to film
The Old Man and the Sea.
Cabo Blanco, Peru
May 1956

Fishermen from Cojimar bringing back a marlin. From
Ernest's collection of photographs.
Cuba
1955

Ernest and Antonio Ordóñez
at a bullfight.
Zaragoza, Spain
October 1956

Antonio Ordóñez has just dedi-
cated the death of the bull to
Ernest, when suddenly the crowd
gives Ernest an ovation.
Zaragoza
October 14, 1956

Pamplona
July 1959

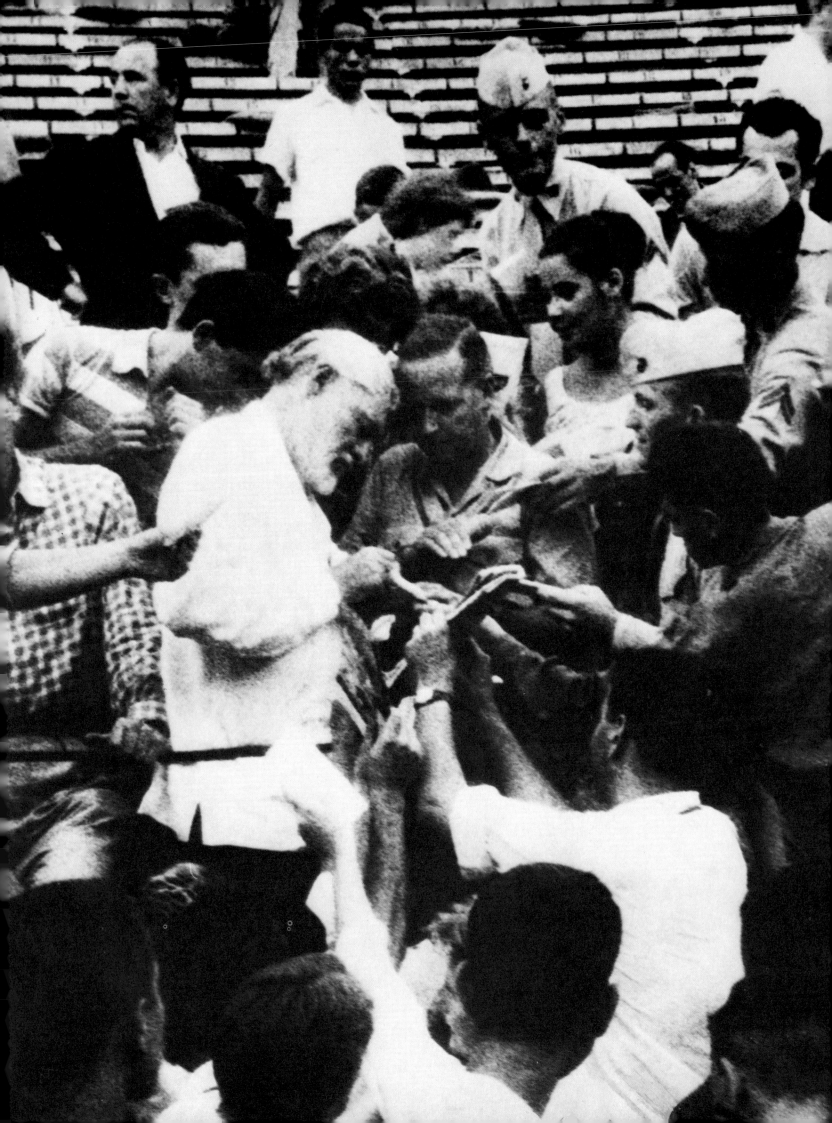

The bullfight is over.
Spain
1960

THE GREATEST THING A HUMAN SOUL
EVER DOES IN THIS WORLD
IS TO SEE SOMETHING
AND TELL WHAT HE SAW
IN A PLAIN WAY.

HUNDREDS OF PEOPLE CAN TALK
FOR ONE WHO CAN THINK,
BUT THOUSANDS CAN THINK
FOR ONE WHO CAN SEE.

TO SEE CLEARLY
IS POETRY,
PROPHECY,
AND RELIGION,
ALL IN ONE.

John Ruskin

Photo Credits